Altered Creatures Epic Fantasy Adventures
Book 5 of the Thorik Dain Series

Prey of

Ambrosius

Historical Date Unknown
(?)

Copyright © 2014 by Anthony G. Wedgeworth

Published by Anthony G. Wedgeworth

Artwork by Frederick L. Wedgeworth

ISBN 978-0-9859159-1-9

Altered Creatures Epic Fantasy Adventures
Historical Date Unknown
Thorik Dain Series
Book 5, Revision 1.0
Prey of Ambrosius
www.AlteredCreatures.com

Printed in the United States of America

No thrashers or Chuttlebeasts were harmed in the making of this book.

Dedication:

I dedicate this book to all the fans
of the Altered Creatures realm
as they have ventured with Thorik
and his companions across the land
through countless adventures.

Acknowledgments:

Thank you to everyone who has been willing to help me
become a better story teller and writer.
It is greatly appreciated.

Thank you for your labor of love and friendship:
JoAnn Cegon, Sarah Wedgeworth, Tami Wedgeworth,
Darci Knapp, Kelly Gochenaur, Pat Mulhern, Jacob Vrieze,
Josh Crawford, Freelance Journalist & Writer Lyle Ernst,
and my dear friend and business mentor Dennis Shurson.

**Altered Creatures Epic Adventures
continues with the following books:**

**Nums of Shoreview Series
(Pre-teen, Ages 7 to 12)**
Stolen Orb
Unfair Trade
Slave Trade
Baka's Curse
Haunted Secrets
Rodent Buttes

**Thorik Dain Series
(Young Adult and Adult)**
Fate of Thorik
Sacrifice of Ericc
Essence of Gluic
Rise of Rummon
Prey of Ambrosius
Plea of Avanda

Prey of
Ambrosius

by

Anthony G. Wedgeworth

Prologue

We've been swept into the magical spheres of the Govi Glade. I know not the fate of anyone else involved, nor do I know if the same sphere captured all of us. What I do know is that I have been separated from my friends and am in another time from when I entered the sphere. I couldn't determine if I've traveled into the past or future until I found a small shack with an old friend living within it.
- Thorik Dain of Farbank

Chapter 1
The Shack

Following the disheveled man into the small broken-down wooden shack, Thorik couldn't believe how much his friend had aged. "Ambrosius, what happened to you? How did you end up here in the Govi Glade?"

Walking into the musty smelling room, Thorik stopped his questioning to gaze upon the thousands of formulas and markings recorded on every wooden plank of all four walls within the small one-room home. Not even a knot or the inside of a knothole was overlooked for a location to write a few more characters of an equation or unreadable note. The writing continued on every inch of the ceiling and rafters, the floorboards, and across the front door in various colors of ink overlapping each other to the point that it was nearly impossible to read anything.

Aside from an ash-covered fireplace and stone hearth, the room contained nothing more than a single wooden table and two chairs resting in the center of the room. Marked-up papers were scattered across the table's surface and upon them sat a thick candle with three wicks; one burning a sky blue flame, one a bright bloody red, and the third a golden yellow.

Ambrosius slammed the door closed and held it firm before snapping his head toward Thorik. "Better question is, what are you doing here in this place and in this time? All was destroyed. The destruction of the Lu'Tythis Tower caused the crystal in its peak to fall. Gravity waves randomly pushed and pulled in all directions. The Weirfortus Dam gave way, the ocean flooded the valley, and the world shifted, changing our weather and landscape. Everyone has been gone for such a long time. And yet, here you stand." With an aged wrinkled face and a crazed twitch of his cheek, he eyed the Num who stood a head shorter than himself.

Startled by the question as well as the glare, Thorik's relief to find an old friend was quickly changing to concern. "I fell into a sphere and landed here just a few moments ago."

"Ah!" Ambrosius barked out with a questioning squint of one eye and scratch of his chin under his mangy beard. "Not likely.

Something here is amiss. It simply doesn't add up. You can't be here, nor should I, and yet we both are." Snapping his head toward a dark empty corner of the room, he pointed a stern finger in the same direction. "Are you behind this?! This smells of your devious plots. What are you up to?"

A long pause by Ambrosius caused the Num to become uncomfortable as the old man turned his attention back to Thorik and stared him down. However, before the Num could gather the courage to speak, Ambrosius continued.

"Something's not right. There are laws of nature that have been infringed upon…no, they have been violated and vandalized. Never before has this been done with so little respect for others and the future of all."

"By who? Who has done this? And…may I ask… what is it they have done?"

Whirling his body away from Thorik, he snapped his fingers and shouted, "This!"

At the command of his snap, all three of the candle's flames became yellow, causing most of the writings on the walls, ceiling, and floor to fade into the background, while the formulas written in yellow ink became bright and vibrant like the flame that lit them; literally lifting off the surface they were etched into and floating inches into the room.

Grabbing his ink and quill off the fireplace's hearth, he began writing an equation on the wall, over the top of blurred prior notes of other colors. "When? When did you fall into the sphere? What was the date?"

Thorik only had to think about it for a short moment before answering. "It was the 9th day of the 10th month of the 650th year."

"Not so loud! I don't want him to hear you. We can't trust him." The old man gave a momentary crusty gaze at the empty corner again.

"I'm sorry."

"Are you sure of that date?"

"Yes. It was the day of the battle. Don't you recall?" He received no answer, for Ambrosius was busy working on something far more important. The Num began to pace back and forth in front of the only window as the memories resurfaced. "It was a terrible battle. We lost so many at the hands of Bakalor and Ergrauth's armies. The rest were killed once Weirfortus Dam collapsed, as you already stated. If it hadn't been for my attempt to dispose of Vesik in the glade, I would have perished as well."

"Vesik? You have Irluk's master book of magic?"

"I had it, but it has been lost. We originally found the book here in the glade in an attempt to use it to save Granna. Avanda then became attached to the book. In fact, I think in a way it took over her thoughts. She started doing things she normally wouldn't. She became obsessed and eventually killed others under its spell." Thorik shook his head at the memories. "Are you going to tell me what this is all about? What happened? Why are we both here and what is the date we now live in?"

Ambrosius worked diligently on his formulas, ignoring what Thorik was saying.

After several more attempts to get the E'rudite's attention, Thorik became tired of waiting for him to answer and began to wander around the small room, avoiding the corner where Ambrosius' imaginary friend sat in. Calculations and notes filled the papers that were randomly scattered about. The only surfaces not written on were the glass windowpanes, where a thick coat of dust had gathered upon them.

Confused and frustrated, Thorik stared out the window in hopes of seeing one of his friends arrive. He so hoped that they were safe. He had no idea what had happened to them once they all got separated just as he was pushed into the sphere. Placing the palm of his hand up on the window to wipe it clean, a tug of memories flashed in his mind the moment the touch of cool glass was felt.

Slowly pulling his arm back he stared at the handprint he had just made in the dust, and yet he couldn't figure out why it seemed familiar. Curious, he slowly approached the window again. This time he took his index figure and wrote his name in the window's dust to notify his friends he had been there.

Stepping back from it, he recognized the writing, but for several seconds couldn't place where he had seen his name and handprint on a window before. "Wait a moment. I think I recall this. But I saw this from outside!"

Ambrosius mumbled to himself as he worked on his equations, stopping for a moment to change the flames to red in order to reference the red notes on another wall. The yellow writing faded into the back and the red scribbling raced forward for his review.

"It's me!" Thorik announced with a sudden realization.

The E'rudite attempted to add the Num's information into his equations. "It's you? I don't understand."

"Yes, it's me! Ambrosius, I approached this old shack when I was originally trying to find Vesik for Granna. At the time I thought I was communicating with a ghost, but it was me all along. It was a future me! So, a past me is just outside the shack looking for answers." His mind quickly raced as to what he should tell the younger Thorik. "I need to warn myself of Vesik's powers and dangers."

Without any forewarning, the front door unlatched and opened, followed by the sound of footsteps entering the shack. Yet no one could be seen causing these events.

A ghostly "*Hello*" could be heard from within the room.

"Hello?" Thorik replied.

The wind blew into the shack, stirring the papers on the floor, catching Ambrosius' attention. "Keep the door closed! No more intruders. There are already too many of us in here," he grumbled. Reaching over with his E'rudite powers, he slammed the door shut and locking it tight. The old man turned back to his writing on the upper wall. "Where was I? Oh, yes…"

Suddenly, the door shook hard from an unseen source, causing the weak shack to sway and wooden timbers from the roof fall. One beam swung down and hit Ambrosius in the head, knocking him to his hands and knees.

A ghostly voice shouted, "*Stop!*" and the shaking of the door did just that. Everything went eerily quiet.

Moving a chair out of his way, Thorik ran over to see if Ambrosius was injured.

Aside from a cut across his forehead, the old man seemed fine. However, he had become angry about the interruption. "Get out!" he yelled to the unseen visitor before glaring at Thorik. "Did you bring someone with you? Trying to filch my formulas for the enemy?"

Thorik shook his head. "No, you don't understand. It's me, from my past." He knew that the glade was a blend of all times crossing paths as spheres of energy roam within it. "I was once here at this shack and now we can witness that visit."

The old man looked past the Num. "Leave us alone, you thief! These are *my* notes. Do your own analysis!" The E'rudite began writing on the walls again at a greater haste, this time using his back to block any visitor from viewing them. Using his unseen powers, he lifted the candle up into the air and over his shoulder for lighting.

"*...you called...*" could faintly be heard from the unattached voice.

Upset with continued interruptions, Ambrosius reached out with his mind and pushed the table toward the same empty corner he had talked to earlier. "I'll discover your secret. I'm smarter than you give me credit. You will fail!" Waving his arm, he caused the papers on the floor to fly about in a chaotic vortex. A cold chill filled the room as papers continued to fly about in an unseen cyclone.

"No!" Thorik attempted to calm the E'rudite with his voice but his eyes were busy watching one of the chairs move slightly on its own. "We need to give my younger self a message of what is about to happen in our land." Pressing his hands on where he would assume the chest was of the uninvited guest if seated in the chair, he hoped to hold his prior self in place until he had communicated with him. Leaned forward, he shouted, "Do not leave. I must give you a warning! You are in danger!"

The chair shifted as though the visitor was going to get up and vacate the shack.

Thorik grabbed the arm rests of the chair, hoping he could prevent the younger Thorik from departing until he could talk to him. "Destroy the book once you use Vesik to save Granna!" he shouted. "If you don't, Avanda will become enchanted by it."

"Do you have him trapped?" Ambrosius asked, leaving his writings long enough to approach the table and chair. Looking down, he could see all of his codes etched into the top of the table. "He's seen my notes!" Enraged, he used his powers to cause the table to explode into thousands of small pieces, spraying in every direction.

Small splinters of wood sprayed in Thorik's face as he fell to the floor. "Are you insane? It's me! I'm here with us!"

"*...danger,*" the soft ghostly voice said.

"Yes," Thorik yelled out to the room. "Vesik will cause you all danger if you let Avanda become attached to it."

"*What...*"

Thorik's mind raced at what else needed to be said. "After you get rid of Vesik, use your coffer to notify Ambrosius that Bakalor is going to destroy the Lu'Tythis Tower! Can you hear me? He must prevent the destruction of the tower or everyone in our land will die!"

The sound of the door being unlocked caught his attention, causing Thorik to run over and hold the door closed. "Do you understand? Stop the tower from falling!"

Noises of rolling on the floor and scrambling about could be heard, but there was no response to Thorik's question.

"Ambrosius! Tower!" Thorik screamed again, hoping to get his message across.

A loud crash of breaking boards near the front window caught Thorik off guard, making him jump back. The sound was clear, but there was no evidence of any boards being shattered, let alone cracked.

Thorik sighed and shook his head. "I hope I was able to get more across this time. Perhaps it will prevent me from ending up here, alone with you," he said, glancing up at the silent old man.

The E'rudite was now staring at the window and the writing on it. "Thorik," he read out loud.

Thorik nodded.

"Thorik Dain of Farbank," Ambrosius said in an inquisitive tone.

"Yes?"

Snapping his head back to the dark empty corner, Ambrosius gazed with wide eyes. A twitch of his cheek returned for a moment. "Don't you see, Thorik? He thinks you're the key. You're the factor that causes the abnormal events and skewed history."

"What?"

Ambrosius rushed over to his latest writings and began drawing lines through the air linking various equations on multiple surfaces. "You are the element that causes the variances in the timeline which eventually puts me here and the end of Australis out there." His pointing to various formulas didn't help Thorik understand it any better.

"Surely you can't blame me for the end of the world. You can certainly see that I was trying my best to convince my younger self and to warn you of your own fate."

Adding the new factor into his notes, he began nodding like a crazy man. "Yes. He's correct. It's you!" he yelled with delight. "After all these years, I've finally solved it!" Hugging Thorik, he picked him up off the ground and twirled him in the air before releasing him down to the wooden floor. "How fortunate are you to arrive on the very day I came to discover this conclusion."

Thorik laughed softly at the E'rudite's jubilant actions. "Yes. Yes I am."

"Excellent! The influence you have had on our history must have been more profound than I had given you credit for."

Thorik nodded softly, trying to be modest about his past. "Saving your life, Temple of Surod, Destruction of Ergrauth's city, and changing of tides in the great war near River's Edge." Standing up with a bit of pride, he smiled at his accomplishments. "I have made my mark on this land and influenced our world."

"That is for sure, my small friend. We don't know which of those acts caused our history to veer off on a forsaken tangent. In fact, you may not have even conducted the catalyst yet." Scratching his mangy beard again, he glanced back at the empty corner and thought for a moment before continuing. "You are very ingenious." Pointing at the corner, he nodded his head and smiled with pleasure. "I understand now."

Following the old man's gaze into the empty corner to see what he was missing, Thorik gave a weary smile. "That's great. Can you explain it to me?"

"Yes. Regardless of what it is you did or will do, if you can be prevented from ever being born, then the timeline will straighten out and all will resume as it should have."

Thorik's proud demeanor suddenly sunk as his shoulders and facial expression drooped down from the comment. "Prevent me from ever being born?"

"Yes." Nodding to the empty corner for conformation, he continued. "The strategy to end your life in the here and now would have to be performed in a fashion that will ripple through time, erasing your existence starting from your conception. The future is more fragile than you may think. We can take the needed steps now that I understand what's happening."

Thorik backed away from the man, still unsure if his words were genuine. "That's pretty funny, old friend. In all seriousness, what are you doing in this shack? What year is this? Who are you talking to in that corner? What exactly is going on here?" He waited only a moment for an answer to any of his questions before realizing that Ambrosius was not joking. "Is it really possible to rewrite history by preventing someone from being born?"

"Yes. However, it is difficult to set the forces of nature back in line by removing the variable, even for a powerful E'rudite, but it's possible. It would take a while for it to catch up to you in the here and now after the process gets started. At first you'll only feel pain."

"Oh, how pleasant to know." Thorik leaned against a wall and shook his head in disbelief. His eyes darted around the room for options as beads of sweat ran down his brow.

"Think of it as a wave that expands in every direction from a pebble dropped into a calm lake. Your influence spreads in many directions. Removal of your existence would cause this ripple effect to interact with more events than you could imagine."

"Will I just vanish from the here and now?" Stalling was his only game plan until he could find a way to escape.

"Yes. Slowly. At first, people you've met will suddenly not know you."

Wiping the moisture from his face, Thorik nodded. "Because they will have never met me in the first place."

"Correct. It's an amazing undertaking to observe."

"Isn't there another way? Isn't there something I can do in order to make things right?"

Ambrosius gave the Num a sinister smile. "Why yes. You can sit very still for me."

A chill ran down the Num's spine.

The E'rudite stared at him like a starving madman who was salivating at the sight of a juicy steak before devouring it. A twitch on his upper lip and another from one eye gave the appearance of insanity. "Thorik, don't you see? Now that I am aware of your role in this historical deviation, I have no choice but to take action." Ambrosius stood up straight and lifted his hands toward the Num.

Backing into a corner, Thorik looked for a way out or a way to prevent the E'rudite's powers. Neither were available.

"My dear friend, Thorik. I'm so pleased you dropped by. Now, please stay calm. I will take care of everything."

Chapter 2
Goodbye

Thorik felt a pressure in his mind like none before. It was less physical and more mental. Experiencing one's death was one thing, but to feel his entire life to be erased from the world was an entirely different feeling. One memory after another became blocked. It was less painful and yet more terrifying as each moment in his life played back in his thoughts. Curling up in a ball on the floor, the horror raced through his mind that his parents would never love him and he would have never felt their touch once Thorik Dain of Farbank was prevented from being born.

Oddly enough, through his suffering and screaming within his own mind, he heard voices in the distance, voices he recognized.

"We must leave immediately, father!" the first voice yelled.

"Not now, I must finish what I came here for." The second voice definitely came from Ambrosius.

"There's no time to discuss this. Darkmere and Bredgin have found you and will be here in moments."

"I'm not finished here!"

"You are now."

The voices immediately disappeared, leaving the shack absolutely silent. The painful thoughts in Thorik's head immediately began to vanish as Thorik speculated if Ambrosius had been successful on some level to rid his existence from this world or if any side effects from the old man's attack would cause him future grief.

Still suffering the emotions from the earlier sensations, he waited a few more moments before opening his eyes and glancing out into the room. It was empty except for a thick three-wick candle on the floor and broken furniture.

A large inhale was followed by a swallow and a large sigh of relief. Unsure how, Thorik had survived Ambrosius' attack.

Glancing at all the writings on every surface, he squinted his forehead. "How could *I* be the problem when I'm the one trying to solve the issues?" A second sigh of relief shook out the cobwebs in his mind of the E'rudite's powers. "I think it's time to leave this place before he returns."

One last look around at the wooden shack caused him to halt his movement and to stay ever so silent. The wooden door and floorboards near it appeared to start turning gray even under the light of the three wicks in the candle. In fact, the light itself seemed to struggle to even reach the front door. The color of the wood and the writings upon it faded to various colorless shades.

The door not only turned a shade of black but it also began to crack and split right before Thorik's eyes. The snapping of the lumber sounded distant even though it was but a few feet away and the hinges rusted and broke apart from the door's weight. In less than a minute, the door fell from its frame and crashed upon the floor, sending fragile dry wooden splinters and ashes across the room's floor.

Thorik couldn't move any farther back into the corner if his life depended on it. Shaking with fear, he taxed his brain for options to escape.

With the candlelight struggling to shine upon the shack's entrance, a human figure stepped into the room. Tall and thin, this dark outline of the man gave little detail even with Thorik's naturally powerful Polenum eyes. However, he was able to make out the shape of the bald man's head and a few facial features.

Thorik had met this man before; the first time was within the Southwind mines, and the final time in the Temple of Surod. It was Darkmere's son, Lord Bredgin, who Thorik thought had been killed during the collapse of the temple. His death was obviously inaccurately presumed.

Memories of the heartless man flashed into Thorik's head; dreadful and painful recollections. Thoughts so terrifying that nightmares had festered in his slumber long after their initial confrontation.

Lord Bredgin stepped into the room and between the candle and the Num. An aura of darkness shrouded his body, subduing light from passing. Scanning the lit side of the room, he focused upon the writings on the walls and ceiling. "It appears you have been very busy, Uncle."

Without expression, Bredgin methodically rotated his head, stopping at the Num hiding in the corner. "Thorik Dain of Farbank, I do believe."

Shivers ran down Thorik's spine while hearing him speak his name. Frozen with fear, his mind raced through various options for escape, none seemed the slightest bit realistic.

"If I recall, it was you who trapped me in the Temple of Surod to die. I will now gladly return the favor." Stepping forward, he expanded his shroud of darkness out from his body and toward Thorik.

Moments after the candlelight faded away, Thorik could feel the stinging touch of Bredgin's powers. The icy chill of the air could support no warmth or life. The Num's outer layers of skin closest to the E'rudite died upon impact and deeper tissues began drying up and becoming lifeless. Thorik let out an excruciating scream from the biting pain of the darkness.

Pressing his back against the corner of the room he felt his leather boots begin to crack and fall apart as the knees of his pants ripped away from their sudden aging. He had to escape. And he had to escape right now. To jump forward to attack Bredgin was suicide for he would be nothing more than bones by the time he reached the man. His only other choice was to sit still while being tortured to death. This was not an option he was willing to take.

It was at this point when he heard and felt a crash as the entire shack exploded. Everything over a few feet high had been leveled to the ground including the fireplace and Lord Bredgin.

Covered by debris, Thorik had been below the destruction impact height and had survived the blast. Pushing a few boards off of him, he looked around for answers. Had the explosion been caused by Bredgin? Had it been Ambrosius returning to finish the job? Had it been some new threat? Regardless, Thorik took full advantage of this change in circumstance and jumped to his feet in order to run for safety.

Before his third step was taken, a series of massive thuds hit the ground before him in the dark of the night. This was followed by a deep heavy breathing of a mammoth sized beast, something the size of a Chuttlebeast.

Thorik stood motionless as he weighed his options. However, before he could, the creature reached out with its head toward the Num. The small bit of light allowed Thorik to see the white teeth of a dragon's open mouth come at him. It was immediately followed with a slap of the dragon's tongue, which knocked the Num onto his knees.

Thorik jumped back up and hugged the dragon by its neck. "Chug, you found me!" Knowing that the dragon's destruction of the shack wouldn't keep the E'rudite down for long, the Num leaped upon the back of the dragon. "Fly! Quickly!" And with that, the two flew up into the air, away from the shack as well as the Govi Glade.

Chapter 3
A Curious Path

Thorik's Log:

I know not the year of when I write this, for in my effort to hide the book of magic, Vesik, my friends and I were swept into the Govi Glade spheres which links us to other times of our past and future. I have only seen my muted dragon, Chug, since this event and am unsure if the rest of my party even fell into the same sphere as I did. They very well could be living hundreds of years before this time or after it. I have seen Ambrosius and Bredgin and they both look much older, so I must conclude that the Govi sphere took me into the future. Unfortunately, Ambrosius now believes I must be removed from history in order to save it. I am very confused.

A glimmer of bright light blossomed out from the mountain peaks, shining upon Thorik's face. The south side of the Cuev'Laru Mountains was different than any place Thorik had ventured. Mile high layers of thick stone slate sheets leaned up against the mountain as though a stack of giant panes of opaque glass fell north against the mountains and fractured. The fissures left horizontal cracks across the otherwise flat surfaces as well as jagged points across the edges as they jutted high up into the sky.

Dirt filled cracks within the vertical rock slabs allowed for growth of trees and grass along the mountainside. Horizontal fractures ranged from a finger's thickness to several yards, one of which is where Thorik awoke from his slumber.

The calm freezing mountainside night had been shielded by the warmth of his large sleeping brown dragon friend, Chug, whom he had ridden during the battle against the demons Ergrauth and Bakalor.

"Wake up." Thorik nudged the dragon. "It's time to see if anyone else made it through the same Govi sphere and landed in our time. Once we know, it would be wise for us to leave this place before any more encounters with the E'rudites."

Stretching his neck and front legs, Chug yawned before he began shaking his head, and then neck, and then torso. The process continued down his body until his massive tail snapped back and forth before ending in a long stretch and a final eruption of brown smoke, sound, and odor out of his backside.

Coughing at the stench, the Num waved his arms back and forth to clear the air without any success. For a moment he laughed at the thought of using the power of a Runestone to clear the air. Rarely did he use the powers of the Runestones due to the badgering from his Uncle Brimmelle over their unnatural mystic abilities. However, seeing that his uncle was not around and clean air was seen as vital at the moment, he smiled and quickly grabbed a Runestone out of his backpack and then held it before him with both hands while still holding his breath. Concentrating on it for a moment, electrical shivers ran up one arm and then down the other back into the Runestone. A few seconds later the air around them was quickly purified.

It had been the first time he had used such powers for something so trivial. In a way it felt playful and mischievous. A feeling he hadn't been allowed to have in a long time due to always being on the run and always under his uncle's supervision. This sensation felt good. He felt young again, even if it was just for a few moments.

Laughing at his friend's stomach issues, he tossed the Runestone back into his sack, only to see an odd sight. The crystal in the center of one of the other Runestones was glowing. He had never seen any of them activate on their own. Touching it with both hands and focusing on it was the only way to activate their powers. With his laughter abandoned for curiosity, he reached in and plucked the Runestone from the rest. It was the Runestone of Endurance, and one of the many he hadn't had a chance yet to determine its capabilities. "Now is as good of a time as any."

Holding the item out before him, he grabbed it with both hands, as he normally did to activate a Runestone. However, this time the electrical tingling, which normally ran up one arm and then down the other, shocked his fingers so bad that he was forced to drop it. The pain had been too much to maintain a grip.

Inspecting the layers of dead flaky skin coating his own arms, he could see the damage caused by Lord Bredgin's attack from the prior night. Perhaps Thorik had to heal himself before he tried that Runestone again. Carefully picking it back up with only one hand, he tossed it back into his sack.

Rolling up his blanket and tying it onto his badly worn backpack, he noticed a procession of people walking up a steep path carved into the giant slabs of rocks leaning against the mountain. No more than a foot or so across, the windy trail continued up and then into a cavern toward the middle of the leaning rock.

A dozen men and women slowly walked the dangerous path up to the cavern. Covered with old torn cloths, no conversations took place as they preceded forward, heads hanging low.

Behind them was a large Krupe; a tall bulky creature covered from head to toe in black armor. Thorik had seen these creatures before and yet had never actually seen what one looked like under their thick black armor. They were the slow and sturdy infantry of the Del'Unday.

In a way it seemed almost silly that a dozen humans would be corralled by one cumbersome Krupe, for they could easily push his unbalanced body off the thin path and down the steep incline. Yet, it looked as though the people had been so beaten that the fight was no longer within them.

"Perhaps our friends were captured and taken as well. I'm going to have a closer look to find out." Checking to make sure he had flint and a makeshift torch for the dark cavern, he glanced up at his friend. "Chug, stay here." The warm air from his breath caused a misty cloud of vapor to form in the below freezing temperatures.

The large brown dragon slapped his tongue upside Thorik's face, smiled, and then started forward, toward the humans.

"No, Chug! You need to stay here. They'll see you. I can sneak up on them to see what's going on without them knowing I'm there. Do you understand?"

The happy dragon smiled and shook his head before stretching out his wings in an effort to take flight.

"No! Chug! Pull your wings in! They'll see you."

Looking confused, he pulled his wings in and sat down like an enormous puppy waiting to be petted.

Thorik reached over and scratched him behind one ear. "Good boy. Now stay. Stay right here. I'll follow them into the mountain to see what they're up to and then I'll be right back."

He knew Chug understood this time by the sad expression on his face and the drooping of his ears.

"It will be fine. Just wait here." Turning back toward the procession on the path, he could see that it was time to go by the few people left to enter the mountain tunnel. "I shouldn't be more than an hour."

And with that, the Num skillfully traversed the awkward terrain to reach the tunnel only moments after the Krupe had followed his parade into the mountainside.

The tunnel was more of a series of large holes in each layer of the slabs of rocks leaning against the mountainside. Wooden beams straddled the openings between each of the slabs, spanning chasms from one to seven yards. Dew had settled on the wooden beams and condensation on the vertical rocks dripped down, collecting in frozen puddles at each end of the timbers. A fall from any of the beams would lead him to a bed of sharp jagged rocks.

After multiple rock slabs and chasms, the tunnel was eventually carved directly into the mountain. Although the walking surface was uneven, there was the benefit of it being somewhat straight. Gentle bends to the right or left kept Thorik hidden as he followed them deeper into the mountain. Hiding behind the frequent support post, he quickly found that leaning against the supports caused rocks to fall from the ceiling.

Avoiding ceiling rocks from falling on him wasn't the biggest challenge. It was that the sunlight was slowly fading from use and his powerful Num eyes would only help so far. Even Nums can't see in the pitch black. He considered using his flint to light a torch, but he decided against it in order to prevent the Krupes from spotting him.

Gliding a hand along the wall for direction, Thorik continued on at a slow pace until he heard a bone-chilling scream of terror followed by a cracking and stones slapping together. Screams of fear filled the tunnel in front of him as dozens of humans began to cry out.

Momentarily terrified by the sound, Thorik considered running back to Chug, but his curiosity forced him forward to determine the cause of their pleas for help. Slow movements forward toward a lit section of the tunnel periodically stopped as the screams and cracking increased, and yet it only took a few more minutes for the Num to see what was happening. It was here that he came to a complete stop.

"It can't be," he muttered to himself. "You're dead."

The large cavern before him was a blend of a natural cave and a carved out structure. On the far wall a lava flow slowly fell into a crusted-over magma pool. A structure had been built of columns and headers around the fiery mere. It was the only structure in the open cavern.

Large metal grates covered the majority of the floor. In the center of the grates was a short metal pole as thick as one of Chug's legs. The pole bore a heavy metal chain linked to a creature nearly eight yards tall, made of stone and mud as a green burning oil lubricated the joints between the rocks and boulders.

"How?" Thorik racked his brain on how Bakalor could possibly be alive.

The massive rock creature reached over and grabbed one of the men who had been led to the creature's den. Tossing the man into his mouth, he easily crushed the human with his powerful jaws. The cracking of the man's bones echoed in the cavern and blood shot out of the beast's mouth before running down his rock face.

The remaining men and women screamed with fear as they tried to leave the cavern. The well-armed Krupe blocked their path with a few swipes of his spear, cutting those who strayed his way.

With the death of Bakalor's victim, a deep swallow ensued. The soft green flames at the beast's joints suddenly increased in size and power as the thick oil oozed down his body, past his feet and through the grates. It was only a moment later that the beast used his large diamond eyes to look for the next meal. Green flames flicked from behind each eye causing a spectrum light to shine wherever he gazed.

People scattered as the beast approached. However, the thick chain only allowed Bakalor to barely reach the far walls and a few of the humans were able to hide in the cracks just out of reach. Unfortunately, there were too many people and not enough cracks in the walls.

Dragging the chain clamped onto the beast's ankle, the stone creature quickly snatched up another two people and tossed them into his mouth at the same time. Outside of his mouth, legs kicked and arms grabbed for freedom as the beast chopped down on them both, ending their flailing.

More oils extruded from the giant beast and poured down its legs, through the grates, and into the angled walls below which funneled the captured oil into a small hole and pipe.

"This can't be. I already killed you." Thorik was mesmerized at the sight and struggled to understand it.

Grabbing two and even three at a time, the beast finished off all of the humans he could reach. It was up to the Krupe to prod those crammed in the wall cracks out of hiding for the creature to feed upon.

Once complete, the beast was filled with energy as its flames raced high above his head and oil splashed to the floor as Bakalor let out a mighty war cry, shaking the cavern walls. He looked unstoppable if it weren't for the chain holding him prisoner.

Thorik had seen enough and knew it was time for him to leave before getting caught. However, before he did so, he saw a man walk into the cavern from a tunnel that didn't exist moments earlier. This man had semitransparent dark gray flesh which almost looked liquefied under the skin's surface. With soft features, his eyes and nose looked misshaped compared to a human and his neck and fingers appeared too thin and long.

"Good morning, Bakalor," the man said in a soft-spoken calm voice that seemed to emanate from all directions instead of his mouth.

"Deleth!" Bakalor loudly announced the man's name while he stood up tall in order to tower over the uninvited guest. The sound shook the tunnel Thorik had come in and small rocks and sand fell from the ceiling.

Just the sight of the oddly shaped man wielded fear and paralysis in Thorik's body, for Deleth was one of the three Oracles, the only three survivors of the Notarian race after being defeated by the Mountain King. Deleth created the Del'Unday and was Darkmere's master. There was no greater dark power in all the lands than this being, and yet Bakalor treated him with such little respect.

The rock monster pulled at his confines. "Unchain me!" he ordered. "I am ready to leave here. You have nothing else to teach me."

Scoffing at the idea, Deleth stepped closer. "No, you are not ready." His quiet mellifluous voice could be heard clearly as though the Oracle's mouth was only inches from Thorik's ears.

Pulling the chain tight, the demon stomped over to the man, who was but a fourth of his own height, and leaned forward to intimidate him. "How can you say this? Nothing can stop me."

"I can say this because you are an idiot."

Bakalor roared with anger at the comment. "If I'm so stupid, then why are you preparing me to take over the world?"

"If you were stupid, then you wouldn't have the capacity to do my bidding. I, on the other hand, called you an idiot, which means you have intelligence but simply make poor decisions."

Growling at the intellectual brow beating, Bakalor defended himself. "Say what you want, but I am ready to rule the land in your name. No challenger could defeat me."

"You have failed me before and I've spent great personal resources to rebuild you correctly this time. I will not let you leave until I am sure you are ready."

"And for this failure you chained me to this post, treat me like a slave, and experiment upon me?"

"Experiment? You call the gifts I give you experiments? I've given you the powers to withstand the forces of nature as well as the unnatural. Powers of space and time now have no effect upon you, as well as myriad of other abilities. I continue to give and you continue to impatiently complain."

"For how long, Deleth? How long am I to be held hostage?"

"Until I have finished preparing you. There are many more skills to give and tests to run. Exposure to various elements without being properly prepared for them could cause permanent danger from such elements. I must ensure you are resistant to all chemicals and forces before you encounter them. I am not willing to risk everything on this only to have you meander off and destroy all I've put into you."

"So, I am to stay here as your slave while creating urns of your living oil?"

"Yes. The natural byproduct of your digestive system is of great value to me. It brings my stone art to life and provides me with needed entertainment. I fail to see any inconvenience to you by capturing it," he calmly said while gesturing toward the funnel below the floor grates. "Besides, once you're free to roam, I know the likelihood to gather more oil from you is very improbable."

"That is for certain," Bakalor growled. "Once I'm free to roam out in the world, I will never be captive in a cave again. I loathe living underground."

"Speaking of you roaming free, I have designed a high frequency whistle into your design. Simply cover you right nostril and blow as hard as you can while keeping your mouth closed. Assuming you can keep your trap shut long enough."

Bakalor growled at the insult. "Why would I need to do such a thing?"

"Assuming you cover the correct nostril, this sound will cause a frequency that I can hear regardless where I am. It can be used to alert me that you are in distress and need my assistance."

Forcing out a laugh at the thought, the rock creature shook his head. "I will never need you or anyone else once I escape this prison. I am all powerful! And if I am not, then it is once again your failure in design!"

"Cease with your childish drama. We have work to do." Dismissing the creature's attitude, Deleth walked toward the pool of magma surrounded by a half wall and a circle of columns. "Were you well fed today? Do you feel up to another test?"

"Tests! That is all we do. It is time to fight and conquer this land." Stomping his feet, he smashed his fists together to display his aggressiveness.

"I will take that as a yes." Stepping up to the half wall, he glanced down at the crusted-over magma which buckled and cracked and rolled from the stirring of the new lava pouring into the pool. "Now, break off your toe."

A moment of silence followed as the two stared each other down.

Bakalor was the first to break the silence. "Break off your head."

"Your pathetic attempts at verbal assaults only demonstrates your juvenile aptitude, which indicates you will run amok in your personal conquest of our lands. Therefore you are not ready yet. Therefore, detach one of your toes and toss it into this diminutive cirque tarn of flaming molten rock."

"If your test is to see if I am gullible enough to do something foolish, than I have passed. I am not damaging myself for your amusement."

"Bakalor." Deleth's voice was stern and commanding for the first time. "Stop wasting my time and follow my instructions. This is not a request."

"No! I will not cause myself pain for you or anyone else."

The creature had not even finished his sentence when Deleth reached up with his hand toward Bakalor. An unseen force lifted the massive stone creature up in the air until his chain went taut. A moment later he was slammed down onto the floor, bending a half-dozen metal floor grates. Then, with a wave of his hand, all of his flames went out from his neck down.

Bakalor's eyes grew large as his body failed him. The green flaming oil on his head kept him alive. However, his body was nothing more than a pile of rocks now that the life blood of oil had lost its fire and light. He was essentially paralyzed from his neck down.

Deleth watched as the burning oils slowly dripped off his head and down to the creature's body, reigniting the lifeless oils. "I'll personally amputate one of your digits off, if you are too reluctant to facilitate it yourself." His voice was once again calm and collected.

Flickering back to life, the flaming oils continued to drip down and spread across his body until eventually he was in full blaze again. Bakalor shook off the attack and slowly rolled up to his knees and then lifted one knee, planting one foot before him. Growling at the man before him, he grudgingly leaned forward and grabbed one of his four toes. Closing his large diamond eyes, he snapped the stone toe backward with a loud crack. A twist was required to finalize the removal of the toe. Bakalor groaned as he tried to control the pain. Eventually he lifted the toe in the air as though he considered throwing it at Deleth. "There! I have disfigured myself for your pleasure."

"I find no pleasure from this, nor do I care about your suffering. It is simply an experiment to ensure you can produce offspring. Besides, a new toe will fully grow back within a decade."

"Offspring?"

"Yes, if you are going to help me rule this world, then you will need some kin to carry out your bidding on multiple fronts. Trust no one but your own species."

Bakalor appeared befuddled. "But there are no others of my species."

"Exactly." Waving a hand toward the lava, he added, "Toss your toe into this nursery I've constructed and we will see if you are capable to producing descendants."

Still poised to toss the boulder of a toe at Deleth, he eventually lowered his arm toward the pool. Unable to reach the half wall, he gently tossed it the rest of the way between the columns.

With a slight splash, the boulder floated upon the crusted-over lava for a moment before sinking underneath and out of sight.

Squinting his large eyes, Bakalor waited for something to happen. "Well?"

"Patience, my servant of destruction. You must learn patience."

"I find no value in patience."

"I know, which is why it is one of your greatest vices." Deleth stepped back from the pool. "Wars are not won on brute force alone. It takes proper planning and the ability to wait until the time is right. If you are to be one of my demons to rule, you must learn these things."

Gurgling began within the pool and increased as time went on. Eventually it stopped and a large ball of magma spun out of the pool and onto the stone floor, which surrounded the grated room. Nearly the same size as the boulder toe that had been tossed in, the flowing ball of liquid rock began to crust over.

"Kin?" Bakalor barked.

Deleth nodded his head slightly. "Yes."

"But what can a ball of lava do for me? Does it speak? Does it even see?"

"No. But it feels vibrations in the ground for its sight and it eats through solid rock at speeds faster than a bird can fly. Try giving your son an order."

Bakalor stepped back, kicked part of his chain out in front of him, and then smiled. "Boy of mine, come and free me from my confines."

A crack across the middle of the magma sphere broke open and a mouth opened wide, exposing a furnace of liquid heat within as flames lapped out of the opening. Additional cracks opened, two on the sides above the mouth and two below the mouth, all of which dripped magma from them which hardened into two arms and two legs.

Bakalor was obviously impressed as he watched the newborn attack one of the links that held the demon as prisoner.

"Excellent. It would appear that you are now capable of creating loyal servants to do your bidding." Nodding to himself, Deleth turned and began to leave the cavern.

Bakalor watched the infant struggle to melt the chains. "I thought you said it could eat through rock. It can't even melt metal."

"You truly are an idiot. Do you think I am a fool and wouldn't expect you to try such a rudimentary escape? I have tempered your metal chains to prevent such attacks," Deleth said while leaving through the hallway that he had come from. Moments later the passage closed up as though no hallway had ever existed.

Thorik Dain was amazed, but it was time for him to sneak back out the tunnel, reach Chug, find his friends, and then inform them that Bakalor had been recreated.

Starting off with a careful walk, the Num swiftly changed to a jog in order to exit as quickly as possible. Following the slight bends of the tunnel he finally saw the opening and the first wooden beam bridge. Without thinking twice, he increased his speed to a full run.

Forgetting about the frozen puddles on each side of the beams, he slipped on his leap up to the wooden crossway and missed his footing once upon it. Momentum carried him across as gravity dragged him down off the side. Falling forward, he reached out and caught himself on the wet wood near the far end. He hung from the beam with both hands, looking down at the sharp rocks over a hundred yards below.

Catching his breath, he calmed himself down before taking any action.

Hand over hand, he began making his way to the far end. The wet wood was difficult to hold onto, and the freezing temperatures caused his fingers to be sensitive to every touch. The wood had not been sanded down, so the raw coarse nature of its texture helped his grip but also caused multiple splinters while shuffling his hands along the way.

Eventually he made it to the side of the chasm. His arms ached, his fingers were burning from the frost, bleeding from the cuts, and throbbing from being over used. So, it shouldn't have been much of a surprise when he shifted his grip off the wood that the cold slick stone floor caused his hands to slip off the surface and for him to fall from the ledge.

His unexpected release sent panic in his mind as he headed for his death. He had so much more to do and he couldn't believe this was his end. Could he have truly made such an error? He didn't believe this event was truly happening until he was caught while falling backward. However, this time it wasn't Chug or any of his other friends.

Instead, it was a Krupe who had leaned over the ledge just in time to grab the Num's wrist. Lifting the small Num up by the one arm he had grabbed, the silent black armored soldier carried Thorik back across the chasm and then tossed him onto the tunnel's floor before taking out his spear and pointing it at him. A second Krupe appeared behind the first and watched from the far side.

Thankful to not be skewered by the sharp rocks within the chasm, Thorik was not pleased to see his current situation. He would have to get past the first Krupe and then worry about the second one once he had successfully crossed the wooden beam. Rolling up to his feet, he tried to make a break for it and run around the closest Krupe, but the sharp blade of a spear snapped into position up against Thorik's neck.

The point was well taken. This Krupe could easily kill Thorik with a flick of his wrist. So instead, the Num turned and was escorted back to Bakalor by both the Krupes.

Chapter 4
Between a Rock and a...

Thorik reached the large cavern coated in sickly green light as the Krupes marched behind him at a steady pace. There was no reason for them to rush, Thorik was running into a dead end. He was trapped.

Thorik hoped the hallway that Deleth had used was truly still there and there was simply an illusion making it look like it disappeared. He would make a run for that location prior to Bakalor having time to see him and react to his presence.

Bolting across the grates, Thorik made quick work of the distance to the far side. Once there, his hands began to explore the cavern walls for a hidden hallway.

A deep growl emanated from high in the air behind Thorik.

Twirling around, Thorik placed his back to the wall as his hands continued the search. "Hello, Bakalor. I bet you're surprised to see *me* again."

With lowering brows, Bakalor leaned over and looked closer to the Num. "Do I know you?"

"It is I, Thorik Dain of Farbank," he replied instinctively. He immediately wished he had not given the demon his name for it might cause him to actually remember.

"Ah, Thorik Dain of Farbank." He nodded a few times before his eyebrows tightened inward and then down in the center. "You're late. I already ate, but I'm willing to have you as a dessert." Reaching down, he attempted to grab the Num.

"Wait!" Thorik yelled out while squeezing into a crack in the wall, just out of the demon's reach. "You truly don't remember me?"

Pulling his chain taut, Bakalor leaned forward enough to poke the Num but not enough to grab him. "No. I don't get in the habit of remembering my meals."

"I was not a meal to you. Besides, why does a creature of rock require the nourishment of the living?"

"I crave your life force. It feeds my flames. And where I have flame, I have life and I have power. This is why I will eat you alive."

"And that is what's confusing. You wanted me dead for something I had done to you in the past. What good would I be to you dead?"

"I have little memory of my prior life, nor will I care to have any memory of you in my future, for you are but a minor snack in a long buffet." Stepping back from the Num, he looked over at the approaching Krupes. "Stay," he told them before turning to his child. "Boy of mine, go prod Thorik Dain of Farbank out of that crack."

Thorik took the opportunity to make a run for the only structure in the cavern. Leaping out of the way of Bakalor's attempt to grab him, the Num rolled under the rock creature's massive arm and right between his legs, before tumbling back to his feet. Jumping up on the structure's half wall, he nearly slipped and fell into to pool of lava. Grabbing a column, he swung himself around and slapped his back firmly on the far wall. "Before you eat me, can you remember why you hated me? What had I done to you that was so terrible that you would wish to kill me?" He knew the longer he kept his enemies talking the more time he had to find a way to escape.

"I don't know who you are or what you're talking about. If I had to guess, I would say you kept me from a meal with your annoying questions."

The arms and legs of Bakalor's child melted back into its body before it began to roll toward the nursery.

Thorik moved along the half wall, toward the lava falls. "If I have done you no wrong, than let me be and I will not return." He knew he was trapped. There was no place to go. The heat from the falls was already felt upon his skin while the demon's infant rolled toward him, unleashing its own inferno each time it opened its mouth.

"Cook him, but don't kill him." Bakalor ordered. "I prefer to eat him alive."

Thorik was stuck. Negotiations had failed him and jumping in any direction was jumping into fire. He could feel his heart pound against his chest like a deep drum, hammering so loud that it sounded external of his own body. He eventually realized that it actually was external and it wasn't his own heart that he was hearing. Something was coming down the tunnel, smashing each and every ceiling support post as it raced through the tunnels toward Bakalor's Chamber.

With a loud crash, both Krupes flew into the cavern, landing and then rolling across the grates. They had been knocked unconscious by a large brown dragon with a female Num rider upon it.

"Chug! Avanda!" Thorik screamed once he saw them skid to a halt inside the main chamber.

"Child! Get that dragon!" Bakalor ordered.

Without wasting a moment, the infant rolled away from Thorik and toward Chug.

Avanda & Chug flew up into the air. One of the dragon's legs pushed off Bakalor's head for extra lift.

Jumping up to grab the dragon's leg, Bakalor missed and landed hard on his feet, bending and cracking several floor grates.

Free to escape the lava pool area, Thorik quickly moved along the half wall before jumping off and landing right in front of the demon's newborn. "No!" he said to himself, wishing he had looked before he had leaped.

There was no time to react as the lava creature rolled toward Thorik. Heat spewed forth from the searing crusted-over viscous ball.

Swooping down, Chug reached out with one of his front claws and grabbed the Num out the creature's path.

Secure in Chug's grasp, Thorik swallowed hard with relief. Hope of surviving the ordeal was looking brighter.

With wings spread wide, the brown dragon arched his body and quickly gained altitude once more. But not before Bakalor was able to once again jump up and grab at one of Chug's legs. This time he was successful.

All of them came back down with another crash, breaking through many of the grates and pinching one of Bakalor's legs between them.

Held by the Demon, Chug fell to the floor, knocking Avanda off his back and tossing Thorik toward the tunnel. The brown dragon flopped unto its back and then front, rolling and kicking to free itself from Bakalor's giant stone grip.

Holding tight to the dragon's leg, the demon struggled to free his own leg from the thick metal grates. Pushing with his free foot, he slowly bent the grate that held his other leg captive. The metal groaned and buckled from the massive stress placed upon it. It was only moments before he was free and able to roll onto his knees and grab the dragon's other leg.

Standing up tall, he used one hand to hold Chug upside down like a giant turkey before being slaughtered. "Who do you think you are to come into my lair and try to snatch my dessert?"

"He's my friend," said a small green dragon flying out of the tunnel and up to the demon's right eye. Stretching his neck and body out long and thin, Pheosco threaded the flaming crack between Bakalor's rock cheek and clear eyeball. Once inside the small green fiery gap behind his eye socket, he pushed with all of his might until the demon's diamond eyeball popped out.

Landing on the floor, the eye rolled across the grate to the far wall, reachable for Bakalor only if he dropped Chug to do so.

Screaming, the demon ignored the loss of one eye and immediately shoved one of his flaming rock fingers into his own eye socket to kill the green dragon. Missing Pheosco, who shot out of the tight squeeze just in time, Bakalor yelled about his own inflicted pain before he removed his finger and turned around to grab the evasive little flying Del'Unday dragon. Keeping his left hand firmly gripped on the brown dragon's back legs, he swatted in the air at the small green winged menace.

"Pheosco!" Thorik was pleased to see another of his party had made it through the Govi Glade.

Never taking time to soar toward the cavern's ceiling for safety, Pheosco dove time after time at the left side of Bakalor's face and torso. Recklessly close calls seemed to make no sense to the Nums.

Even with only one eye, the demon continued to swipe at the dragon as he learned the little creature's pattern while turning to reach for him, each time getting closer and closer. Bakalor finally felt he had the green flyer figured out and added an unexpected element to his little game. He dropped the brown dragon at the last second and used the free hand to stop the green one from getting past.

Plowing into the unexpected giant palm, Pheosco had tried to change his angle at the last moment to avoid it. Unsuccessful, he smacked head first into the top of his rock palm and flipped over the top and down the back of his hand, crashing onto the bent floor grates covered with Bakalor's chains.

Pheosco lay momentarily stunned near Chug as he shook his head clear of the room as it spun in his vision. Both dragons were at the demon's feet and at his mercy.

Bakalor gave a slow deep laugh. "I was designed and destined to be all powerful. You stand no chance against me." Glancing over at his child who patiently waited for orders, he allowed him to have the honors. "Boy of mine, take the first bite."

"Stand no chance? Stand?" Thorik mumbled as he suddenly realized what Pheosco was trying to do. "Chug! Bite the chain and leap this way!"

Always obedient to Thorik, Chug grabbed the chain in his mouth and jumped away from Bakalor, toward Thorik.

Reaching down for the brown dragon before he had the chance to get away, the chain suddenly tightened. It had wrapped around the demon's ankles several times while swatting at the green dragon. As the brown dragon lurched forward, the chain instantly tightened and then pulled him off his feet.

Falling sideways, the demon watched both dragons race down the tunnel with the two Nums riding the larger winged beast. His crash snapped a metal cross-brace, causing Bakalor and half the floor sections to fall into the large funnel that had been collecting the green oils. Not only had he destroyed the floor, but he had fallen and crushed his son, squeezing his soft rock body through the grates into dozens of thin slices. His son was dead.

The tunnel ceiling had been falling apart ever since Chug had arrived, and now the four escapees flew through the debris as new rocks fell from above. Side walls buckled and gave way as they whipped past, just in time. They raced over fallen rocks, around fallen boulders, and beneath sagging wooden beams that still remained standing under the increased stress.

Thunderous cave-ins rocked the tunnel as well as the giant sheets of rock that leaned up against the mountainside. Thin sheets of rock began to break away and fall through the open chasms. The wooden beams spanning the chasms were quickly crushed and knocked down before some of the large tunnel holes began to fill up with rocks, blocking their exit.

Flying out of the mountain tunnel, beyond the first chasm, the passageway immediately became blocked. It was the same location where Thorik nearly saw his own death when he slipped on the ice and fell into the chasm. However, this time he had a friend with wings.

Shooting out of the side of the giant sheets of rock, Chug carried Avanda and Thorik while following his friend Pheosco. Banking up and to the south, they flew a short distance before lowering and then landing in a small opening within the woods, free of danger.

Landing hard, as usual for Chug, Avanda and Thorik were nearly flipped off his back. Hanging on until he had stopped, the two Nums dismounted with ease.

"Avanda! It's you! I didn't know if the Govi Glade sphere dropped you in the same time and place. Then Ambrosius started to prevent my birth, which I thought was working seeing that Bakalor didn't recognize me, and yet Chug, Pheosco, and you still do, so maybe his powers failed." Taking a deep breath from the long-winded sentence, he sighed at the sight of her. "I'm just so glad to see you!" Thorik emotionally stepped closer to give her a hug.

Avanda backed up and tightened her lips. Her stance was rigid and she meant to take care of business. "What did you do with Vesik?"

"Vesik? Who cares about that book? You survived! We survived the Govi Glade and now we can find the others and go back to where we belong."

Stepping forward, she grabbed him by the shirt with both hands and pushed him up against the side of Chug. "We wouldn't be in this mess if you hadn't taken Vesik in the first place. She's not yours to take. She's mine!"

Pheosco scowled down at Thorik, while perched on the brown dragon's back.

Chug's ears and nose lowered in an attempt to avoid being involved in any confrontation.

Thorik made no attempt to free himself or fight back. "It wasn't yours. It belongs to the Death Witch, Irluk, who you have started resembling the more time you spent with that book." He tried to calm the emotions by speaking in an even tone.

She pushed harder against him, driving her fists into his collar bone and his back against Chug. "She's mine until Irluk comes and tries to take her away from me. I refuse to let the likes of you steal Vesik from me. So, where is she, Thorik? Where's my book?"

"It's gone! I must have dropped it when we all got pushed into the Govi Glade spheres. It's now back where we found it. Lost forever, never to cause anyone any more harm."

Shoving him one last time, she released him and threw her hands up in the air. "Are you insane? Vesik is a critical part of who we are. We can't go on without her."

Thorik straightened his shirt and leaned forward, off of Chug. "Why do you say that? Vesik was needed to help bring Granna back. We should have returned it immediately afterward."

"She was one of us. She was family."

"*She* was a book! An object!"

"Don't say that! I need her."

"For what purpose, Avanda? What did Vesik give you that we can't?"

"She protected me. I'm always safe with her at my side."

"We protect you. As family and friends we always protect each other."

"No you didn't! Not always. Not against the vile touch of those I wish not to think of. Not against men who would try to rape me. No, Thorik, you were not always there for me when I needed you, nor was anyone else. I was there by myself; helpless and defenseless."

"Is that what this is all about? When Lucian tried to rape you?"

"No. This is about not allowing *anyone* to ever have control over me again. This is about ensuring that I can handle any threat that comes my way by myself. This is about me finally achieving the security I need and then you ripping it out of my hands."

"I did nothing of the kind. You were becoming addicted to Vesik. You couldn't function without it."

"I could leave her whenever I wanted...but why would I? She gave me what I wanted, unlike you."

"What she was giving you wasn't real. It wasn't love. It was power."

"Well, maybe love hasn't protected me in the past, whereas power has. Love is weak and frail. You proved that to me when Emilen came back in our lives. Your so-called love floundered and wavered. You became distant and indecisive."

Thorik's head drooped at the mention of his old love interest. "True, I acted differently when she was around but I was also trying to be careful to see if she was a spy for Darkmere. But my love never drifted from you. If anything it grew the longer I couldn't express it."

"Vesik was always clear. No games were played. When I opened those pages, power pulsed through my body. I was confident and untouchable. I can't get that from you."

Thorik paused and let her words absorb before speaking. "You're correct. I can't give you that euphoria of confidence. Bad things are going to happen to us and I can only do the best I can." He stared into her bloodshot eyes for a moment. "I can't compete with your need for power and security. I can only offer you my love." He finished his statement with an open hand, palm up, with a blue crystal resting in the center.

Avanda peered at the crystal for only a moment. "How dare you try to play that childish game on me? That crystal meant something special between us once. You can't just display it every time you do something wrong and want to make everything alright. It just doesn't work that way, Thorik."

Turning toward the forest, Avanda gave one last command. "Come, Ralph!"

"Pheosco," the green dragon corrected. The name Ralph was a nickname Avanda had called all of her prior animal companions. However, he was not an animal. Dragons lived in civil societies with languages to communicate with higher life forms such as other Del'Unday. And Pheosco was not just any Del'Unday species. He believed he was the highest species of them all, a dragon; a lineage that dated back to the original lord of the dragons, Rummon, who was created by the ancient Notarians to rule the skies.

Launching off the back of Chug and into the air, Pheosco flew past Avanda to scout ahead. He knew his dislike of the name was shallow seeing that she trusted him with her life and the name simply gave her comfort from past confidants. It was worth overlooking.

Disappointed with the way the reunion unfolded, Thorik didn't know how to resolve it and make it better. She was more than his best friend. He loved her. "Where are you going?" he asked her as she entered the forest.

"Govi Glade," Avanda replied. "You may not want to be around me once I find Vesik."

Nodding to the large four-legged brown dragon to follow, Thorik shadowed her footsteps at a safe distance but never more than a dozen yards. "Have you heard from Grewen, or Brimmelle, or my Granna? Did they make it through the same Govi Glade sphere? Are they here as well?"

He received no reply. In fact, she avoided interacting with him the entire hike. On one hand Thorik was emotionally concerned about her feelings toward him and on the other hand he was so thankful to be free of the attacks from Ambrosius and Lord Bredgin, as well as Bakalor and the Krupes. It had been a very stressful night and morning. A quiet walk through the woods with his friend, Chug, was actually kind of nice. Perhaps Avanda's silent treatment was a blessing in disguise.

Chapter 5
Searching Through Time

Thorik's Log:
*Avanda and I have returned to Govi Glade where we originally
found Vesik, in order to once again attempt to find it. In some ways I
hope we never find it again. And yet, I can't stand seeing Avanda in
pain and hating me for taking it from her. I'm torn as to what the
right decision is for our future.*

Flames crackled in the night air from the fresh campfire. The
valley was much warmer than the mountainside but still had a
wet chill in the air. Slightly moist wood snapped under the heat as
small glowing bark fragments lifted into the air and sailed off into the
Govi Glade. These glimmering splinters of bark eventually fell into
casually drifting transparent spheres or floated past Avanda and burn
out while she searched for her book of magic in the tall grass.

Only a few yards into the forest from the glade, Thorik tended
to the fire. Dissatisfied, he felt the pile of dead branches and limbs
wasn't properly stacked, preventing enough ventilation to keep the
fire burning. Poking and prodding with a long stick, he was visibly
frustrated about more than just the poorly stacked fire wood. "I wish
Avanda had allowed me to place them properly before you started
the fire."

In a nearby tree, Pheosco slowly coiled his long leathery neck
down toward the Num and spoke in a scolding tone. "The day I ask
permission from you to start a fire is the day Lord Rummon bows to
your command."

"No reason to be coarse. I'm just saying that we should work
together instead of against each other. You know, let's help each
other out. We're in this together."

Adjusting his back legs on the limb he perched on, Pheosco
called to the other dragon. "Chug, look at me for a moment."

The large brown dragon had just dropped off another load of dead wood he had found on the nearby forest floor. Swiveling around toward Pheosco, Chug's thick and mighty tail swung quickly with excitement upon hearing his name, knocking Thorik several lengths from where he had been standing.

Thorik rolled to a stop at the edge of the glade. Looking up past the campfire and over Chug, he glared at Pheosco, knowing the little dragon had called Chug's name on purpose to cause the big dragon to knock him over. Sitting up, he shook his head at the green dragon's games.

Grabbing a claw full of leaves, Pheosco lit them on fire with his breath and then crunched up the ashes into dust. "Want to help Thorik out, Chug?"

Smiling from scaly brown ear to scaly brown ear, the oversized four-legged dragon wagged his tail back and forth through the fire without even noticing.

"Yes, I do as well," the small green dragon said with a snarl. Blowing through his claw fist, Pheosco blew the ashes into Chug's face.

Inhaling all of the ash, out of sheer excitement to be a part of something, the ashes tickled the inside of his long snout. It was only a matter of seconds before Chug let out a powerful sneeze. So intense was this sneeze that it caused him to blow wind out his backside as well. This would have gone without much notice if his tail hadn't been pointed directly over the campfire.

A flame shot across the glade, lighting up the sky as though a falling star had crashed into the glade without making any impact crater. The rising firestorm spun up above the trees and dissipated into the night air. Darkness returned.

A few moments went by before Thorik lifted himself from the now scorched grass. His hair was smoldering from the little bit of the blast that came his way and his face and clothes had a singed ash coating to them. Wiping his eyes, he saw before him a raging campfire, ready to withstand any ventilation issues.

"You were correct, Thorik. It does feel good to work together." Pheosco patted Chug on the head for his unwittingly good job. "There's no reason to thank me for the campfire."

"Thank you?" Thorik began to argue.

"You're welcome." The green dragon grinned before the Num could continue.

Grabbing a cloth, Thorik began cleaning himself up while complaining about the dangerous game that had been played. Eventually his grumbling died off as he sat back at the warm fire and looked out into the Govi Glade. "She's walked this glade all day and now into evening, past dusk. How much longer is she going to be out there?"

"Until she finds Vesik…or decides to return to camp and take her frustrations out on you." Keeping a trained eye on Avanda, Pheosco continued. "Any idea as to which one I'm hoping for?"

"Oh, I don't know. Let me see. I would say 'return to camp'. Am I right?" His reply was thick with sarcasm.

"Surely not. What do you take me for?" Pheosco said with disappointment in his voice. "I'm hoping she finds Vesik…then returns and takes her frustration out on you."

Frustrated, Thorik snapped up to his feet and turned toward the little dragon. "What issue do you have with me?"

A sharp look, down from the tree branch, made it clear that he was no longer joking. "My issue with you, my dear Num, is that you broke Avanda's heart and then thieved the only thing that made her feel whole."

Thorik's eyes widened at the allegations. "It's not like that!"

"It *is* like that, whether you meant it to be or not."

"That was not my intent."

"Oh, well, that fixes everything."

"I know it doesn't, but it's still the truth."

"She could care less if it is or not, it still crushed her. And anyone that hurts her is an enemy of mine."

The words bothered Thorik. "I am not your enemy, Pheosco. I am not anyone's enemy. I'm just trying to do the best that I can in this life to help as many others as I can. Is that so wrong?"

Leaning his long thin neck down toward the Num, he tilted his head back and forth as though he was examining the Num's face for sincerity. "What gives you the right to determine what's best for Avanda?"

Thorik didn't have to think twice about his answer. Standing up firm he looked the green dragon in the eye. "Because I love her.

And when I see anything that could hurt her, then I am going to try to save her from it. Even if she desires it...and even if she doesn't see the danger within it."

"Even if it drives her away from you?"

His shoulders fell slightly before answering. "Yes, even if it means I lose her forever."

Crackling of the campfire filled the air as the two stared at each other, sizing each other up. It was soon interrupted by a voice that did not belong to either of them.

"How did you increase them last time?"

Both Thorik and Pheosco's head snapped toward the glade. Exhausted after walking all day and evening, Avanda stood there with slumped over shoulders and fatigue showing in her face. With feet planted firm, they had no idea how long she had been standing there.

"Increase what?" Thorik asked.

"The spheres. I've walked every step of this glade and from every angle. Vesik's not here. So, if she's not here now, then she's in another time. We need more spheres to reveal the glade's past and future."

"I don't think so. Spheres are dangerous. The fewer the better. Too many and they will surely kill you. They approach without noise or warning. They lift up from under your feet and could rip off a leg or arm before you even see them. If you fall in one, you'll fall into another time or place and most likely will never be able to return. The dangers are too great. We are fortunate that this time is not very active with them."

"Thorik," she said with great strength, pulling back her shoulders and lowering her eyebrows. "Vesik is not here and I'm not leaving without her. The more spheres that pass through this glade, the more likely Vesik will show up. So tell me how you increased their frequency."

Shaking his head, he didn't want to help her find Vesik. "I can't help you."

"You can. You're just choosing not to. I heard what you said as I approached. You said you loved me. If that's true then you would help me find what makes me happy."

"I…" Thorik wanted her happy, but not at the expense of her addiction and slavery to the book's powers. "I do love you, and that is why I cannot help you."

"That doesn't make sense," she said. Controlled anger in her voice was showing signs of weakness. "You're just jealous of my powers. You don't want me to be happy. You want me to be weak and at the mercy of needing your help."

"What? Never!"

"Then help me!"

"If you find it, it will start to take you over again."

"No!" she yelled, but after a thoughtful sigh, her emotions switched to a soft plea. "Not this time. I'll only use her powers when we both agree it makes sense."

"How could we possibly handle such decisions?"

"I'll share her with you." Tears ran past her cheeks and down to her chin.

"What?"

Sniffing, she wiped her face clean. "Yes, we could share. And then we would use her powers together when needed. No one could harm us."

"Absolutely not."

Crying and coughing at the response, she looked up at him with tear-filled eyes. "Thorik, you don't understand. I can't live without her."

"Sure you can. Once you spend some time apart, you'll be back to normal."

"No, you don't understand. She is a part of me and me of her. Without her, I am feeling such great pains inside. They continue to grow worse. I fear I will die without her."

"You won't die. Why would you say such a thing?"

"I… made a pact with her that if I stayed with her I could use her powers. Although, if I ever left she could use my energy…my life. And now that we are separated, I can feel her collecting on this agreement. I don't have much time, Thorik."

Thorik was shocked at the new information. "Please tell me this is not true."

"I'm sorry, but it is."

"I wish you had told me this in the first place."

"I knew how disappointed you would be in me. I didn't want you to think less of me."

He shook his head in protest. "Is there no way to end such a contract?"

Her eyes searched the ground in front of her as though she was reading the pact from the book. "Perhaps. Yes, there is. If we can obtain her, I think I can force the end of the contract."

"Releasing you from this?"

"Yes."

Thorik didn't like the idea of finding Vesik, but he also wanted to end this obsession, once and for all. "We need energy."

"What?"

"The more energy and life in the Govi Glade, the more spheres appear and the more rapid they travel."

"How do we obtain more energy?"

"We spend more time in the glade."

"I just spent hours out there and only witnessed a dozen spheres, all moving at a crawl."

Thorik's eyes squinted as he thought about the puzzle before him. "Perhaps we are too far in the future for them to reach. We may need more energy than normal." Looking around for options, he suddenly got an idea. "I don't know if this is the right type or not, but it's worth a try."

Grabbing a Runestone from his pouch, he eyed it for a few moments as he contemplated his idea. "It gave me quite a jolt when I tried this earlier." Palming the item, he took a deep breath before looking directly into Avanda's eyes. "If I can invoke the spheres and you find Vesik, will you promise me that you will end your contract and let it go?"

She looked him in the eyes and agreed with a nod.

Leaping onto Chug's back, he reached his hand out in order to help her up. "Let's see if we can bring some life to this field."

Climbing up onto Chug, she wrapped her arms around Thorik so she wouldn't fall off.

Capturing the moment, Thorik's body relaxed at the feeling of her holding onto him with her body pressed against his back. It had been so long since he felt her soft touch. He honestly didn't want to move and lose the sensation, but he knew he had better head out.

Taking flight out over the glade, Chug landed near the center. Pheosco had followed and was soon gliding in circles just above them, keeping his own watch for the random floating time portals.

"Chug, keep those wings out and be ready to soar into the air, should a sphere approach us from below."

The brown dragon kept his wings out as he drooled from the smile he normally made whenever anyone called his name.

"Stay here," Thorik instructed Avanda before tossing a leg over and jumping down to the soft glade's grass. Once there, he rested on his knees for stability. The last time he tried activating the Runestone of Endurance he had received an electrical shock that he had not expected. His hope was that he could maintain it because it wouldn't be unexpected.

Placing the stone before him in both hands, he concentrated his thoughts on it. A sudden surge of energy ran up one arm, across his chest and then down his other arm. He firmly held on even though it was intense and painful. Electrical sparks expanded from his body, flooding the ground near him with small discharge impacts.

The grass near him began to grow taller before their very eyes. Small mushrooms and fungi sprang forth and worms and insects raced out of the ground and sped in every direction in a crazed fit.

It was then that the first sphere rose from the ground. Inside of it was water, filled to the top, as though it was deep under an ocean.

A second sphere quickly arrived, this one with a thunderstorm in its own night sky as violent winds blew from within.

The two spheres collided, causing a massive crash. Wind and water sprayed out from the intersection of the spheres, showering Thorik and his friends before the spheres bounced off of each other and went their separate ways.

Swiftly rising afterward was a third and fourth portal, quickly followed by a half dozen more spheres.

Leaping off Chug, Avanda began to race about, looking for Vesik in the giant bubble bath of portals in the glade.

Pheosco dove and twisted around the semi-transparent spheres in his own search for the book. The sooner he found it, the sooner he could get Avanda out of the glade's dangers.

Pulling his wings inward to prevent them from being clipped by the spheres, Chug stayed near Thorik. If in immediate danger, he would scoop up Thorik and head out of the glade.

Thorik struggled to hold onto the Runestone as the pain reached out to every part of his body. He screamed internally, while clutching the stone long enough to stimulate the glade into producing enough spheres without his help. Losing control of his muscles from the electrical jolts surging through his body, he couldn't remove his hands from the Runestone if he had wanted to.

Spheres filled with calm days and nights shared the glade with ones filled with battles, snow storms, and forest fires. Chaos quickly filled the open terrain and the air just above it.

Chug became nervous at the sight and marched his legs in place, waiting for Thorik to give him permission to leave. Pawing at the Num to get his attention, he accidently knocked Thorik over. Electrical sparks snapped at the dragon's body until the Num fell to his side and dropped the Runestone, ending the stone's powers.

Extremely depleted, Thorik used his last bit of energy to grab the Runestone in one fist so as not to lose it. Collapsing from the ordeal, he was defenseless from any approaching dangers in the glade.

Reaching his thick wings out to his sides, Chug grabbed the fallen Num and lifted up into the sky, just above the range of the spheres, before heading to the safe harbor of their camp.

Below them, they could see Pheosco and Avanda frantically searching among the unpredictable glade. Immense waves of energy and sounds sprang from the sphere clashes, lighting up the glade as though a celebration was in play.

The search continued as the danger mounted. Both of them nearly ended up inside spheres of unknown times, many of which would have meant immediate death. Stable ground opened into sinkholes as spheres breached the surface of the ground. Open paths one moment were blocked by trees and brush the next moment. It seemed like an endless maze that constantly changed paths each time a sphere modified the landscape in its path. It appeared hopeless. They couldn't keep up the pace of all the environmental transformations and exhaustion would eventually cause them to make a mistake. However, just as Pheosco had decided it was time to talk her out of the glade before they were killed, he heard her voice filled with excitement.

"I see it!" yelled Avanda. Within a rising sphere was the book, Vesik, cradled within the arms of a large tree's thick branches.

Racing forward, she dodged a few other spheres before reaching the one she was looking for. Once there, she dove into the sphere without thinking twice. Climbing the tree was of no challenge to her as she latched onto the book and turned to leap back out. Unfortunately, the portal was rapidly moving too high for her to return if she didn't act immediately.

Holding Vesik close to her chest, she considered not going back through the portal. She had what she needed. Staying would prevent her from having to argue with Thorik about her keeping it.

Chapter 6
Was It Worth It?

A chaotic scene of bouncing semi-transparent spheres, filled with everything from lightning storms to a magical war, covered the entire Govi Glade. Light of various colors flickered against the slight haze that hung above them. The display could be seen for miles in every direction.

Within one of the spheres was the Num, Avanda, sitting on a tree limb on a hot summer's day. An internal struggle continued within her whether or not she should return or stay within the sphere to start a new life. It was a valid option until she noticed the odd sounds below her.

Her presence in the tree had awoken the apparent owners of the tree trunk and roots. Tens of thousands of red ants swarmed the bottom of the trunk as they moved quickly up toward her in a unified wave.

Climbing as quickly as possible, while holding onto the book, she ascended as far as she could. With the weight of her and Vesik, the top of the tree pitched to one side. It wouldn't be long before it would snap.

More ants flooded out from holes at the base of the tree, frantic to fend off or kill whoever had invaded their home. Coating the trunk and every limb with a living sheet of red, the collective endeavor to capture and eat their enemy would leave no branch unsearched. Those limbs that fell to the ground were immediately swallowed by the ring of red that spanned out as far as the tree's own branches. This species of ants had developed an incredibly sophisticated system to acquire their victims.

There was nowhere to escape or to hide. The wave of ants reached both of the branches she stood upon.

Shifting her weight onto one branch, she kicked the other limb and knocked hundreds off before stepping back on it and doing the same for the other one. This continued as the ants worked their way up to the limbs she held onto for her balance.

Applying the same strategy, she held onto one limb while slapping the other. Back and forth this went at her feet and her hands, but she was losing the battle. More and more were staying on the limb as well as on her boots and then hands.

Reaching the skin on her legs and arms, they began biting. A few bites quickly became a few dozen as the swarm infested over her boots and one of her hands.

The pain from the bites was getting worse and she knew the ants were winning this battle. Leaping out as far as she could and rolling away from the tree was her only hope to survive. The odds of breaking an ankle at that height were very high, but she had to do something. Her only option left was to…

"Jump!" was heard, not far above her head.

Avanda looked up to see Pheosco poking his head through the small remaining opening of the sphere's portal.

Instead, she tossed Vesik to him, knocking him back through the shrinking gateway. Stepping firmly on two ant covered branches, she quickly followed Vesik with her own leap from the tree.

Ants flew through the air, some from the snapping of the tree limbs while others from her own body. Those remaining on her broke off their attack once they no longer had a physical connection to the rest of the colony. Those that flew through the portal with Avanda quickly became disorientated and unaggressive.

Once clear of the portal and back in Thorik's time, Avanda was pleased that she was free from the ant army attack, at least until she realized she was falling from a tree that was no longer there. Tumbling onto the grass and soft moist ground, she only needed a few moments to catch her breath before looking for Vesik.

A few yards away sat Pheosco upon the book. "Avanda, we need to leave here immediately!" he yelled over all the clashing of spheres.

She nodded while running over and grabbing the book before racing around spheres emerging from the ground and those falling back to earth. Weaving back and forth, she followed Pheosco's twisted flight out of the glade and back to the campfire.

Lying next to the fire was Thorik's motionless body, still depleted from what he had endured with the powerful Runestone. Chug stayed next to him, protecting him from the night's cool air with his wing.

Reaching safety, Avanda fell to her knees with Vesik held tight to her chest. She had succeeded in her task and now felt comfort and security.

Pleased that she was safe, Pheosco attempted to engage in conversations with her, but she kept her distance in camp, physically as well as socially. He had helped her obtain what she wished for, but even he was unsure if she should have it. "Chug, my friend, it looks like we're on our own for dinner tonight. Thorik will survive without you for a while, so go see what you can find for the two of us to eat."

Happy to be involved in anything, Chug jumped to his feet and then flew up over the trees in search of food.

After a few hours of reacquainting herself with her lost companion, Avanda eventually cuddled up with Vesik to have her first good sleep in several days.

Meanwhile, the dragons shared a wild boar, Chug's favorite meal, before they settled in for the night. Silence fell upon the camp aside from the rustling of the fire and the clashing of spheres in the glade, which slowed every minute that went by.

Perched back up on the limb, Pheosco kept a watchful eye for danger for hours into the night. "I feel as though we're not alone," he muttered to himself.

Moments passed of tense calmness, only to be interrupted by the arrival of two male voices in the woods, moving closer to the camp.

"Who approaches?" Pheosco asked in a commanding voice. "Announce yourselves, or my enemy you will be."

Avanda snapped awake at the sound of his voice and instinctively grabbed Vesik tight to her chest to protect it. "What's going on?"

Walking out of the woods, a very old man and a middle aged man approached the camp as they argued openly with each other without a care as to who would overhear them. The verbal disagreement between them and their lack of interest in those around the camp was completely unexpected and a very dangerous way to enter a camp in the middle of the night when they were not invited.

"Ambrosius! Ericc!" Avanda shouted to the E'rudites. Her excitement suddenly changed to concern and she quickly hid Vesik under a blanket in case they had come for her book of magic.

Disregarding her, Ambrosius pointed an old shaky finger at Thorik. "There, see, just as I said. He's a predictable creature for sure. I knew he'd return to the glade," he said to his son as they walked directly toward Thorik, ignoring the others. "Only Thorik would create such a dazzling display of lights high in the air above himself while at the same time trying to avoid being found."

"I still do not feel it is safe returning here, father. Evil still lurks about for us, waiting to kill us all at our first mistake. Your fortune at finding the Num could easily be a trap to ensnare us."

"Ambrosius?" Avanda pushed her pack on top of the blanket covering the book. "How is it that you're here?" She received no response from him. "Why are you so old?" she said with disappointment and in a softer tone. Impatient for an answer, she raised her voice. "Do you not hear me?"

"I hear you fine," he replied without much interest. "Keep your tongue silent. Thorik is my interest for now."

Chug leaned his thick neck and head over the top of Thorik in an attempt to prevent the approaching men from touching his friend.

"Easy now, friend. No need for any trouble. We're here to finish what we had started." Using his powers, Ambrosius casually pushed the large brown dragon back away from protecting the Num.

Chug resisted and began to dig his claws into the ground for traction. He was not going to walk away quietly.

"Ambrosius?" Thorik muttered from his exhausted half-conscious state.

"Leave him alone!" Pheosco announced. His small chest pushed forward and his wings widened to make him appear larger and more dangerous.

Ericc sighed. "We don't have time for this."

"I'll take care of the dragons, son. Just keep your eyes open for more formidable intruders." Lowering himself down to one knee he placed a hand and his attention on Thorik while casually pushing the large brown dragon back further into the woods. "Stay calm, Thorik. It will be over soon enough."

Depleted of energy, the Num stared up at the man he once called friend, unaware of what was to happen next. His weak attempts to sit up or raise an arm were quickly prevented by the E'rudite's unseen powers.

Chug growled and churned up the forest floor as he continued to be pushed backward. Roaring in anger, leaves shook off the nearby trees. The brown dragon's sense of loyalty was being tested, and a rare side of him was starting to reveal itself.

"He's making too much noise." Ericc cringed each time a brown dragon let out loud roar or slapped a tree with his tail. "Let me take care of this before it gets out of control. I know a place on the mountain pass that should be far enough away."

"I think not!" Pheosco shouted as he sprang from the tree branch and dove at the younger E'rudite. Claws out and ready to shred a few layers of skin from the man's face, the little green dragon was more dangerous than he looked.

Reaching his target, Pheosco racked both claws down across Ericc's eyes, only to find the man had literally disappeared from existence upon contact. The unexpected vanish disrupted his flight plans, causing him to flail about for a moment. And in that time, Ericc's hand reached around the dragon's neck from behind him.

Before the green dragon reacted, he and Ericc were no longer standing near Ambrosius. Instead, they were near the large brown dragon, who was still in a full battle against the elder E'rudite's powers.

"Chug!" is all Pheosco got out before Ericc touched the brown dragon and all three of them disappeared.

Silence fell over the camp. Ambrosius started preparing Thorik, while Avanda looked on with total confusion as to what her old allies were doing and what they wanted with Thorik.

Appearing out of thin air, Ericc stepped near his father. "There, that should keep them out of our way for a while." He waited for a response, but received none. "You're welcome." A mumble and slight nod from the elderly disheveled man was the best he would get, even though it very well could have had nothing to do with Ericc. "You still haven't explained what this is all about. Why are we risking ourselves out here? What's your plan and strategy this time? You move us around like pieces of a game against your enemies. Perhaps I could help if you would tell me the goal."

"It's finally become clear that Thorik's life has caused or will cause the disruption in time. Therefore the strategy is to prevent Thorik from ever existing in the first place. A very unique solution that is difficult to perform and even harder to prevent." Scratching his chin under his mangy beard, he sighed at the task before him. Yellow campfire light danced across his face as he intensely studied the powerless struggling Num below him. "I'm ready now. It is time to get started. Our task will take some time so keep your eyes open for our enemies."

Ericc searched the woods for immediate danger. "Why so long?"

"My nephew would make easy work of this, for this is one of his trade skills. I took another route in my academics, so it will take much longer to ensure success."

"In that case, we should take him somewhere else to perform this." Ericc scanned the area for intruders. "Are you certain that removing him from history is the resolution?"

Ambrosius repositioned his fingers upon Thorik's head. "I've worked countless years on those equations. I'm telling you that he is the key factor that causes the disturbance and the variance in time we experienced. We must take care of this before it's too late. Now, watch my back. I need to concentrate."

Thorik's attempts to escape were pointless against the E'rudite. It felt as though gravity had tripled and his body was strapped down to the earth. Breathing became his top priority as he struggled to keep his lungs working under the massive pressure.

Avanda gazed at Thorik and then at the two men with disbelief. "Ambrosius, what are saying? Are you talking about killing Thorik?" Her eyes darted from the scruffy man to his son. "Ericc, stop him. Don't let him do this! Thorik saved your life. Now would be the time to return the favor." She may have been upset with Thorik, but she still felt some love for him and wasn't going to allow anyone to hurt him, except for her.

"Quiet! I need to concentrate," the old man grumbled as he prepared to perform the dangerous task. Focused, he didn't take time to look at her when speaking.

Avanda shot her view over to Ericc. "What did you do to my friends?" Standing up with her arms at her hips, she had become agitated at their lack of respect to her. It was obvious that they had no interest in her or what she had to say. "Fine." Picking up the blanket covered book and a stick from the fire to use as a torch, she walked a few steps toward the forest.

"Stay here. I need to know friend from foe in these woods." Ericc's words were instructive and unemotional, providing only a moment of eye contact to ensure she had heard him.

She stopped only for a moment to glare at him. "So do I. Right now I can't tell which stands before me." Turning away, she walked off into the dark.

Once she felt she no longer was under the watchful eyes of Ericc, she removed the blanket and opened the book of magic. "Vesik," she said while softly tracing the page with a gentle finger. "I need your help. We need to stop them from killing Thorik." Energy surged through the spine of the book and across the front and back cover. "I know. Thorik is the one that stole you from me and tried to keep us apart. But he is also the one who brought us together...twice."

The pulsing of energy felt like a heartbeat to her as she waited for an answer. Swirls of light snapped from the edges in a final reply. "Yes, you're right," she said. "He still wants you gone...but...I can't leave him to be killed. I do owe him that. Once we free him, then we can go on our way."

Again, the pulsing continued until eventually a page softy rolled from right to left. It was followed by another, and then several more, until it stopped abruptly at a blank page.

Holding tightly to the book, she stared into the blank page until words and symbols slowly filled the sheet. "I see. Yes. I understand. Thank you, Vesik. I will begin gathering the components at once."

Cries from Thorik echoed across the Govi Glade for several minutes. The intense E'rudite powers were more than he could endure.

Returning to the camp with Vesik in hand, Avanda began reading out the spell while crushing various items in her free hand. She could see Ambrosius leaning over Thorik with a smoky pulsing mist between them. It was causing a distorted view of both of their heads and the space between, as though looking through a shifting liquid prism.

Ericc glanced over at Avanda and then back into the darkness of the night. "Avanda, you need to step away and let Ambrosius finish what he's started." He had never seen Vesik before and knew not of its powers. His father was far too busy to notice the book, giving her the advantage she needed.

Throwing a handful of crushed pinecones, mushrooms, bird feathers, and insects into the fire, she continued her rhythmic chanting. With a bloody hand, from a recent self-inflicted cut, she reached out, allowing the flames to lap between her fingers. The pain was intense as she held firm until the spell took effect. Her other hand shook as she held Vesik open. The stinging grew and blisters formed on her outstretched digits. Soon, a swarm of small creatures materialized from the fire, allowing her to step back from the heat. Blazing hot fiery bodies lifted from the heat like cinders with collective thoughts. More continued to rise from the burning logs, hanging above their heads, waiting for her command.

"Attack!" she shouted, pointing at Ericc.

The fiery embers dove down at the E'rudite with unexpected speed. They were on him and burning his exposed skin before he realized what was happening. His clothes burst into flames as more coated the man.

As quickly as they had attacked, the man vanished from underneath the flames, leaving a swarm waiting for their next victim.

"Now, him." Avanda said with spite in her voice, glaring at Ambrosius. "No one touches me or my family without my permission."

The flying cinders rushed forward at the E'rudite, piercing beneath the exposed skin on his arms and face, causing heat blisters to form and burst.

Attempting to keep his concentration on Thorik was nearly impossible as his skin peeled away from his body from the internal burning.

"Release him, or deal with my powers! No one hurts Thorik as long as I'm around." Avanda announced with pride, watching her spell take its effect on the mighty E'rudite. No longer fearful of anyone, she was once again powerful and dangerous to those who wished harm against her or her friends. "I am no longer the vulnerable little girl you met in Farbank, and I demand your respect, old friend."

Ericc appeared from thin air, directly behind Avanda and grabbed the book of spells out of her hand. Before she realized what was happening, he threw Vesik out into the glade, causing the spell to end and the cinders to fade to ashes.

Avanda erupted with anger at Ericc with both of her fists. However, the moment she reached him, he was no longer there. He had disappeared from that location and had returned just behind her again.

Grabbing and holding her arms tight to her sides, his slight smirk of success faded as he looked past her. "Father, we *must* leave!" he shouted, squinting his eyes in the night to make out a shape approaching from the glade.

Avanda never hesitated in taking the opportunity to escape. Kicking him in the shin, she broke free and bolted out into the glade to save Vesik. Her journey was cut short as a sphere under the ground caused the surface soil to sink in from below her steps. Rolling off to the side, she narrowly saved herself and yet fortunately landed mere feet from Vesik. However, before she could crawl over to it, she noticed the grass around the book was quickly wilting and turning a gray hue. Even the yellow campfire could not add color to the grass. Vesik, on the other hand, was the only thing that maintained its colors. Frozen with fear, Avanda stayed on the ground, motionless.

Lord Bredgin stepped out of the darkness that had been encasing his body and glared down at the book with curiosity. Reaching down, he picked up the object to inspect it. It preserved its colors in spite of the shades of gray that surrounded it.

Filled with fear and anger at the sight of Bredgin holding Vesik, Avanda screamed out at him. "Don't touch her! She's mine!"

A slight glance her way was all that was needed for his powers over darkness to lash out at the female Num, forcing her from her position.

Shocked by the blast of frigid lifeless darkness, she had leaped out of harm's way in time to escape the small section of glade that had been instantly killed with his skills. Temporarily drained of strength, she watched in terror as he held her book. "Don't! Please!"

Confused as to why the book retained its palette of colors, Bredgin focused on Vesik and grasped it tightly, pushing his energy at the resistant book. It took both hands and great focus before darkness finally seeped into the leather cover and then pages within. A dark hole in space eventually encircled the relic, and once this dark void faded away, the book was a series of gray tones. It was now without color and beauty. It was just a leather bound stack of papers.

Pleased with his efforts, he dropped the book near Avanda and walked past her. To be more specific, he headed toward Ambrosius.

"Time to leave!" Ericc shouted, moving into Bredgin's path.

Continuing to kneel on one knee, his father held a hand firmly on Thorik's head. "Hold his darkness at bay," he commanded.

Strong forward steps led Lord Bredgin into camp. All living grass and weeds on the ground before him curled up and died prior to him stepping forward and crunching their remains into dust. The logs within the campfire nearest to him immediately lost their flames, color, and strength as the wood fell to ashes by the time he stepped on them. A trail of darkness followed him, not as smoke or a cloth train, but instead as light struggled to reclaim the path in which he had walked.

Still in the Govi Glade, Avanda picked up the dead gray book and gently held it to her chest. It slowly cracked and crumbled away under the pressure from her arms. Rocking back and forth, she began to cry at her loss.

Ericc grabbed one of the still sturdy logs near the fire and vanished, reappearing behind Bredgin. Swinging the log at the man, the timber immediately decayed and lost its strength prior to the impact, sending dust fragments from the weakened attack.

Lord Bredgin didn't sway from his target. He continued at a steady methodical pace toward Ambrosius. His dark presence encroached upon the elder E'rudite, fading his clothes and skin tone. Nearly on top of him, Bredgin stopped and reached down to grab his victim, who was by now feeling the pain of the darkness that emanated from the man's body.

Ambrosius cringed in pain while keeping his focus on the Num. He refused to stop.

Frustrated with his inability to stop his nemesis, Ericc leaped at Bredgin. His outstretched fingers lost sensation as they penetrated the darkness before his palms slapped upon his shoulders. Upon touching him the two disappeared, only to reappear again a few thousand feet up in the air. The moment of contact ended quickly and Ericc vanished again, leaving Bredgin to fall by himself.

Materialized back in camp again, Ericc was in great pain. The momentary touch of Bredgin and his darkness had severely injured the E'rudite. Rolling up into a ball, he screamed from the pain within his arms and hands.

Breaking his concentration, Ambrosius looked over to his son and then up to the darkness that was falling from the sky directly toward him. There was no time to think. Ambrosius reached up with both hands to push with all his powers against the falling man. To even his surprise, what should have been an easy task of batting him away, took everything he had just to slow Bredgin's descent.

Falling to earth, the darkness around him appeared to absorb most of Ambrosius' forceful energy. There was no flailing about in terror as one would normally do when dropped unexpectedly from a half a mile up in the air. Instead, his body was controlled, his face was concentrated on his victim, and his own mysterious powers were using Ambrosius' own powers against him by slowing his return to earth and preventing a deadly crash into the ground.

Focused upward, the elder man was too late in realizing the return to camp of two dragons. The first was a small green one who immediately landed near Avanda, while the large brown dragon rushed in and grabbed Thorik and his backpack. In doing so, his tail accidently knocked over Ambrosius, releasing his powers upward.

The wind had been knocked out of Ambrosius, but not his will to survive. Above him, Bredgin fell fast and hard while expanding a net of darkness to capture him. Thorik had escaped and could be seen dangling from a front claw of Chug as they flew over the Govi Glade with Avanda riding on top. Ericc was still screaming in pain from his momentary touch of the dark E'rudite. "Best to flee and fight another day," the old man spat out.

Ambrosius refocused his powers, causing Ericc's fetal positioned body to rapidly slide across the camp over to him. "Get us out of here." And with that, the two vanished from sight.

Chapter 7
Back on the Ledge

Returning to the mountains, Chug attempted to set his cargo down gently. However, while focusing on Avanda, he bumped a wing along the mountainside and dropped Thorik a few feet to the moss-covered terrain with a thud.

Landing near them, he covered Thorik to protect him, as drool spilled from his panting mouth and onto Thorik's neck.

Clutching his head, Thorik eventually woke up and felt the pounding from the inside his skull. The headache throbbed and his body parts objected to his mistreatment with twinges and muscle cramps. Even his vision was blurred as he started to realize that they were no longer in the glade, nor was it night. In fact, the surroundings looked very familiar, for he was waking up in the same place he did the prior day. The only difference was that Avanda and Pheosco were now with them.

Avanda was still in tears as she rocked back and forth with the remains of Vesik against her chest and her arms wrapped around it. Now only shades of gray, she found that the pages inside were empty, void of spells and magic. The cover corners had turned to powder and dissolved away, the paper had become brittle and would snap off if not handled just right. Dry as a bone, it was inert and nothing more than an empty lifeless book. Vesik was dead.

"Avanda?" Thorik recognized the difference in the book's texture and color. "Did you have to kill the book to free yourself from the contract?"

She didn't respond.

With slits for eyes and exposing his teeth, Pheosco glared at Thorik. The green dragon sat with her, protecting her, providing her with the time she needed to grieve over her loss.

Gathering his senses and staying clear of the small dragon, he finally fully sat up and wiped Chug's saliva off his neck. "Thanks, Chug."

Happy to hear his name, the brown dragon slapped his thick tongue across Thorik's head, causing half of his head of hair to point straight up in the air.

"That's enough," Thorik responded, pulling himself up to his feet while using Chug's snout for support. Peering down the mountainside he searched for clues. "What's our next step?" he asked the brown dragon, knowing he couldn't respond.

"Onward, to your destiny," answered a voice directly behind him.

Startled, Thorik snapped his head around to see who it was, his legs nearly buckled and his brain felt as though it had continued to spin inside his skull from the sudden turn. In spite of the unexpected imbalance, he was happy to see his grandmother perched on Chug's back. "Granna? I can't believe it! You have no idea how thankful I am that you survived the Govi Glade sphere."

Not much larger than Pheosco, the orange and red bird swiveled each of her oversized eyes in different directions. "You made it through. Why wouldn't I?"

"I had no idea of who all did, and even if they landed in the same time that I had." Tears of joy pooled in his eyes as he rushed over to hug her. "I thought I had lost you, Granna! Where have you been?"

"Waiting for you to join us," Gluic replied while her grandson finished the emotional hug. "You certainly took your sweet time."

"I'm sorry, but I didn't know where to meet you."

"Well, of course you didn't, dear. That's why I told Chug to bring you here. Of course the first time he dropped you off you didn't stay put, did you?"

With his tongue hanging off to the side of his mouth, Chug nodded his head with pleasure, knowing he had carried her instructions out correctly twice.

"He's a bit sharper than you have been as of late," she said with a laugh. "Come now. It's time to become the person you were meant to be. I've been waiting a long time for this."

Rolling up his sleeve, he showed Gluic the newly formed soul-markings that had finally graced his skin during the battle of Doven. A few dark skinned lines ran up his wrist to his elbow. "Look, Granna! I've already grown. I've matured. I made it."

"Made it?" Bright orange feathers raised up on the top of her head. "A seed can pop its head out of the earth, but it is not yet a tree."

"But...I finally received my markings. I thought you'd be proud."

"Proud? Why would I be proud of how you look? That never meant anything to me."

"I know, Granna." His eyes lowered slightly from his prior excitement. "It's what's inside that counts."

"No, wrong again, my grandson. What value is having good thoughts and good intentions inside if you never act upon them? It's what you do that counts. Your actions are what defines you."

Thorik reflected on the statement and smiled. "You're amazing, Granna."

"Yes, dear, I am." Her beak lifted and turned back into the valley. "Speaking of amazing, did you see those lights out over the forest and glade earlier? Now those were incredible." Her eyes rolled independently in opposite directions as she talked.

"Actually, we received a pretty close view of them. A little too close, if you ask me."

"Good. For a moment there I thought I was seeing things, especially after eating those luminescent vomit-tasting slug bugs."

"Yuck! That sounds awful."

"You weren't there, dear. It was either them or me."

Laughing at the thought, he glanced back out over the valley. "Do you have any idea whether Grewen and Brimmelle made it here?"

She nodded yes, scrambling her eyes as she did so.

Thorik waited for her to continue with more information until he eventually gave up and asked. "Do you know where they are?"

She nodded again.

"Can you take us to them?" he asked, this time without hesitation.

Her eyes finally came together and focused upon him. "You sure take forever to get the right question."

"Yes, I know. I'm trying to get better at that."

"Follow me!" Gluic leaped into the air and then stretched out her wings before falling down onto a lower mountain shelf. "Stretch wings and *then* leap," she scolded herself.

Reversing the sequence she became airborne before swaying to one side and then the other as though she was fighting wind gusts of a hurricane.

Feeling nothing more than a slight breeze, Thorik waited for her to stabilize and gain her bearing before finally leaping up onto the back of Chug to follow. Once on, he reached out a hand to Avanda. "We must go now."

Pheosco growled at the extended hand and could have easily snapped a few fingers off of it, but instead he gave the needed warning before turning to Avanda. "We can't stay on the side of this mountain. We need to seek shelter. Once there, you can have your peace. I promise."

A silence followed before Avanda finally nodded with closed eyes. "Thank you, Ralph."

"Pheosco," he mumbled under his breath to correct her. Helping her to her feet, reluctantly placing her hand in Thorik's so he could help her up onto the brown dragon.

Once she was securely seated, Chug lifted off to follow Gluic who was still weaving a serpentine flight pattern back and forth along the side of the mountain.

After several minutes, Gluic's path straightened out. Heading directly toward a small cave, she focused in on the spot and eventually flew right into it, disappearing from view.

The cavern entrance was only about half the height of Thorik, so there was no way Chug's monstrous size would fit in more than a single leg. Knowing this, the brown dragon landed near the hole in order for Thorik to investigate.

Leaping off his back and onto the slippery wet moss-covered mountainside, Thorik poked his head into the cave. "Granna? Is this the only way to find Grewen and Brimmelle?"

Not hearing any reply, he got on his hands and knees to climb in and ask the question louder. "Granna?"

"Who's there?" she asked back from the dark.

"Granna, it's me, Thorik."

"What are you doing here?"

"I'm following you."

"Why?"

"Why?" he asked about the odd question.

"That's what I asked," she replied.

"Because you were going to lead us to Grewen and Brimmelle."

"I already did that."

Thorik paused, wondering what he was missing. "You did? When?"

"On my way here."

"Granna, we followed you directly here from when we left. You never stopped anywhere along the way to show us where they are."

"No, I didn't stop. I signaled to you as I flew over it."

"You did?"

"Yes."

Thorik taxed his brain trying to recall any such sign. "How did you signal us?"

"I couldn't have made it any more clear. I began flying erratically and spun my eyes around all crazy."

"Yes. Well, I don't know how we missed it." He gave off a slight uncontrollable chuckle. Is there any chance you could show us again?"

"No."

Taken aback, Thorik was so surprised by the answer that he sat up, bumping his head on the small cave's ceiling. "Why not?"

"Because I'm not decent."

Laughing at the thought, he gathered his self-control before responding. "Granna, you're a bird. How can you be indecent?"

"I'm sorry, Thorik, but you're going to have to leave." Her voice was clearly serious.

"I'm sorry. I meant no offense," Thorik responded quickly.

"None, taken, dear. Granna has a friend over and needs a little grown-up time. So, you need to go play outside."

For a second time, Thorik's head cracked against the ceiling. "But-"

She quickly interrupted him. "On your way," she ordered before giggling and softly whispering, "You're so wicked."

Thorik groaned at the thought and started backing out of the cave. Once back out, he looked up at Avanda and Pheosco sitting on Chug's back.

It was obvious that Pheosco was impatiently waiting for an update.

"She was...um..." He struggled to figure out what to say. "Granna said she flew right over the entrance we need to take. This one is just for her."

Climbing back up onto Chug, they retraced Gluic's weaving flight pattern instead of the more direct and straight one they had taken. It wasn't long before they noticed a large cavern entrance flanking the forest border that would have been undetectable from most angles.

Trails of wagon wheels and footsteps from multiple species ended at the hard, cold, and wet surfaces that proceeded up into the long winding tunnel. An empty guard station protected the entrance, but appeared to be recently abandoned. Barrels and crates of fresh food and supplies were stacked neatly in place near an open set of gates.

Landing at the mouth of the cave, Thorik dismounted and inspected the wagon wheels impressions in the dirt path leading from the woods. "I think we've found them." For the first time, in a long time, he felt as though he was going to have his family pod back together. The safety and comfort of the thought gave him a rush of adrenaline throughout his body.

In a way, it felt like he was returning home. At least it did until he also noticed the tracks of Krupes. He had dealt with these Del'Unday before.

Waving at Chug to follow him, Thorik cautiously entered the cavern.

Chapter 8
No Color in Dolor

Water dripped down the walls, collected on the stone surfaces, and slowly wandered down the center of the large cavern until it ran outside and into the forest. Skulls hung upside-down from the walls, filled with oils that fueled the bone lantern's wicks. Cool damp air blew down and out of the dark mountain hole with the periodic skull lanterns being the only light source.

Thorik led Avanda and the dragons up the incline of the smooth cave as the path swayed to one side and then the other while they advanced into the heart of the mountain which was in the form of a city. Not a heart of a beating, living, thriving thing, but a cold creatively-vacant environment. The city of Dolor stood before them.

Enormous spires of sharp limestone rock shards reached up from the stone floor throughout the city which rested at the base of a hole in the mountain. The entire area had been carved out by the glacier that still loomed around the city's stone borders, high above.

Built along every vertical stone wall that could be found, thousands of gray wooden structures were stacked upon one another as they lined the uneven stone city streets. Flumes of steam billowed up from cracks in the street causing pockets of heat where citizens would gather to warm their exposed hands and faces.

A mile-high glacier had once filled the area. Melting from the heat being release along the streets, it was now a gaping hole in the mountain with shark teeth shaped rocks rising into the air, pointing at the skies above. Water dripped down the sheer rock walls as a reminder of the glacier that still surrounded the city's upper rim of peaks.

This vertical hole in the mountain was now the home to a city filled with creatures of every Ov'Unday species Thorik had ever seen as well as some new ones. However, most were humans and Polenums.

Stepping out of the tunnel and into the city, they passed between two turrets built into the city's wall before entering a large busy market place selling meats, fruits, vegetables, cookware, lanterns, clothes, and many raw materials for home needs. The grand open area had one major street leading straight into the center of the city and several small streets leading in multiple directions.

Structures were built for function and no obvious cultural or religious influences appeared to be added. Most were two stories with small windows and just about every roof and windowpane had a layer of dark brown dust on it. At the base of most buildings, trash and waste had built up in small piles along the sides of the streets.

The market area was filled with locals slowly going about their mundane activities. Each and every one of them wore dirty brownish-gray clothes which blended in with the stone streets and buildings. Only a few of them gave Thorik and his crew a second look. It almost felt as if they were invisible until eventually one Polenum, covered with an ankle-length thick leather coat, came limping forward.

"Gansler is the name! What might yours be?" shouted the male Num, flailing his wooden cane in the air with excitement as he approached. Soul-markings painted whimsical dark skin lines around his wrists and neck. He also had a set of markings across his forehead that was lost in his hairline just above his ears on both sides. His red hair curled up and about in a chaotic mess upon his head and lined his chin with a patchwork of clumps amid his beard.

"I am Thorik Dain of Farbank, and this is Avanda, Pheosco, and Chug."

"Excellent! Welcome to my city!" His arms pointed and gestured to various parts of the city. After each motion he stopped and nodded with pride with an awkward moment of silence. "Isn't it wonderful?"

Thorik glanced at a few of the locations he had pointed. All buildings were shades of gray and brown. As with the structures, clothes and decorations were also designed more for function than for beauty or any type of artistic value. Simply put, the city lacked any kind of color or vitality.

Always enjoying the unique music of each new culture Thorik entered, for the first time in his travels there was none. "Your city is very nice. Exactly what city is this?"

"Mine."

"Okay. So this is Ganslerville or something?" Thorik chuckled at his own joke.

"Ganslerville? Excellent choice. We'll call it that."

Thorik glanced over at Pheosco to see if he was hearing the same thing. Once he saw the green dragon's head shake, he realized his Num ears were working just fine. "What is it that you do here, Gansler?"

"Well, here in *Ganslerville*," he nodded to Thorik for the use of the name. "I run this city. These are my citizens."

"So, you're something such as the Sovereign?"

Gansler smiled from ear to ear. "I like the sounds of that. Yes, that is correct. I am the Sovereign of this great society." He stood up tall and confident. "I am Sovereign Gansler. It is a pleasure to meet you Forik of Tharbank."

"No, it's Thorik of Farbank."

"Of course it is." With a smile, he tapped the side of his nose before looking about to see who else had heard. "I'll play along with your little charade."

Before Thorik could respond, two of the many local citizens stopped near them. Both were male. However, one was a human and the other was a Polenum who was a head shorter than the first.

"Hello, Gansler," the man said in a dry tied tone. As with most humans, they stood about a head taller than the Polenums.

"Kuta, don't you mean Sovereign Gansler?" Gansler corrected.

He sighed before responding. "Oh course, Sovereign. My apologies. We need your services at our home."

"Absolutely. I'll come by once I help these travelers settle into our city."

Kuta turned to greet them in an emotionless tone. "Welcome."

"This is Korith of Barfank," Gansler said with a touch to the side of his nose again while smiling at Thorik.

"It's a pleasure," Thorik responded.

"We're always in need of additional labor. We could use your help." Kuta said before turning back to Gansler. "Don't arrive too late."

"Understood." Gansler nodded and winked at the man before turning to the Num who had arrived with Kuta. "I've heard from your wife that your family is need of my services as well, Ren."

The second citizen piped up. "Within the next few days. I don't need the wife any more troubled than normal, so please do not speak to her about it beforehand."

Gansler made an oversized wink, which didn't provide any level of discreetness that the Num was looking for.

Thorik watched Kuta and Ren lower their heads and quickly blend back into the crowd, washing away from his view before asking the obvious question. "You need *our* help?"

"I do?" Gansler asked. "For what?"

"Kuta said, 'we could use your help.'"

Looking up and searching his memory, Gansler shook his head. "I don't recall that. Then again, I talk to so many people about so many things that it's hard to keep track."

"But it *just* happened."

"What did?" Gansler whipped his head back and forth to search for something that had just happened.

Wiping his face with his hands, Thorik tried to shake the entire conversation from his thoughts and start anew. "We are in search of some friends. Can you help us find them?"

"I can introduce you to many. Only time will tell if you'll become friends with some of them."

"No, no. These are old friends of ours that we want to reunite with. We believe they are here in your city."

"Really?" Stretching his neck, Gansler looked about for them. "I don't see them."

"You don't even know what they look like."

"Well, that will make it more difficult, won't it?"

"Yes. Yes it will." Thorik's voice was louder and his words sharp.

Gansler thought deeply for a moment. "Who do you think could help us find them?"

"What? I haven't even talked to anyone that lives here other than you and Kuta."

"Kuta? What makes you think he knows where your friends are?

"I have no idea if he would know."

"Then why did you bring up his name out of the thousands of residents that live here?" Gansler glared at Thorik, questioning his reasons for this.

"He's the only one I've met except for you. And I thought you might know something about what's going on here in this city."

Still eyeing the Num, he tilted his head. "And why would you think that I would know this?"

"Because you're the sovereign of this city."

Taking a moment to process the statement, he erupted with excitement. "I *am* the sovereign. Sovereign Gansler," he said with a smile before turning and shaking a hand of a citizen walking along the street. "Sovereign Gansler," he announced again to another. Turning, he shook three more hands while proudly announcing his name before he spun back to the travelers. "How do like my city?"

"To be honest, I'm not very fond of it so far."

Gansler looking genuinely surprised. "Why? It's clean. Most of the trash is picked up."

"True, but I'm looking for my friends and I'm not getting any assistance."

"Oh, I'm sorry to hear that. Perhaps I can help you."

Thorik took in a heavy sigh. "I'm not feeling that's possible."

"Sure it is. I'm in charge of scheduling the work details. If your friends are here, they will be working. Everyone pitches in and works."

"I thought you were the leader of this city."

"I have a lot of responsibilities here." Gansler glanced over at some trash along the side of the street. Picking it up, he held it up to show the Num. "We all have to pitch in. No titles and casting of duties here. We're all equal."

Frazzled by the entire conversation, Thorik suddenly saw a glimmer of hope in Gansler. "So where do we start?"

Glancing around for a place to dispose of the trash, he answered with his own question. "Start what?"

Thorik's face tightened. "Where do we start in order to find our friends?"

"Oh, that. I thought you meant where do we start cleaning the trash. You can really start anywhere you want, but I think we have workers that already do that," he said as he tossed the trash back down on the street and dusted his hands off on his shirt. "Follow me." He then turned and started walking away.

"Where are we headed?"

Not missing a beat, he slowly walked away. "You're a forgetful little guy, aren't you? We're going to look at the work logs to see if they are on it."

Sighing, Thorik nodded to his group to follow Gansler.

"I think not," Pheosco replied. "We're not going to follow some lunatic around the city."

"Pheosco!" Thorik scolded, with eyebrows crunching together above the bridge of his nose. "Don't call Gansler names. He's trying to help us!"

Calm and collective, the green dragon grinned out of one side of his mouth, exposing his sharp teeth. "Who said I was talking about him?"

"I just...Why do you always have to...Forget it. Stay here in the market area and see what you can trade for some food. I'm going to see what our new friend has to show us."

Instead of taking the large main street into the center of the city and then turning on the only other large street to the right, Gansler led Thorik through a series of back streets in order to reach their destination faster.

Shaking hands and introducing himself as Sovereign Gansler along their path through the city streets, they finally arrived at the entrance of a large structure carved out of the mountain wall. Three doorways provided access to the structure, each with their own unique characteristics and purpose.

The first set of thick wooded doors were twice the height of most humans. Propped open, a slow moving line of locals entered while another line of exhausted locals left the structure. Those leaving where coated with dirt and soiled clothes. That is not to say that those standing in the line entering were clean by any stretch, just cleaner than those leaving. Beyond the doorway was an open area that housed a large pit where the workers slowly descended a long spiral ramp that clung to the wall of a deep round hole. A second spiral ramp provided a path for the ascending out of the pit and then out of the doorway, back into to the city.

Two massive doors stood nearly ten yards high and just as wide, providing the second entrance to the structure. Firmly closed, there was no way to see what was behind them, however it appeared that these larger doors had a straight shot to the pit's ramps.

Walking past the long line of humans, Polenums, giant Mognins, sloth-like Gathlers, and all the rest of the creatures that paraded into and out of the building, Gansler led Thorik past the giant massive closed doors to the third entrance to the structure. It was a smaller locked door designed for those the size of a human.

Gansler firmly knocked on it and waited. There he rested his bad leg and leaned against his cane while waving at those passing by.

No one waved back.

"What is this place?" Thorik asked.

"It's the entrance to the mine, of course. Well, actually it's the entrance to the mine shaft pit which then leads down to the mine far below us. Where else would the work logs be kept?"

Before Thorik could respond, the door opened and a large Krupe stood in the doorway, filling it from side to side. He had to lower his head to see below the doorway header. The large and husky creature wore the dull black full-body armor and helmet that all Krupes were known for. It served its purpose to protect the Krupes as well to intimidate others.

Thorik's initial reaction was to run. However, instead he stayed calm with heightened awareness of his surroundings.

"Sovereign Gansler here." He pointed at himself with a wiry smile.

Thorik figured that this was the end of the man's hoax and prepared to make a run for it.

Stepping to the side, the Krupe allowed them to enter.

Thorik followed Gansler into the carved out entrance before the Krupe closed the door behind him. As was with the streets, the internal work areas were lined with litter. There was much to be desired for their waste management.

The rooms beyond were etched into the mountain. To one side was the parade of local city residents entering the structure and registering in logs before walking down a spiral path into the huge pit. This was an enormous cavern room that housed several entrances, including the two massive closed doors Thorik has seen from the outside, which were strategically placed nearby for large imports or exports into the pit. Wagons of food could easily be wheeled in and onto a platform that could be lowered down into the pit to feed those working in the catacombs below.

Gansler led the Num past the registration logs and up some steps to an observation post jutting out over the pit.

Looking down over the ledge, Thorik could see faint lights nearly a mile down at the bottom. "What are they mining for?"

"Here, carry this," Gansler said, handing him some trash before picking up some himself. "Lead by example. Everyone should help out."

Passing several more Krupes, the two continued deeper into the carved out building until they entered a large room filled with piles of registration logs from floor to ceiling.

Thorik was spellbound by the endless stacks of logs. "Where do we start?"

Quietly shutting the door behind them, Gansler tossed the trash on the ground and nervously watched the hallway. "I would suggest you find them in the correct log the first time so we don't have to waste time reading through all of them."

"Wow. What a great idea. I wish I had thought of that." The sarcasm in Thorik's voice was thick.

Nodding, the man smiled and pointed at himself. "That's why I'm the sovereign. Sovereign Gansler."

Thorik shook his head and picked up the top log closest to him. "This is crazy."

"Did you find their names?" Gansler asked as he grabbed a log of his own to start going through.

"No. It's crazy to think we're going to find their names in these logs among the thousands that are in this room."

"You know what's even crazier? I think I just found them," Gansler said with excitement in his voice.

"How can you have found them?" Thorik's shoulders fell with defeat. "You don't even know their names."

"Oh." His voice had lost a lot of enthusiasm. "Well, I don't recognize this name so I assumed it was someone new to the city."

Turning the page, Thorik scanned another log. "Are you saying you know everyone by name in the city?"

"I know more of the residents that live here than you do."

"True. I only know Kuta."

"Shoot!" Gansler slammed the log down.

"What's the matter?"

"That's not the name on the log that I thought was your friend."

Thorik shook his head. "That's good. We're not looking for Kuta?"

"Why? I thought you said he was the friend you were looking for."

"No. He's the only one in this city that I've met aside from you. We're looking for the names Grewen and Brimmelle."

"Is that spelled with one or two L's?"

Thorik turned another page of the log. "Does it really matter? Do you have a lot of residents named Brimmelle?"

"No. But this one is spelled with two L's."

"What?" Thorik ran over and looked at the log, finding both of his friends names recorded on one of the pages within the very top log book. "You found it!"

"Of course, it's my job," Gansler said with beaming confidence. "Besides, they always stack the most recent logs over here on this stack."

"That information would have been helpful to know."

"And it was," Gansler said, very pleased with himself.

"So now that we know they are here, how do we find them?"

"We wait."

"Wait for what?"

Gansler pointed to the date and time on the top of the log. "For them to return. They are on duty down below."

"Can't I go down and find them?"

"You can, but by the time you get through the line and reach the bottom they might be on their way back up. You can wait for them at my home until they return. I'll notify the guards to send these two over once they return to the surface."

Opening the door, Gansler tucked the log under his arm and marched down the hall, back to the entryway and over to one of the few humans standing with the Krupes near the registration desk.

Thorik followed close behind and kept quiet, trying to avoid too much attention from the Krupes. They continued to make him very nervous.

Pulling the log book out from under his arm, Gansler opened it and pointed to the names. "Durren, please have these two workers report to me when they return from the mine."

Turning away from his work and toward the two Nums, the man smiled. "Well, if it isn't General Gansler."

"Sovereign Gansler," he corrected the man.

"Well, congratulations on the promotion," Durren said with a sarcastic laugh.

Gansler stood proud of the accomplishment and winked at Thorik.

Durren grabbed the log out of his hand. "What do you need with these two?"

"Forik of Tharbank…" He glanced at Thorik and touched the side of his nose, "…is looking for his friends. These two workers are them."

"We've talked about accessing our logs before, Sovereign. Haven't we?"

"Have we? I don't recall."

"Yes, we have. I should report this, you know."

Gansler shook his head. "No need to bother yourself with that. I'll report it myself later."

"Will you, now?"

"Of course. I'm always willing to do you a favor." Smiling, he nodded for a few moments. "Now, can you just be a good man and send those two my way when they return?"

"You always make me smile," Durren said with a laugh. "Drop by my place within the week and we'll call it even. My children have noticed items missing again."

"I'll be there," Gansler agreed before leaning toward Thorik. "There just isn't enough of me to go around."

"Be there after my shift ends," Durren replied.

"Absolutely. And while I'm here, why don't you let me help you out." Scooping up an armful of trash near the worktables, he led Thorik out of the large carved-out pit area and back into the city before dumping his armload of garbage onto the side of the street. Wiping his hands off on his shirt, once again, he sighed at the sight of the garbage and muttered, "What an eyesore. I really wish people would clean up after themselves."

"General?" Thorik scoffed as he followed him to out of the area, back toward the market area. "So...*you* were a military leader?"

"Oh yes, I was the general of a great army once. Seems like a lifetime ago."

"Really?" Thorik attempted not to sound too skeptical. "And who did you fight?"

"We rose up and fought our repressors; the prior landlords of this fine city; the Overlords who made us work as slaves. We rebelled against them. And because of that, we have the peace and harmony you see here today."

Walking up the crowded streets, he continued to introduce himself to each passersby with a handshake, introducing himself by saying, "Sovereign Gansler."

Thorik attempted several times to ask more about the city but his voice was lost within the crowd. Eventually, he gave up and just followed the man who appeared to be running for some political office.

Returning to the market place, they met back up with Thorik's friends who hadn't had much luck shopping. Nothing they had seemed to hold much value to these citizens. Pheosco was frustrated, Chug was hungry, and Avanda continued to cling onto to her dead book as she wished for it to come back to life.

If there was any chance of anything coming back to life, the odds were even more against it in the drab city of Dolor. Without any vegetation in sight it appeared unnatural for even the residents to exist among the cold stones, steam vents, and endless dripping water from above.

The two Nums and two dragons fell in tow behind Gansler as they continued through the dark brownish gray city. Thorik noticed slight changes in the structures the farther they journeyed from the entrance. They were heading into an older section that had received much less maintenance. Piles of trash sat unattended to, unlike the cleaner section, near the market, where they had entered the city.

Rounding a final corner, the street opened to a large cul-de-sac filled with mounds of oddities along the building walls. Chair legs, broken wooden planters, worn out wagon wheels and the like were stacked higher than a Num could reach. All were wet and decayed with green moss and tan fungi growing on them, while steam migrated up through the piles from cracks in the street. As much of a heap of junk that it was, it was first sign of plant life they had seen inside the city walls. The sporadic splash of color from the moss and fungi was a welcome sight.

The dead-end street supported several home fronts, all of which had the wooden junk piled high against them. These dwellings were obviously abandoned, except for one that had a clear pathway leading to a set of large old wooden doors, which opened upon their arrival to the cul-de-sac.

A female Num stepped out from the doors and into the street. Age had started taking its toll on her once dark red hair and crisp soul-markings that traced her eyes and nose. Her pleasant smile added a comfort to her demeanor that appeared to calm others. "Welcome home, Gansler." She held one hand firmly under her large pregnant stomach. The other hand and arm held a young child, only a few years old, who was straddling her hip.

"Sovereign Gansler," he corrected, sharply striking his cane to the ground and puffing out his chest.

"Ah, I see. How fortunate am I to be married to a Sovereign."

"Very fortunate," he said with pride before relaxing his shoulders and giving the small child a smile. "How was Revi today? On her best behavior like normal?"

Setting her daughter, Revi, down so she could race over to her father, Gansler's wife glanced at the group before her. "Who are your friends?"

"This is Tharbank of Foric and his friends," he said, tapping the side of his nose. "They are new to the city." Catching his daughter on a full run, Gansler tossed her in the air and then caught her in a tight hug.

She nodded at Thorik. "I'm Narra. It's a pleasure to meet you."

"It's actually Thorik of Farbank. And this is Avanda, Pheosco, and Chug."

"Would you like to come and join us for a meal?"

"If it wouldn't be too much trouble. We're famished."

"Please join us," she said, gesturing for them to enter their home. "I'll bring out something for your large friend as well."

Chug lowered himself, allowing Avanda to step off and enter the home with Pheosco. Thorik followed after giving Chug a strong scratch behind the ear and telling him lie down and wait for them.

Narra beamed as she watched her husband play with their daughter in the courtyard, while rearranging a few of his piles of miscellaneous wooden garbage in order to cause the clouds of steam to break apart and travel in different directions prior to rising above and then out of the area.

She then turned, following the other Nums inside.

Chapter 9
Gansler & Narra

Thorik's Log:
We're out of the forest and in a secure city. And yet I don't feel that the safety of this city has provided its residents with the sense of happiness it should have. Gansler is the only happy Num we've met. However, he has more than a few holes dripping from his mug. Surprisingly, his family seems nice.

Soup was made and bread was broken for all to eat as they kept dry and warm by the large open fireplace. It was a meager meal and poverty settings, but Narra had made the most of what they had.

The dark gray walls, ceilings, and floors of their home were not due to poor cleaning. It was more of the materials used and the lack of funds to decorate. Also at play was the absence of creativity and vitality for life. The entire city showed a sever deficiency in color in their gloomy environment, reflective of their attitude toward their lives.

In the main room a thick wooly rug lay before the large open fireplace as two old chairs sat facing the lapping flames. A desk in the corner was covered with notes and diagrams and rolled up documents overflowing onto an old wooden chest. This appeared to be Gansler's area of the house, for it was the only area not neat and tidy.

Doorways to the kitchen, a closet, and a spare room exited the main room, as well as the front door and a staircase up to the second level. Only the fundamentals of living existed in each room. That is not to say that shelves were empty, for cups and plates and needed tools were stacked neatly upon racks and other surfaces. However, no luxuries or art were seen anywhere. This matched the atmosphere of the entire city.

Sadly, no toys were seen either. Not a single doll or ball of string gave any signs of a child living in the home. And yet the house was filled with calm joy and pleasant love from those who lived here.

"I'd like to make a toast to our new friends," Gansler announced as he lifted his old metal goblet in the air. "Welcome to our beautiful city. May you enjoy the virtues we have to offer."

Thorik raised his goblet as well. "Thank you. We truly appreciate you taking us in, and we'll do what we can to help pay for the food and lodging."

Gansler waved his hands and shook his head. "Nonsense. You're our guests. We were once one of the wealthiest families in the city and we have enough stowed away plenty of tokens for hard times. We'll be just fine."

Entering the room with a tray holding several cups of hot liquid, Narra overheard her husband's last comment. "We do not discuss finances at the table, dear." Changing the subject, Narra asked, "Would anyone like some tea? Gansler always enjoys a few sips after his meals." She proceeded to set a cup of hot brown tea in front of Gansler, Thorik, and Avanda.

Slapping his Goblet to the table, he rubbed his hands together with anticipation for the tea. "Cleans the pallet and settles the stomach. Isn't that right, Thorik of Farbank?"

"Thank you, Narra. That is very kind," Thorik replied to Narra, smiling at the fact that Gansler finally said his name correctly. "Avanda, would you like some as well?"

Still in grief about the loss of Vesik, Avanda had eaten very little. Shaking her head, she excused herself from the table and took her remaining soup outside with her. Pheosco accompanied her and perched on the outdoor steps as she walked down to them and emptied her meal into a plate for Chug.

The large brown dragon had already emptied a full helping, but was always happy to receive more.

Sitting down on the steps next to her green dragon, Avanda plopped her head down into her hands.

"Where's your head?" Pheosco asked. "You've changed. You are no longer the spry and adventurous Num I first met."

"I don't know. I'm so conflicted between anger, revenge, sadness, disbelief, and sorrow that I don't know how to react to anything. I'm numb on the outside and dead on the inside."

Pheosco smiled ever so slightly. "You're a numb Num?" His joke received no reaction. "Listen, Avanda, there is a saying we

dragons live by that may help your situation. During the battle of
Er'Que Kalla, Lord Rummon had outlived everything he loved and
became a recluse. He lost the desire to befriend anyone, knowing he
would outlive them and end up watching their death. He became hard
and cold to the virtues of companionship. This continued until one
year, during the dragon's annual celebration of the West Winds,
when Lord Rummon showed up unannounced. Fear struck all that
witnessed it, at least until he searched the eyes within the crowd. He
then said, 'A fulfilled life requires happiness when alone as well as
with others.'"

Avanda glanced over at him. "How does that help?"

"When you feel that pit in your stomach from a loss and you
question if you ever want to open yourself up again, you must seek
inner peace within yourself as well as external peace with others.
You cannot shut out the external when trying to repair the internal.
They both must be in balance for either to be mended."

Avanda thought about his statements while watching Chug
continue to lick the bowl just in case he had missed a droplet of soup.
She wished her life was as simple as it was for the large brown
dragon.

After placing Revi to bed upstairs, Narra returned to the room
with two cups of hot tea, setting one down for Gansler and the other
for Thorik. "So, Thorik, where are you from? Where is this
Farbank?"

"It's a small village along the King's River and surrounded
by the colorful wooded valley walls. There are fish in the river, deer
in the woods, and crops to harvest. Pleasant and calm, Farbank is
peaceful and we are content, like a warm blanket on a cool night."

She smiled at his explanation. "Is it a good place to raise
children?"

"Absolutely. There are children running and playing all the
time. I always enjoyed walking down my path to find several of them
barefoot and fishing from the piers on warm summer days. I even
teach our youth a class on... Well, I used to teach a class."

"On what?"

"On the Runestones. Their names and meanings. You know.
The basics."

Confused, she shook her head.

"On the sacred scrolls and Runestones."

"I have not heard of these. Would you have the time to tell me about them?"

"Of course," he replied before turning to Gansler. "Speaking of wanting some time, what did Kuta want you to do over at his home tonight?"

Narra peered at her husband. "Did you make a promise to Kuta?"

"I um…I don't recall." Gansler looked up in the air in an attempt to remember.

Pulling the cup of tea from his hands, she was visibly upset about his forgetfulness. "If you need to go to take care of business, then you get it taken care of. That family has helped us many times in the past."

"It will be fine," he said with confidence. "We dropped by on the way home and took care of it."

Thorik's head snapped back and forth from Gansler to Narra. "No we didn't. We made no such stop to help anyone on the way home."

Narra placed a kind hand on her husband's knee. "Go on. I'll wait up."

"Yes, dear," he replied with a pout before he excused himself from the table.

Thorik also stood. "I'll go with him."

"That's not possible. It will be dark soon and he won't be back until afterwards." Seeing confusion in his face, she continued. "Not only is it dangerous to be out in the streets after dark, it's also against the law. There is a curfew. Violators may be sentenced to death."

"Then why is Gansler going?"

"He is the only one allowed to travel after dark," she said to Thorik, before giving her husband a hug and looking him square in the face. "Be careful. Be compassionate. And return to me, my love. I will give our guests directions to some lodging."

"Oh…well…Thorik and his friends will be staying with us until I can find other accommodations."

Narra's eyes widen and her face flushed. "I don't think now would be a good time for them to stay with us. There is still enough daylight to make their way to the boardinghouse."

"They won't be in the way. I promise."

"With our son on his way, this house will be in disorder. There will be screaming and mayhem."

Thorik smiled at her extended stomach before looking back up into her face. "I've seen child birth before and know what it's about. In fact, we can help if needed."

Glaring at her husband, she continued. "The crying, the lack of sleep, the constant cleaning up. Thorik and his friends are not from here. They simply don't understand."

Gansler placed a gentle hand on his wife. "Trust me. It will all work out. I have a good feeling about Thorik and his friends. They are here to help us." Kissing her softly, he grabbed a few items from his upstairs bedroom, including a long sword, before heading to the front door.

"A sword?" Thorik was confused at the sight of Gansler with a weapon.

Giving Thorik a wink, he patted the weapon, now sheathed at his side. "I won't be back until long after dark. Stay inside, and I'll see you in the morning." And with that he headed out the front door, past Avanda, Pheosco, and the now sleeping Chug with all four of his legs up in the air.

Only a few moments passed before Avanda and Pheosco stormed into the home. "Did you see what Gansler was carrying? Where is he headed? Is there trouble?"

Upset about her husband's promise to let them stay in their home, Narra pointed to one of the side rooms. "There are blankets in the closet. You're on your own for the night. Do not come upstairs." Grabbing her stomach from a pain or perhaps a kick from the unborn child, she took a few deep breaths before continuing in a rigid tone. "Under no circumstance shall you walk up these steps. Is that understood?" She waited for a nod from Thorik before gathering herself and then walking up the staircase and out of sight.

Chapter 10
The Truth is Hard to Hear

The room went silent after Narra gave strict orders to stay downstairs, prior to retiring for the night on the second floor. Thorik, Avanda, and Pheosco stood quietly, watching the fire lap upward and the occasional spark pop out into the room.

"I like them!" The voice came out of the dark directly behind Thorik, causing the Nums to jump. Pheosco, however, leaped in front of Avanda to protect her from the intruder.

Stopping himself before tripping into the fire, Thorik turned to see Gluic ruffle her feathers as she shook the water off them.

"Granna, you've got to stop sneaking up on us like that," Thorik said with great relief in his voice.

"They seem like such a nice couple." Gluic walked between the Nums and turned around once she was near the fire, spreading her wet wings. "Ah, that feels so good."

"Where have you been? What exactly was going on in that small cave where I last talked to you?"

Gluic leaned forward and spoke softly into his ear. "How much do you really want to know, dear?"

He backed off quickly before he heard something he wouldn't forget.

"I thought as much."

"We found Grewen and Brimmelle," Thorik announced. "They are here, in the city."

"Yes, I know," Gluic responded. "That's why I showed you the entrance to the cave."

Thorik nodded. She was correct.

With eyes glancing in different directions, his grandmother checked out the room. "So, what are your plans once you find them?"

"Plans? Well, we will leave this city and then…"

"How do you plan to leave the city?"

"The same way we came in."

Gluic shook her head. "You'll never make it past all of the Krupes. They prevent anyone from entering or escaping."

"There were no armed guards when we arrived."

"That's because they were chasing my friend Ep into the forest and trying to find him. Never a faster bird will you meet."

"And your friend just happened to attempt an escape right before we happened to show up? Seems like quite a convenient coincidence."

"Surely you don't think they would chase a typical bird out into the woods...unless he stole their keys to the tunnel's gate. It was a little favor I had asked him to do for you."

"I see. Well, we owe him our thanks for his help."

"Trust me, dear, I've thanked him enough for all of you," she said with a wink.

"Eww, Granna. You didn't!"

"I may have been turned into a bird, grandson, but I'm not dead." A sudden shiver rushed through her body, causing all of her feathers to shake. "Then again, I never let death hold me back either."

Attempting to get some self-created pictures out of his thoughts, he asked, "So what will it take to have Ep help us one more time so we can escape?" He then cringed at the thought of her potential answers.

"Oh, poor Ep didn't survive."

Thorik's shoulders fell slightly. "I'm sorry to hear that. The guards caught him and killed him?"

"No, Ep was too strong and cunning for that. He teased them for hours until he was sure they were far enough from the entrance that you had plenty of time to make it in before they got back."

"So what happened to him?"

"Apparently I underestimated my own ability to tease."

"Granna!" Thorik shouted. "I don't want to hear that."

"Then you shouldn't have asked, dear."

Wishing he had never started the conversation, he quickly changed it before it became a permanent memory. "What is up with this city? I can't get a straight answer out of anyone. The only one that has taken us in can't tell us the truth if his life depended on it."

Lowering her feathers tight against her body, she stepped up to her grandson. "It would appear that he's not the only one that lies."

Thorik became defensive. "What? Not us. We have been true to our words."

One of Gluic's eyes rolled about until it stopped toward the female Num. "Look at Avanda, for example. She blames you for her pain."

"What?" she said, slowing coming out of her introverted self-absorbed state. "I have nothing to lie about. Thorik thieved Vesik from me and tossed her into the Govi Glade. Now I have nothing more than a corpse of a book. There is no lie in these words. Her death and my unhappiness is the result of Thorik."

"True," Gluic said in a light tone.

"Granna!" Thorik began to argue but was stopped by a wave of her wing before she addressed Avanda head on. "However, this is your responsibility just as much as it is his."

Shaking her head, she glared at Thorik. "I was happy with Vesik."

"No, dear. You felt safe. There is a difference. Ever since Lucian nearly raped you, you have always felt unsafe and Vesik finally gave this security back to you."

"What's wrong with that?" she argued.

"It is false to think we are ever safe. We are always at risk of being hurt physically or emotionally. That is life. To have Vesik give you that absolute security is a lie and it prevents you from ever having to grow."

"That's not true!" Avanda argued. "I became stronger with Vesik."

"Is that so, dear. Would you roll up your sleeves for me?"

"What? Why?"

"Pacify an old bird's interest, please."

Pulling up her shirt sleeves, it was obvious that her once bold soul-markings were now faded and difficult to see. Stunned, she stared at her arm in shock.

"Once Vesik gave you the euphoria of believing there was nothing to fear, you not only stopped growing as a Num, but you began losing the lessons you had learned earlier in life." Gluic stepped closer to Avanda, placing her beak near Avanda's nose. "Pain can be a good thing in life. It helps us mature to be better and teaches us to handle issues in our future. It also helps us enjoy the times without pain so much more."

Avanda softly traced the cover of the book she held onto while thinking of what Gluic had to say. "I don't want to feel vulnerable. I don't want to be a victim again."

"I know, dear. None of us do. But if you don't face your problems head on and force yourself to grow and flourish into something better, you always will be a victim of your own making."

Thorik had been listening intensely, waiting for his turn to step in and help. "See, Avanda. We're here to help. That book has filled your head with lies."

Turning her head, both of Gluic's eyes snapped in his direction. "You lie just as much as the rest, dear boy."

"What? How can you say that?"

"Sometimes people lie to others and sometimes they lie to themselves. You are currently in a middle of lying to both."

"How? In what way?"

"First of all, you've enabled her. You not only gave her access to Vesik, but then you asked her to use it."

"But Granna, if I hadn't asked her to perform a specific spell then you would have died. Instead, we were able to bring you back to life. Unfortunately, we only had a bird's body to place you in at the time, but I was hoping we would have the time to correct that mistake."

"And how would you do this?"

"We would use...Vesik."

"So you would have her use the very book you know is hurting her?"

"I don't know. We never had the time to discuss it." Thorik tried to think of how he could prove he was doing the right thing. "Once I knew Vesik had taken control of her, I tossed it into the Govi Glade to free Avanda of it. I took actions to save her, not enable her."

"And then when she struggled with her pain from your actions, did you help Avanda through her hardship or did you give in and pacify her urge?"

"What do you mean?"

"Thorik, you then took her back to the Govi Glade to help her find Vesik, after knowing the danger you were putting her in. You felt it was less painful for you to enable her than to feel her anger toward you."

"I was losing her! She was going to leave. I'd never see her again."

"You were going to lose her anyway, once she had Vesik back."

Thorik wiped his face with both hands, knowing he had done wrong. "We had to go back. Avanda was in pain. She needed to find Vesik or she would die."

Gluic laughed. "You are so gullible sometimes."

Thorik looked confused and glanced up at Avanda.

She couldn't look him the eyes. "I felt like I would die without it."

"There was no contract?" Thorik asked.

She shook her head no.

Grappling with the new information, Thorik turned to his grandmother to defend himself. "I didn't know she lied about her deal with Vesik."

"Of course you did, dear. You knew it wasn't sound, but it was an excellent excuse for you to rush back in and pacify her need to make her happy...and to get you back in her good graces."

"Granna, I seriously didn't know."

"Did you question it? Did you challenge her story?"

After a delay, he answered. "No."

"Then deep down you already knew it wasn't true." Gluic moved back over to the fire while one eye continued to watch Thorik. "So, permitting her to have and use the book while condoning it was your first lie."

Thorik looked slightly off kilter as he waited for more. "What else could I have been lying about to her? She knows that I had feelings for Emilen at one time, but that has passed."

"You blame the book Vesik for your relationship with Avanda."

Avanda nodded slightly in agreement.

Thorik raised his hands while defending himself. "You don't understand. The book was starting to control her. It was taking over her mind and making her do things that she wouldn't normally do."

"All true," Gluic said.

"Then, how am I lying?" Thorik looked back and forth from Gluic to Avanda.

"You're blaming Vesik for your personal issues with Avanda. You're saying the book was evil. That is your defense when she says you took it away from her."

"It is, or at least was. What am I lying about?"

"You're lying by not admitting to the responsibility of your actions."

Thorik was obviously dumbfounded by the statement. "I'm feeling the responsibilities of them constantly! Avanda is the love of my life and she won't forgive me!"

"Then tell her the truth."

"I don't know what you're asking me to do. What am I lying about?"

"Instead of justifying your actions by blaming Vesik, take ownership of what you did. She blames you for stealing Vesik and you have yet to accept this act and how it hurt her. Instead you justify your actions."

Thorik didn't know where to start or if he even understood what she wanted. "Yes, I hated that book!" he shouted. "As much as I hate saying it, *I* am responsible for causing you the pain you feel from your loss and the disappointment you have that I betrayed you. I took Vesik from you and I'd do it again. Is that what you wanted to hear?"

"Close enough," Gluic said while casually warming her back feathers by the fire.

Avanda glared at him while still clutching the dead book to her chest.

Pacing the room, he continued. "I made the decision to do this, so you are right in blaming me. I did this because I love you too much to see you waste away, hiding alone with nothing more than your book for friendship. Vesik was preventing you from being part of the world and to experience the good as well as the bad in it. It gave you a false sense of security that would have led you to feel powerful and unstoppable which would have made you a monster."

Thorik stopped pacing and took a deep breath before looking into Avanda eyes. "I did this knowing it would cause you pain. I'm sorry I hurt you. I want you to know that it kills me every time I hurt you in any way. However, I love you too much not to fight for you even if it rips us apart." Lowering his head, he turned and walked back outside and sat down on the front steps, under the overhang of the front doorway.

Gluic rustled her feathers one last time. "Well, that went well. I'm all dry and warmed up now. Time to head off. This is now between the two of you. It's not my place to get involved."

Avanda glanced at Pheosco and then to Gluic. "But…you just arrived."

"Oh, I'll be back."

"Where are you going?"

"I'm going to see if Ep has any brothers."

Chapter 11
Thorik's Job Training

Thorik's Log:
I sit here in the city of Dolor, at the bottom of a mountain's hole, surrounded by a glacier which constantly drips down upon us. The hot steam vents in the streets keeps us from being frozen over and the mines below us keep the people busy. Is there nothing more in life for those who live here other than working for food and shelter? Is it too much to ask for more when many don't even have the essentials to live? Are the basics to exist worth risking for the chance of freedom and the risk of not being able to survive on our own?

A t the base of the hole within the glacier and mountain itself, dark of night filled the city. A few fires shined near the entrance to the city and the mine. Other smaller ones shined in the empty streets of the marketplace.

Thorik swallowed the rest of his tea and gazed up past the surrounding rock and beyond the ice walls, into the star-lit night, wondering about his journey since he left Farbank. Had he made the right decisions? Had his efforts been in vain? Had they caused more problems than they had solved?

He was questioning everything, as he watched the stars begin to move about in a dance that kept his attention. Swirling and chasing one another, they playfully pranced in the heavens until he closed his eyes and heard his uncle's voice say, "Stop your daydreaming! Stars can't dance." And so the voice he heard from inside his head was correct. Gazing back up, the stars stayed fixed in the normal positions. It had been so long since he had a good night sleep, his senses were starting to play tricks with him.

Realizing he was extremely drowsy and fighting sleep, he wiped his eyes and listened to the moans of the winds throughout the city. It was then that he recognized he hadn't felt any breeze. The moans he was hearing were from the distant homes within the city.

His natural instinct was to leap up and investigate. "There I go again, thinking it's my responsibility to investigate and fix…only to mess things up more."

Listening for a few more minutes, they faded away. With eyes struggling to keep half open, he decided to call it a night. "I have no weapon and I don't know these streets. I think I'll wait until the morning and ask Narra. I'm sure everything is fine."

Standing, was the next challenge. His legs buckled and his body swayed as he used the railing to gain control.

Entering the house, he was light headed and yet in very good spirits. Seeing Avanda and Pheosco curled up by the fire, he staggered his way over and sat near them.

"You know, Avanda, we are so lucky. So few of our people from Farbank have ever left the village, let alone the King's Valley. We've done both. Not at the same time. One before the other. We left the village first, obviously." He talked softly so he wouldn't wake either of them.

"We then saved the Dovenar Kingdom from being flooded, saved Ericc, destroyed Ergrauth, revived Rummon, and won the war against the demons." Swaying back and forth while sitting, he was very proud of himself, as his eyes were now only open a sliver as he fought off his body's attempt to sleep. "Yep, we're pretty amazing. We're an unstoppable force. Nothing can stop us. Hence the unstoppable term I used prior."

It was then that a crash of glass was heard upstairs.

Thorik grabbed the arm of his chair to stabilize himself. "Did you hear something?"

Words were spoken from upstairs as more items where broken.

"Sounds like Gansler must be home and Narra isn't pleased with his actions," Thorik laughed as he fought his eyes from fully closing against his wishes.

A few more outbursts could be heard with some muffled screams and begging, along with chairs and tables being toppled.

"They do have a temper…" Thorik said as he fell asleep sitting up, before falling to one side. Slumber had won the battle over interest and curiosity.

He dreamed of good friends and good times, the Farbank's market and Harvest Fest contests, the children playing in the fields, and the sight of Avanda's face as she grew up from a young student of his into a self-reliant woman. All things were good in his world.

The closing of the front door jarred him awake long enough to watch Gansler come in for the night. Taking a detour before heading up to bed, he walked over to cover Thorik up with a blanket before climbing the stairs.

Barely lucid to what was happening around him; Thorik was struggling to separate his dreams from reality. For a moment he even considered warning Gansler about the earlier fight that Gansler was involved in with his wife in the bedroom, but he figured the husband would find out soon enough. Unsure how Gansler was able to come home after already being upstairs, Thorik fell back to sleep. It all somehow made sense in his groggy state of mind.

The next morning Thorik woke up on the hard floor in front of the chair he had fallen asleep in. Gathering his wits, he could see that Avanda and Pheosco where gone from the room. However, Gansler was finishing his morning meal at the table.

"Slept well?" Gansler asked, before taking his last few sips of tea from his cup.

"No. Not really. I had the oddest dreams. You and Narra were in one of them…and I think you were fighting."

"Really? That's odd. It's been a long time since we had verbal badgering with one another. Tell me, who won?" He smiled, hoping he was the victor.

"I don't recall. Not that it matters."

"It does if you're the one who's fighting." Setting his cup down, he pulled on his long coat, collected his cane and then walked into the kitchen to kiss his wife before heading out to work for the day. "I love you, Narra. Be good to your mother, Revi."

"Don't take any chances. I want you home safe and sound."

"I know, dear. Every day you ask the same thing, and every day I tell you that I would never do anything that would risk our lives together."

Stumbling into the kitchen, Thorik walked in on their conversation, only to gasp at the recent cuts across Narra's cheek. "Are you hurt?"

Embarrassed, she hid her cuts with her hand. "I'm fine. I tripped last night and cut myself while falling."

Thorik was very concerned about the scratches as well as his dreams from last night. Narra wouldn't look him in the eyes and Gansler looked oblivious as to any wrongdoing.

Kissing his wife and their daughter one more time, Gansler turned. "I'm off to work."

"Wait," Thorik said to Gansler, while dodging out of Revi's race past him and out the front door. "Can I join you today?"

"Sure, if you don't mind listening to a bunch of officials arguing about policies."

"No, not at all. Maybe I'll learn something." Thorik grabbed a piece of bread and his gear before heading out. "Gansler, I have some unanswered questions that I was hoping you could help me with."

"What is it you would like to know? I'm a wealth of knowledge, you know. Did I happen to mention that this is my city?"

"Yes you did." Stepping outside, Thorik saw Avanda playing with Revi on top of the large brown dragon in the open cul-de-sac, while Pheosco kept a sharp eye on them from his perch position above one of the stone window frames. Thorik had hoped that their talk with Gluic had helped Avanda and his relationship, but he had received no indication from her if that were true. "Avanda, we're heading into town. Would you like to join us?"

"No...I have some thinking to do today."

"Understood." He nodded with an accepting soft smile. "Take whatever time you need." Walking past them, Thorik glanced up to see the bright sun attempting to burn off the fog that had settled in the lower parts of the city. As they turned down various streets, from their higher elevation, the city looked like jagged rocks and rooftops where floating in a sea of clouds. Clearing his throat, as they descended into the fog, he finally decided to ask the question he had wanted to all morning. "So...What really happened to Narra last night? How did she get hurt?"

"Why would she lie about something like that?"

"To protect herself from further beatings."

"Beatings by who?"

Thorik bit his lip for a moment before blurting it out. "From you."

Gansler laughed heartily at the accusation. "I love my wife and daughter. I would never do anything to harm them. My entire life is about protecting them and being there for them when they need me." Shaking his head with a smile, he laughed again at the idea. "That was an easy one, what other questions do you have?"

Knowing he wasn't going to get any further with that subject, Thorik allowed the subject to change. "What is the main industry of your city?"

"Farming. We are all hardy people with our hands dirty from working the earth to feed each other."

"Really?" Thorik hadn't seen so much as a small garden. "What about the mine?"

"What mine?"

"The one we were at yesterday when we looked at the log books."

"Oh, you shouldn't look at the log books." His body shivered at the thought. "We can get in terrible trouble from doing that."

"From who? I thought this was your city."

"Yes. Yes it is. How do you like it?"

Thorik was getting nowhere. "Who is in charge of the mine?"

"Was," he corrected. "That mine was closed after we won our rebellion. I was the general, you know. Once we obtained control, we shut that mine down."

Thorik walked slowly to stay with sync with Gansler's strides using his long spindly cane. "We were just there yesterday and saw citizens enter it while Krupes controlled the process."

"It does seem like yesterday, doesn't it? How time flies."

Sighing, Thorik decided to play along. "So what was the mine for, prior to your rebellion?"

"Oh, it was a dirty hole that we all had to work at in order to get daily feedings. No one was exempt from working. If you became injured or too frail to do your part then you were cast out of the city and never seen again."

Entering the lower streets, the lifting fog still limited Thorik's vision to only a few city blocks. "And being cast out of the city would be bad?"

"Absolutely. Beyond the turrets and the egress tunnel, there is no one out there to work for. And if you're not working, then who would feed you?"

"But just outside your city is a beautiful forest filled with plants and animals. There is an endless amount of food available, as well as land to harvest your own produce."

"No. It's a dangerous place filled with horrifying creatures and frightening terrain. It is best that we stay here and tend our crops. Those that cannot or will not work are sent out of the city and sacrificed to the creatures beyond, ensuring there is enough for the rest of us to eat."

"So you still send out your weak," Thorik asked, piecing the puzzle together.

"Yes."

"Gansler, I know what happens to those people. They are being eaten by a creature called Bakalor. Your people are feeding a demon."

"Oh, perhaps in the past. But now it's more of a metaphor." He then turned down into an alley and grabbed two brooms and tossed them into a large cart. The cart itself had two large old wheels on it and two long handles out front for pulling. "Grab a side," he told Thorik.

Doing so, they pulled the cart down the alley to their first stop before scooping up a pile of garbage near the backdoor of a home.

Thorik helped. "So, this is your real job? You are a garbage collector?"

Gansler laughed. "No, surely not. We all help each other from time to time so I surely don't mind pitching in. Besides, if I did this all the time I would put someone else out of their job. I'd never be able to sleep knowing I did that."

Thorik decided to call his bluff. "And whose job is it to be the city's garbage collector?"

"Well, yours, of course. You're in training, which is the only reason I'm sticking around to help you out."

"Mine?"

"Sure. Everyone has to pitch in. That's what we fought for and gave so many of our lives for. Winning our freedom came with a price. We all need to do our part to help each other."

Thorik knew what freedom looked like and he didn't see it in the citizens of Dolor. "Is there any way to convince you that your battle for freedom failed?"

"Nonsense. Look about you!" He randomly pointed to several buildings and distant unseen towers with no commentary to accompany. "Surely this could not be accomplished without our success." He then picked up one of the cart handles and waited for Thorik to do the same to the other.

"Lift with your knees," he said, leaning against his cane, waiting for Thorik to start working. "You're going to have to learn a better work ethic if you're going to make it as one of my city's workers. You're representing me now, and I expect you do so in a proper way." His smile was glowing at the excitement of the new day.

Thorik shook his head as he placed handfuls of items into the cart before lifting his handle. "I'll do my best."

"That's all I ask. Say, did I ever tell you what the Overlords were mining before the revolution?"

"No."

"Oh." Seeing citizens in the street, he dropped his cart handle, as well as his conversation with Thorik, and limped over to them, introduced himself as the Sovereign Gansler. After shaking their hands, he gladly picked up his handle and continued on his way.

Silence followed, shy of the sound of the cart's wheels rolling on the stone streets.

Thorik took this time to consider other approaches to obtain the information he was looking for. Frustrated, he focused on picking up garbage and pulling the cart all over the city.

Eventually the fog faded and the sun gleamed upon the sweat beads covering Thorik's face as he pulled the full cart down another street. He had collected trash all morning while Sovereign Gansler introduced himself to the locals, shook their hands, and ate their gifts of fruits and baked goods, never offering any to his partner who did most of the work dragging the cart and collecting the trash.

Resting the cart handles on a street railing, Thorik was able to let go and rest his arms without tilting the cart and dumping the load. Walking away from the cart, he stepped up to his coworker, who was still presenting himself. "Gansler, I'm exhausted and need to rest and eat."

Gansler looked upon the busy people in the street before shaking his head. "We all need to pitch in. You can't just relax while everyone else is hard at work."

"Yes, but I was working while they stopped and ate lunch."

"Then you should have stopped and ate while everyone else did."

"I suggested that, however you wanted me to finish the last two streets prior to stopping. Now that I've done that it's my turn to rest."

"Honestly, how would that look? Would you feel comfortable sitting down and eating right here on this active street while everyone else is busy? Many of which have no food for themselves. Seems shameful."

"I don't care. This is your city, correct? Then make it happen."

Puzzled, Gansler glanced back and forth at the locals on the busy street. "Understood. I'll cover for you. Sit down and eat." He then pulled a piece of fruit from his side pouch and handed it to Thorik. "I'll make sure they don't notice you," he said with confidence before walking around to the front of the cart.

"Thanks," Thorik replied, before hopping on the back of the cart to take the pressure off his feet. Enjoying the breather, he leaned back on the trash they had collected and scanned the city to see if he could find any clues as to who the overlords were and what they were mining.

Halfway through his piece of fruit, he noticed the locals starting to stare at him. At first he thought he was imagining it, but when they started yelling at him he realized that they definitely were not happy with him.

Unsure what the issue was, he yelled over the cart's trash pile. "Gansler! What seems to be the problem with everyone?"

Instead of an answer, he heard a cough from the far side of the wagon. Hopping off the back, Thorik moved away from the locals before they became violent. Halfway around, he realized what the issue was.

Pulling with all of his might on one of the cart's handles, Gansler acted as though he had been trying to pull the cart up the street all by himself. The load was obviously too much for the older

Num, especially one needing a cane just to walk. It didn't help that Thorik has sitting on the back of the cart eating instead of helping him.

"Gansler, what are you doing?"

"Distraction technique."

"Distraction? Everyone on the street is now feeling sorry for you because you can't move the cart up this next street."

"Exactly. They will all be looking at me and no one will notice you taking a short vacation."

"It worked."

"Perfect. How's your lunch?"

"Everyone also noticed that I was resting while you appeared to be hard at work."

"You *were* resting. I warned you about how that would look."

Giving up on the argument, he took one last big bite of fruit before he grabbed the other cart handle and started pulling it up the street, away from the disgusted crowd.

Up the slight incline and then down a few more streets, they headed off to dump their full cart. Gansler never missed an opportunity to release the handle and introduce himself, even if it meant placing the full cart weight upon Thorik on a steep slope. One of those times, the slope was so much that the weight of the cart pushed Thorik all the way to the end of the street, knocking over local residents along the way. Trash had been lost from within the cart on more than one occasion. Gansler was oblivious to any challenges he was causing Thorik.

When the two Nums eventually reached their destination, they started to unload the items out of the cart and into a large hole in the street, near the mine's entrance. Approximately a yard across, the stone pipe below had been battered over the years from various items bouncing down its unending tunnel. Warm steam billowed from the hole, carrying a nasty smell of rotted food and waste.

Thorik stood on the cart, tossing items off of it and into the dark depths of the stone-lined hole. "Where does this go?" he asked before throwing a large broken clay pot.

"In the hole," Gansler answered.

"What? No, not the pot." He dropped the item in and then listened to it bounce back and forth on the way down. "Where does the hole go?"

"It goes down to the garbage pile in the mine."

Thorik smiled. "Any chance you could tell me what the purpose of the mine is?"

"What an odd question." Gansler looked from the cart to the hole a few times. "Isn't it obvious? It's to put trash in."

"No, I mean the original use of it."

"Oh, the Overlords were looking for something."

"What were they searching for?" he said, tossing a cracked oak bowl toward the hole.

"Wait!" Gansler yelled, catching the bowl before it went in. "I can use that," he mumbled before setting it aside. "Don't toss the good stuff."

Glancing down at the pile he stood on, he asked, "How do I know the difference?"

"The good stuff is good and the rest is junk," he answered.

Not understanding, he got in the habit of showing the items and getting a head nod from Gansler prior to disposing of them, which ended up being specific wooden debris for his pile back home. "So, what were they looking for?"

"Who?"

"The Overlords," Thorik reminded him.

"Where?"

"In the mines."

"Oh. You know about that?"

"Not yet. I was hoping the Sovereign of this city would tell me."

"Hey, I'm the sovereign! I should be able to tell you."

"Yes, how fortunate we ran into each other here at the trash hole."

"Very. Normally I'm busy drafting community guidelines and rarely do I visit this area."

"So, what were the Overlords looking for in the mine?"

"We sent thousands of our residents into that mine to find a giant stone, the Keystone to be specific. They say it's the size of my home." Gansler stretched his arms out just at the thought of it.

"Why were they mining for a huge stone?"

"Because the Overlords told us to."

"No. I meant, why did the Overloads want it?"

"They didn't tell me. But I did overhear what they planned to do with it."

"Really? That's wonderful. What did they plan to do with it?"

Gansler took the time to search in every direction in order to make sure no one else was listening. Stepping over next to the cart, he motioned for Thorik to lean down so he could tell him with a quiet tone. "I overheard them talking about their strategy once we found it. They were going to fully uncover it and then remove it from the mine and then out of the city."

Thorik nodded as he listened. "Yes, and then?"

"Then what?"

"They were going to remove it from the mine and city, and then…"

Gansler's eyes widened with excitement. "Yes, and then what?"

"That's my question. Then what?"

A look of disappointment crossed Gansler's face. "I thought you knew."

"No. I don't know!" Thorik shouted.

"Then don't lead me on like that. You had me on the edge of my wits waiting to hear. It's not very polite to tease."

Frustrated, Thorik raked his fingers through his hair. "You really don't know what they planned to do with the Keystone?"

"You mean after they found it?"

"No, *before* they found it," he replied with a thick layer of sarcasm coating his words. "Yes, of course, *after* they found it and removed from the city."

"I thought they said something about a barrier or fortress. Perhaps they are going to use it to block something," Gansler said very seriously. "Why all the games? You should have asked me that in the first place."

A large sigh escaped from Thorik. His shoulders and chin drooped down as though he had just finished an exhausting battle. "You wear me out, Gansler."

"Sovereign Gansler," he said, standing tall and pointing to himself with a wide smile and a wink of an eye before reaching out a hand for Thorik to shake.

Several more trips through the city were made by Thorik and his often missing work instructor before the work day ended. Exhausted and hungry, Thorik slowly pulled the cart all the way up the sloped streets to the far outskirts where Gansler and Narra lived.

Once there, Gansler was greeted by his wife and daughter before he began showing them the amazing treasures he had found during the day to add to his collection. Gazing at the piles of trash as though they were some great piece of art, he waved his hands around while explaining his vision to his family. Each piece was placed in specific locations to change the flow of steam from below and rain from above.

From what little Thorik overheard, it was a bunch of nonsense. A collection of thoughts that had no ties to each other or even to the items he pulled from the cart to add to his artistic junk pile. He highly doubted that the artifacts would influence anything more than his own storytelling.

And yet, even though Gansler was filling his family with drivel and twaddle, he was genuinely happy. And his family was happy as well. They had rushed out to see him when he came up the walk, and now cherished the time he gave them, regardless of the nature or importance.

Thorik found himself envious of the halfwit, jealous of what the man had received compared to himself as he stood alone in the courtyard. No one came running out to praise his return. No one welcomed him home. Time after time he had risked and sacrificed so much and yet at the end of the day, he was alone.

Chug was even gone, therefore it was logical to assume Pheosco and Avanda were gone as well. There was no telling where they went, most likely into the market area to gather supplies. However, for a terrifying moment he wondered if they had all left the city. Avanda could easily ride on Chug up and out of the city, past the surrounding glacier, and then back down into the forest. Chug wouldn't even realize that they weren't coming back until it was too late. And yet it was best not to go down that line of thinking, for it would only cause him to become depressed at the very thought of living without them, especially Avanda.

Leaving the courtyard, Thorik dragged his sore muscles up the steps to the front door and into the house before grabbing his items to clean up before dinner. Once inside he noticed his sack of Runestones lay untied on the floor, with a few of them spilling out, as though the bag had been tossed aside.

Picking up the loose Runestones, he tied off the sack and placed them back in his worn backpack with a chuckle. He marveled at how the pack was holding together with all the rips and tears over the years. The pressure of all of his gear inside should have breached its capacity long ago. But to get a new one was like giving up an old dear friend. Each and every scratch and discoloration on it reminded him of an adventure in his past. He would keep that old pack until the day he died.

The other essential item found out of his pack was his old beaten up wooden coffer, filled with notes and maps from his journeys. In some regards, it was another companion of his. He had entrusted his deepest feelings and thoughts into it. Allowing someone else to open and read what was inside was perhaps the most vulnerable feeling he had ever had. And yet here it sat, still latched, but out of his pack. His heart sunk for a moment as he pondered the idea of someone opening it while he was gone.

Again, dwelling on these thoughts would only spiral him into a depression. Something he simply didn't want, nor could he afford. He had to keep his wits about him. Ambrosius was trying to prevent him from ever being born. Plus, he still didn't know when in history they were currently living.

After removing some clean clothes, he placed the coffer and his other items back in his pack and hung it up on the coat rack before stepping into the next room to wash his face, hands, and arms before dinner.

Taking off his shirt, he could see his soul-markings across his chest in a pattern similar to a shield, but much less rigid in design. He had waited all his life for his markings to appear, as they are to show one's true character. Most Nums received them in years of later childhood, and he never fully understood why his came in so late. He first noticed them after he took charge in the battle against the Demons at the Dovenar Wall near River's Edge and the Doven Province.

Washing his face clean, he realized that he had forgotten a towel and made his way back into the main living area. To his surprise, his pack was lying on floor below the coat rack. His coffer was once again out of pack and exposed. And his sack of Runestones had been tossed. With the sack untied, several Runestones were scattered across the floor.

Pausing at the sight, he called out. "Gansler? Narra? Are you in here?"

There was no reply, and a quick investigation out the front door confirmed they were all still playing with the new treasures Gansler had acquired.

There was no one else in the house.

The hair on Thorik's body stood on end and he gazed down at the sight of items in nearly the same configuration as he had found them when he returned home.

After a few calming breaths, he knelt to investigate. A deep sigh extinguished his concerns when he realized one of the straps on his backpack had ripped apart. It was reasonable to assume that the frail strap ripped from the pressure and the pack fell from the hook, causing his items to be flung out.

It just seemed odd that they all landed in a similar pattern. "I've seen stranger things happen," he justified, picking up his gear once again. This time he brought it into the other room with him as he cleaned up.

Later, Narra served bland soup that took more than a few dashes of salt to make it palatable. It wasn't that she was a bad cook; she simply didn't have much of a selection of ingredients to choose from. That said, she always made sure there was freshly made bread and a hot cup of tea to end their meals. It was better than nothing.

Retiring to the large fireplace, Revi hopped up in her father's lap and snuggled up to his warm chest. The two looked as though they would be falling asleep within minutes.

"Narra, have you seen Avanda and our dragon friends today?" Thorik asked as they all sipped on their drinks in front of the warm fire.

There was a delay in her response as she cherished the sight of her husband and child nestled in his chair. "Only this morning. They gathered up their items and left."

Thorik eyes dropped at the thought. "Did she say when they would return?"

"No. In fact, she mentioned that she wasn't sure if they would."

Closing his eyes, he took in a deep breath. "So, she's left me."

Pausing from sipping her black tea, she shook her head. "No, she said something about trying to give her book back to its origins."

"She's gone back to the Govi Glade?"

"I don't know what that is or if that is true. She didn't mention that name."

Thorik stood up and grabbed his backpack. "I wish you had mentioned this before. I need to go after her."

Calmly, she stood up and placed a soft hand on his shoulder. "I've warned you before that the streets are not safe after dark, and even if they were, there is a curfew making nighttime travel illegal."

"I'm willing to take the chance. I'm light on my feet and hide in shadows well. I can make it to the city's egress."

"You'll never make it past the guards on the far end of the tunnel. And even if you could, you don't want to be outside of the city, especially at night. There are creatures beyond the city limits that will hunt and kill you."

"Avanda is in danger out there by herself."

"She has two dragons with her. You are the one that will be alone."

Thorik looked over at Gansler to see if he had made enough of a friendship and a bond to have the man help him in his time of need.

Gansler laughed, causing Revi to reposition herself. "Don't look at me. I'm in for the night. Once I put my slippers on, there's simply no leaving the house until morning."

Narra's expression showed great gratitude in her husband's response.

"But I need your help. Avanda needs our help."

"And we will help where we can. But not until morning."

Knowing she was right, Thorik set his pack back down and resolved to stay the night.

The room stayed quiet as they all watched the flames dance under the hearth until Narra decided to wake Gansler. "Let's take Revi to bed. And we should do the same. It's getting late."

Thorik didn't move from his chair as the others made their way upstairs and out of sight. His thoughts were elsewhere, wondering what Avanda was trying to accomplish and if she was in danger. It wasn't long before he fell asleep in his chair as he pondered endless scenarios in his head.

Dreams of saving her played in his mind until a noise abruptly woke him from his slumber. It was his backpack. Once again, it was open on the floor, next to him with the coffer lying near it. And his sack of Runestones were off to the side, untied and several tossed about.

"Hello?" Thorik rubbed his eyes to quicken his awareness in the very dim light of the now nearly red ashes that remained within the fireplace.

No response was expected, but he heard a set of footsteps walking up the staircase, and yet he couldn't see who was making them. They continued to the top and then down the hall. A door then could be heard slowly opening.

Thorik sat on the edge of his chair, waiting to see if anything else would occur. Had he dreamed the entire event, such as he assumed he had the night before?

The door upstairs slammed shut, followed by the shattering of glass and Narra screaming.

Leaping out of his chair, Thorik ran over to the staircase and paused, knowing he had been specifically told never to go to the upper floor.

An argument could be heard from a room above him. Both Narra and Gansler's voices were involved, but muffled and unclear. Movement within the room sounded on the first floor's ceiling.

Thorik's heart raced as he waited with one foot up on the first step, waiting to charge up the stairs and into their room. However, the screaming had been replaced with discussions, and sobbing, and pleading. Not knowing what to do, he simply waited for a scream in pain to rush forward.

A third voice joined the married couple's exchange. Hot tempered and rough, his voice carried throughout the house in a mumble that shook the items on every shelf. The three bantered in waves of soft discussion and yelling anger. It went on and on until the sound of a sword being removed from its sheath was heard, followed by a moment of silence, and then a body falling to the wooden floor above Thorik.

Thorik was in shock, had he just overheard a murder? Who had died? Was he a witness to a crime?

Upstairs, Narra could be heard crying as Gansler consoled her.

Taking the moment upon himself, Thorik slowly worked his way up the stairs, but stopped as he reached the landing, peeking out to look down the hall at a slit of light glaring out from under a door. Shadows moved within the light, and soon the door opened.

Gansler stepped into the hallway, sword in hand. His clothes and weapon covered in blood. "Make sure Revi is still asleep. If she's still sleeping then go downstairs to make sure Thorik is as well."

Ducking down to avoid detection, Thorik was in the nearly pitch-black staircase while Narra stepped out. Bloodstains coated her nightgown as she rushed farther down the hall and entered a room, closing the door behind her.

Stepping back into his bedroom, Gansler reached down, and grabbed a young Num's wrist, and dragged the dead body out of the room, into the hall, and then into a third room. The corpse was difficult to see, but what Thorik's strong Num eyes could see from Gansler's bedroom lantern light, was a disfigured young man nearly sliced in half with a long blade.

The far door opened and Narra stepped out. "Revi is still sleeping. I'll check on Thorik."

Panicking, Thorik didn't know if he would be next if caught spying on them, especially after being told never to come up the stairs. Quickly, and as quiet as possible, he made his way to the bottom on the staircase and then to his chair. Pretending to be sleeping, he kept his eyes open just a thin slit to see if they would come after him next.

Gansler's voice could still be heard from the top of the steps. "Disposing of the body will be difficult. Perhaps I'll send Thorik on an errand in the morning to give us time."

"I told you not to have him stay here. I knew this would happen." Narra's whispering was stern and clear.

"Just make sure Thorik is still sleeping. I'll take care of him tomorrow."

"You better, before this happens again. They seem to be nice people. I don't want them caught up in all of this." Her voice became quieter as she walked down the stairs; looking to see the red embers in the fireplace's ashes shine a hint of light upon Thorik's sleeping body. "Tomorrow, Gansler. Take care of him tomorrow, or I will."

"Yes, my love."

Chapter 12
I Like it Raw

The sounds of knives being sharpened jolted Thorik awake in his chair in front of cold dead ashes that resided in the fireplace. He had stayed up most of the night until exhaustion finally undermined his attempt to be on the lookout for Gansler's arrival to do him in. Jumping up to his feet, he immediately checked his wellbeing and then the locations of his items. All seemed to be in order.

Metal knives could be heard again, along with pans and spoons. The kitchen was busy with activity and a smell of fresh meat wafted into the main living quarters. Thorik quietly made his way to the doorway and peered into the kitchen, and what he saw made him nervous. A large chunk of meat, nearly the size of his own torso, was being cut up into sections for eating. Some were already in pans being fried up, while others were being placed into a wooden crate. The protein was fresh and blood poured from the cuts they had made into it.

Sprinkling salt onto a freshly washed cutting board, Gansler used lemons to scrub it clean. His duties were done for the moment as he was cleaning up his work area.

Narra was busy cooking up a feast, enough to feed the three of them for a few days. She was also cutting some of the larger cuts and dicing them into bite-size nuggets before tossing them into a large pot of boiling water.

"I need to leave before they try to feed me the man they killed last night," Thorik thought to himself. Stepping back from the doorway, he collected his items and quietly moved to the front door. Upon grabbing the handle, the handle unlatched by itself and then flung open, nearly knocking Thorik onto his back.

There in the doorway was Avanda, with Pheosco perched on her shoulder. Standing firm, she looked him over. "Where are you going?"

"Avanda? I'm so glad to see you. Where have you been?"

Before she could answer, Gansler and Narra walked into the main living area with plates of food to set at the table. "Good morning. Please have a seat for breakfast."

There was no hesitation by Avanda. Walking past Thorik, she quickly sat down with Pheosco sitting next to her.

Waiting until their hosts returned to the kitchen, Thorik dashed over next to Avanda and whispered into her ear. "Don't eat the meat."

She protested loudly while impaling a large slice with her fork and slapping it on her plate for inspection. "Why? What's wrong with it?"

"There's nothing wrong with it," Pheosco growled, tearing a second bite off of the piece he had taken for himself.

Thorik felt ill at the thought of them eating the meat from a dead man. "You don't understand. It's not right to eat it. I'll explain later."

"Thorik, sit down and have yourself a hearty breakfast." Narra said, while bringing out a pitcher of water.

Uncomfortable about the situation, he eased himself into a chair and poured himself a drink. "This doesn't seem like your normal breakfast meal."

"Oh, that is an understatement. I'm not sure the last time we had such a feast."

"It would have been nice to have had it as a dinner last night," Thorik prodded to uncover the secret.

"Indeed, it would have." Narra placed a large piece of meat on Thorik's plate for him.

Waiting only a few moments, while staring at his still bleeding rare-cooked slab of flesh, he continued the conversation. "So why didn't we have any of this last night?"

"Because we didn't have any. It was an unexpected surprise that we had some this morning."

"Really? Unexpected delivery of this lovely...antelope?" Thorik questioned.

Narra gave him an odd look. "Yes, unexpected. But wrong species." She chuckled for a moment and waited for him to try some. "Taste it. You'll know what it is once you've tried it."

With all eyes on him, Thorik reluctantly grabbed a fork and knife and cut a small bite sized chuck of meat of the slab on his plate. Stabbing it with his fork, he slowly raised it to his mouth. He simply couldn't get the grim visual images from last night out of his head, and all he could wonder was what part of the dead man's body was on his fork.

"Go on," Narra pushed. "It's better than my soup from last night."

Placing the fork near his open mouth, he began to gag at the thought, coughing and choking on the concepts of eating the meal before him. Grabbing for his water, he washed away his cough. "Narra, before I can take a bite, I must know what this is and where it came from." He knew he was taking a huge risk in calling her bluff. But he had to do it in order to prevent himself from eating the flesh of a dead man as well as preventing Avanda from eating any more of him.

"You'll have to ask Avanda. She arrived this morning with it."

"Small bovine," Avanda commented between bites. "Chug caught it for us in the valley, and then we flew back here for everyone to have some." She took another mouthful. "Since when are you so particular about your meals?"

A huge sigh of relief came over Thorik, now realizing the meal before him was not the evidence of a crime. Smiling, he placed the cut of beef in his mouth and savored the flavor. "Thank you, both. It is wonderful."

"I'm glad you enjoy it," Narra said, before returning to the kitchen.

All went quiet in the dining area, before Thorik whispered to Avanda. "Where have you been? And don't get too comfortable here because we're not staying long."

Avanda slammed her fist on the table. "Don't tell me what I can and can't do!"

"It's for our own safety..." Thorik stopped in mid-sentence as Narra, Revi, and Gansler came out to join them at the table. Revi made sure she sat next to Avanda.

The conversation was very minimal and usually contained a question followed by a single short answer. No one seemed to be in a talkative mood, except Revi, who jabbered nonsense words in endless sentences as though others could understand her baby-talk.

"Did you sleep well last night?" Narra asked.

"Well enough." Thorik replied before returning to his plate. "However, I heard some commotion upstairs last night. Is anything wrong?"

"No. Revi sometimes has night terrors."

Long pauses continued between the pointed questions and lies for answers. There was nothing to be learned at the table.

Finishing up, Narra poured Gansler his tea and asked if anyone else would like any. Somehow tea didn't seem to go well with the beef, so the others declined.

It wasn't long before Gansler prepared to leave for work. "Thorik, are you ready?"

"No, not today. I have errands to run."

"It won't look good for you to take a day off while still in training."

Thorik chuckled to himself about the whole idea of himself being trained as a garbage collector after traveling the world and fighting in so many battles. "I know. I'll be there tomorrow. I promise."

"We all need to do our part. No one job is more or less important than another. We are shorthanded and it takes all of us to keep my city functioning. I'll cover for you today, but after that you'll have to become a productive member of our society. Besides, our extra reserve of tokens will run dry if you don't start working for your own."

"I understand." Thorik nodded. "Thank you, Gansler." He noticed that Gansler always seemed more reasonable late at night and first thing in the morning compared to the rest of the day. Perhaps less crazy would be the best way to phrase it.

"Sovereign Gansler," he replied while shaking Thorik's hand as though they were meeting for the first time.

Thorik speculated if he was too quick to judge the man's sanity, as he watched him grab his cane and head out the door without any boots on.

Narra quickly went running after him with his boots in hand.

Vacant of its owners, the house was filled with more babbling from Revi as she talked her pretend language to Avanda, who nodded as though she understood while lighting a new fire in the fireplace.

Trying to help, Revi quickly coated her fingers with ash before placing a firm palm print on Avanda's cheek. The sight caused the little girl to giggle uncontrollably until she wiped her own nose before realizing she still had soiled hands.

Laughing at the dark puppy nose on Revi's face, Avanda took her own dirty finger and traced thick eyebrows on the small child.

Making faces at one another, the two howled with laughter as they continued decorating each other's faces in dark wood ash.

Thorik stood back and watched. In spite of Vesik still being at her side, the sight of Avanda laughing was one he hadn't seen for some time and he held his body still in order to treasure the moment.

He hadn't seen her playing with other Num children since she herself was a child back in Farbank during the Harvest Festival. It seemed so natural for her, and suddenly he could see her as a loving and caring mother. The idea of them married and having children played in his mind as the happiest days of his life.

"What are you looking at?" Pheosco said to Thorik, breaking his daydream.

"Nothing," he replied, changing topics in his mind as quickly as he could. "I was just wondering why she didn't let me know where you were going yesterday and if you were coming back."

Stretching his thin long green dragon neck, he replied in a clear and crisp tone. "You don't own her. She does not report to you. You are no longer her Runestone instructor or her boyfriend, so she owes you no such information. I don't recall you letting her know when you stole Vesik from her and left us to destroy it in the Govi Glade."

No matter how many times he had heard these words, they still hurt him like the stabbing of a blade into his ribcage. His chest tightened, his shoulders rolled forward, and his eyes lowered. Turning, he walked out the front doorway and sat on the front steps just as Narra passed him on her way back in.

Steam wafted through stacks of odd wooden items that leaned up against the front of the other structures in the circle of buildings which shared a common street. With no gaps between the buildings, the only area that Gansler hadn't stacked the trashed goods was along the entrance to his own front door.

The morning soft fog collected heavy dew on some items, causing them to lean. Tiny random water canals moved the cumulative dewdrops together and carried them into small spillways off the junk piles and into the street. In every street was a stone channel to move the water out of the area.

Laying on his back, in the center of the cul-de-sac, Chug scratched his back over a steam vent on the stone street by shifting his upper and lower body one way and then the other. All four legs stayed bent and pointing to the sky while his tail flung about, knocking over pieces of moss and fungi covered trash. Happy and content, the brown dragon was delighted just to be alive.

It was good to see Chug again, but Thorik's thoughts fell back on Pheosco's words and his mind wandered. He watched the process as heavy dew finally gave way on the top of another pile. He was slightly chilled, more by the humidity than the temperature. Yet he wasn't ready to walk back inside. He once again wasn't sure how to make things better with Avanda. Perhaps he couldn't.

"Feeling down, little man?" asked a deep voice from down the street. Walking around the corner, a giant man-like creature entered the area. Standing well over twice Thorik's height and easily four times his width, the unexpected guest easily weighed over a ton. Oversized feet and hands, even for his size, made it obvious that this creature was a Mognin. Each hand had three fingers and two thumbs on each side while thick brown leather skin covered his body and bald head. The twelve foot tall Ov'Unday was carrying an elder Num with dark hair and a few very thick soul-markings running down his neck and arms. The massive giant approached with a grin.

"Grewen!" Thorik yelled as a flood of emotions raced through his body. "You're alive and well! I was so worried about you and thought I'd never see you again!" His body shook with excitement as he tried to control his excitement.

"You still worry too much, little man." The giant Mognin grinned down at his dear friend. "How long have you been here?"

"We just arrived yesterday. I would have traveled down into the pit to search for you but was advised to stay here and wait for you to return. I know you always tell me to control my concerns, but I was sure I had lost you for sure this time." Taking a breath to calm himself, Thorik glanced down from Grewen's comforting facial expression to the Num the Mognin was carrying. "Is Brimmelle hurt?"

The elder Num started to slowly sit up. "No reason to worry about me. It's just been several long painstaking days of being tortured. But enough about my ills, I'm glad you are so elated to see that Grewen is of good health and spirits." Brimmelle never did attempt to hide his sarcasm.

Thorik didn't allow his uncle to deplete his excitement. Running out into the cul-de-sac, he jumped into Grewen's open arm before hugging him around his thick neck as soon as he was lifted up high enough. It was a feeling of comfort that he dearly missed.

Avanda opened the door to see what all the commotion was about.

Quickly at her side, Pheosco darted his head back and forth, searching for danger.

After releasing Grewen's neck, Thorik leaned down to give Brimmelle a welcoming hug as well. "I thought I had lost both of you." After as quick squeeze and a pat on the back, he quickly released his uncle.

Grewen continued to walk toward the doorway where Avanda stood. Once he got close enough he noticed that she was still holding onto Vesik. Stopping, he wasn't sure what this meant. "The last time I saw you with that book, you were burning down a camp with the soldiers still in it."

"No longer," Avanda spoke softly. "Vesik is dead. I am no longer under her power."

"Good riddance." Brimmelle frowned as he noticed the sadness on her face from the comment.

Grewen took a moment to look at Thorik before looking back at her. "How do you feel about your book of magic being gone?"

"I don't know. Angry. Lost. Scared. I'm not sure what to do now."

Grewen grinned. "It sounds to me like you are starting a new journey. Good thing we are all back together to help you with it."

Revi walked up to the open doorway next to Avanda. Upon seeing the giant Mognin, she quickly reached up for Avanda's free hand.

She smiled at Revi as well as Grewen's comment. "Yes, I'm lucky to have my family pod back together. Even Brimmelle." Helping Revi down the steps, she made her way toward Grewen.

"Even me? What does that mean? That is Fir Brimmelle to you, young lady," he complained while climbing out of Grewen's hand and onto the street. Straightening his worn and torn vest, he stood before her with his chest up and shoulders back. His once elegant clothes had been through so much that it was difficult to see what color many of the fabrics originally were.

"Fir? It's been so long since anyone has spoken about the Mountain King, let alone spent time teaching them," Avanda responded.

Standing much broader than Thorik, Fir Brimmelle was a heavier Num than most. He was not obese, but he was definitely wider and had more girth in his arms and legs than Thorik. "And that is the problem with the world. They aren't learning about the Mountain King or they are ignoring his teachings."

"Mountain King?" Narra asked, standing in the doorway. She had followed Revi out to see what all the fuss was about.

"Goodness, my lady. Have you not heard of the Mountain King?" Brimmelle asked.

"No. Should I have?"

"Absolutely!" Pausing to introduce himself, he cleared his throat. "I am Fir Brimmelle Riddlewood the Seventh of Farbank, senior advisor of the Mountain King's teachings."

"It is an honor to have you join us." She gracefully played to his ego. "I am Narra. Would you care to come into our home? We have some fresh steaks left over from breakfast."

"I would be delighted. Do you have some place I could wash up?" Brimmelle nearly had a bounce in his step as Narra escorted him into her home to discuss his favorite subject.

Thorik smiled. "I don't think I've ever see him this happy. Grewen, did anything happen to him once we split up at Ergrauth?"

"Yes, little man. He had time away from the rest of you to relax his responsibilities long enough to grow." Setting Thorik safely back to the street, he reached out toward Avanda. "How about a hug from my little spell caster?"

Showing him the dead book of magic, she replied. "I'm not a spell caster any longer."

"Oh, I see. So you're giving it up completely, are you? I find that hard to believe. You were casting spells long before you found Vesik."

Nodding in agreement, she smiled. "You know, you're right." A warmth came over her that could be seen in her posture and facial expression. "I sure missed you, Grewen." Letting go of Revi, she leaped up into his massive arms.

"I missed you as well, little lady." Giving her a big hug he then asked Thorik, "Any chance there's more food inside? I'm starving."

"I've never known you not to be hungry. There are fresh bovine steaks for the taking. In fact, I think there is a crate of raw ones coming out for Chug, if you'd like to share."

Grewen grimaced at the comment. "I would prefer something that grows out of the ground."

"They don't have cupboards filled with food here. Then again, they don't seem to have anything growing out of the ground."

"I know. I was just asking."

Turning and walking up the short staircase, Thorik opened the large doors to make way for his friend. "Let's see what she has to offer you. I'm sure Chug is pretty hungry as well."

By this point the large brown dragon had fallen asleep on his back with all four legs in the air and his tongue hanging out of his mouth, drooling onto the street.

"Yes, because he looks like he's famished," Grewen said half-heartedly, lowering his head to enter the eight foot tall double doors.

"What have you been doing since you arrived?" Thorik asked, escorting him to the great room.

"Working in the mine. We needed to eat so we joined the workforce in order to get free meals. Apparently most of this city works in the mines."

"What is it they are mining for?"

"I'm not sure. The Krupes never talk, as you well know, and the mine bosses only seem to know where to dig. I wasn't even able to find out who's mine this was."

"Seems awfully secretive."

"Thorik, I know that look. You're curiosity is heightened and that usually ends up getting us into trouble."

Thorik smiled at the statement. "Grewen, I'm so glad you're back."

"From my perspective, I never left." He gave his typical grin.

Motioning to sit near the fire, Thorik stepped to another doorway. "I'll see if we can find something for you to eat. I have some plans for all of us today. It should prove to be an interesting day."

Fed and cleaned up, Thorik surrounded himself with most of his Family Pod in the cul-de-sac. Chug gnawed on a large bovine bone while Grewen, Brimmelle, Avanda, and Pheosco listened to what Thorik had to say.

"What's this about?" Brimmelle insisted.

"We need to determine where we are and what our plans are. We came through the Govi Glade and now are in this captive mining city. We can't leave. We are warned it's not safe after dark, plus there is a curfew after dark with potential death for those who are caught. We have a choice to stay here or find a way out."

Brimmelle puffed up his chest. "Well, I'm not going to work in those mines again."

"So you're with me to find a way to escape."

"I didn't say that. These people have never heard of the Mountain King and his teachings. I think it's clear what needs to be done. I am a Fir."

"But why stay under these conditions? We need to escape."

"To where? You don't even know where there is to escape to. Farbank might be long forgotten and abandoned by now. These people here need my help. The choice is obvious. We stop this endless dangerous venture across Terra Australis and settle down."

"But these people are not free. How can we live like this?"

"I'm willing to not travel at night or cause problems. In return we receive free food. Sure, it might not be the best, but it's safe and it's secure. Do we really need anything more?"

Thorik couldn't believe his ears. "What happens when they don't need us anymore? Do you know what they do when we can't work or we become ill? They lead you out of the city and up into Bakalor's lair where he eats you."

"Bakalor? What have you been dreaming? We saw him die!"

"He has been brought back to life by the Dark Oracle, Deleth."

"If this is true, than we had better stay in good health. I for one am tired of risking our lives every day by traveling across this endless series of dangerous terrains. These streets seem safe enough from what I've seen."

"Perhaps today. Maybe even tomorrow. But the day will come that you will understand the hazards of living in such a society. Besides, I *can't* stay here. Ambrosius will eventually find me here and attempt to finish what he had started by preventing my birth."

Avanda nodded. "It's true. He wants to prevent Thorik from ever being born in order to change events in history."

Brimmelle chuckled at the idea. "I've wished that myself a time or two in the past, but I don't see how that is possible."

She agreed. "We don't either, but there are a lot of things that E'rudites can do that we can't explain. Thorik is in trouble."

Grewen considered the idea. "I struggle to believe Ambrosius would do such a thing."

"He's changed. He's gone insane in his old age. I don't understand it myself," Thorik said. "At some point I will have to face him if I stay around here."

The Mognin glanced around the Nums and dragons. "Is there anything else we should know?"

Thorik peeked toward the doorway to the house and lowered his voice. "Yes…We need to watch out for Gansler and Narra. I don't know if we can trust them."

"That is enough." Brimmelle tossed his hands in the air. "I'm not listening to any more of this. They are willing to open their home and feed us. How dare you accuse them of not being trustworthy. What gives you the right?"

"Someone broke in last night and I think our hosts murdered him." Thorik spoke a little louder than he had planned, and hushed himself for doing so.

"While you and their daughter were in the house?"

"Yes. I heard noises, but I was too late."

Brimmelle wrapped his arms around his chest and looked through his thick eyebrows at the Num. "Did you see a dead body?"

"Yes! It was very dark, but I saw enough to know what happened to it."

"What did you say when you confronted them?"

"I…didn't. I ran back downstairs and pretended to be asleep so I wouldn't be their next victim."

"Thorik Dain, have you seen these two frail Nums? She is days away from giving birth and he struggles to walk without a cane. And knowing this, you're telling me the two of them were able to murder an intruder in the middle of the night and quietly dispose of the body without anyone else knowing about it? Besides, Gansler doesn't seem to have the backbone to stand up to a grazer, let alone an invader wishing to do them harm."

"I know it doesn't seem likely." Thorik tried to lower his voice so Brimmelle would do the same. "Hang on, how do you know Gansler?"

"We met him on the way here. He introduced himself as Sovereign Gansler."

"Yes. That would be him."

"He's as dangerous as a worm. I'm not listening to any more of this. My time is better spent educating the locals on the Words of Wisdom and the Mountain King's scrolls." Disgusted, he turned to walk away.

"Please don't tell them what I said about them."

"Well, of course not. I'm not going to get us tossed out of a place to sleep and eat just because you're a fool." The Fir stomped up the front steps and then into the home.

Pheosco smiled at the tongue lashing. "That was enjoyable. Who's next? Thorik is still standing."

"What's your suggestion, Thorik?" Grewen's deep voice was softer than normal, trying to ease the tension. "Now that we're all back together, there is the option of simply leaving this city. Chug could fly all of you up and out of the city. I think I'm about double his weight limit, so I'll be staying here unless the front egress isn't guarded."

After a quick glance up to the rim of the glacier above the city, escaping to freedom had never felt so hollow. "No, I'm going to leave without you, nor are we going to turn our head from the wrongs being done here. First of all, we need to find out if we are truly prevented from leaving. Everyone fears the night curfew and the egress from leaving, and yet I have not seen any dangers greater than a few Krupes. Are these people brainwashed to fear what is not there?"

After a quick pause Thorik continued. "I'm also curious as to what they are mining for. What's so important down there that this entire city was created to collect? Surely it has to be more than a single Keystone. And yet I haven't seen any gold, silver, or gems removed from the mines. Also, where are they getting their food? I have yet to see any farms. None of this makes sense to me."

Proud of his friend's desire to help others, Grewen raised one of his large eyebrows as he listened to Thorik's thoughts. "That certainly is a list of tasks before us. I'm willing to return to the mines and see what I can uncover. The work fits my natural abilities and they feed me well."

Leaning up against Chug, Avanda tossed her grudgingly support in as well. "I suppose we could fly above the city to see if there are local farms out of our current view."

Her lack of excitement didn't kill the moment. Thorik was pleased that she was at least willing to help. "Thank you," he replied to his friends. "I'll go to the front gates and see what I can learn."

Grewen cleared his throat to get the Num's attention. "Is it safe to leave Brimmelle with Narra?"

Thorik glanced over to the empty doorway. "It's going to have to be. We'll never convince him to leave with any of us as long as Narra is willing to listen to his tales of the Mountain King."

Chapter 13
What is Going on Here?

S pending most of the day investigating would prevent Thorik and Avanda from receiving their daily food rations, but they felt it was worth it. After many hours of talking to locals, Thorik had come to the conclusion that this city was created and populated for only one objective, to support the mining of an artifact known as the Keystone. And yet no one in the city knew what this item was for. Surely it must have some unique powers in order to justify spending such great resources in finding it. Taxing his brain, Thorik was baffled as to its purpose.

The citizens simply did their jobs and existed. None were willing to discuss any battle Gansler had supposedly led. And the few that had answered his question about curfew simply warned him to obey it. Questions about the egress tunnel to the outside world would typically end discussions, as few were willing to discuss the idea of leaving.

Food and supplies were imported into the city from the outside. Transported on wagons, it was brought in through the egress and then the majority of it was taken down into the pit for the miners. The little amount of goods that remained could be obtained by small copper tokens that served as tender, and fortunately Thorik had a few in his pocket from the prior day when Gansler gave him a handful to buy his meals for the week. From what Thorik could gather, all workers received the same amount of tokens for each day they provided services to the city, such as working in the market, garbage collection, repairs and maintenance of structures, and so on. The amount given for a day's work was enough for a single meal a day. Citizens had to work in the mines to truly eat well and support their families.

Two wide and straight main streets existed in the city. Both intersected at a strong angle in the center of the city, one leading from the front egress and the other from the mine's pit. The rest of the streets and alleys were much thinner and rarely straight for more than a block or two.

The closer Thorik walked on the main street toward the city's egress tunnel, the busier it became. Not just with the local citizens, but with more store fronts with homes stacked one on top of another above. The main market was built up against the very wall that housed the exit which tunneled its way to the forest on the far side, and yet no one acted as though the opportunity for freedom even existed. On each side of the egress tunnel entrance were turrets built into the mountain wall, hanging over the market area, possibly created for speeches to those below.

Within this market area, stores sold basic needs of cooking gear and clothing. Everything was about function and no special colors or styles were available.

The streets themselves became wider to handle the influx of traffic with more street lantern poles, more steam leaking up through the ground, and multiple drainage ditches carved into the streets. The water eventually flowed into the cracks between the cobblestones or out through the main entrance cave.

It was a welcome sight to see no guards were preventing anyone from approaching. And yet, it seemed odd that no one appeared to notice the cavern tunnel at all, as though they didn't even see it.

"Excuse me," Thorik asked a man in typical gray clothes with a dull look upon his face. Then again, that could describe just about everyone walking past him. "Is that the only exit from the city?"

The man stopped, looked at the egress and then back at Thorik with a confused expression.

"The cave, right there." He pointed to make sure it was clear. "If I walk through that cave, would I find the forest and valley beyond?"

Gliding his eyes back and forth a few times, he finally nodded yes slowly.

"Have you or anyone you know gone through to the other side?"

The man's eye's grew, in the first true sense of emotion since the conversation started. "No!"

"Well, why not?"

"It is far too dangerous out there. There are wild animals and beasts. There is no shelter or food provided. We would starve."

"But you could hunt and find your own food. You could build your own homes to shelter yourselves."

Shaking his head, he was obviously fearful of the concept. "We are better to stay here."

"But here, you are not free."

"We are fed. We have shelter. We are safe." The man adjusted the items he was carrying. "The cost of freedom is too high. We will not make that mistake again," he said over his shoulder as he walked away from the Num.

Thorik stood in the center of the street assessing the city and its inhabitants, deliberating how they had given up hope on being happy, creative, and inspired. Had they given in to work without goals for their entire life?

As he pondered, a large wagon pulled by four two-legged Faralopes came out of the tunnel and straight at the Num. Filled with barrels, the heavy load nearly ran over his toes as it passed by, driven by a human cloaked in the gray attire.

Over a dozen more wagons followed the first, all with various foods and raw materials. One after another roared into the city; the last few stopped at the local shops to deliver raw materials of leather, cotton, and metals, as well as fruits and vegetables.

Inventories of goods delivered were taken as they were dropped off, giving Thorik a feeling of security that he wouldn't be noticed if he entered the egress. So he did.

A slow calm walk at first, he increased his speed as he made his way past the skull lanterns that hung in the passage. The closer he came to the exit, the more crates and barrels of goods were stacked up along the walls. Eventually, he couldn't go any farther without being detected by the human and Krupe guards.

Inching to within hearing range, he hid behind a few crates to listen to their conversation. What he heard startled him to a point that he bumped a sack of potatoes, knocking it to the ground.

The guards turned.

Thorik ran.

Chapter 14
Mognins in the Mine

Thick veins of minerals and crystals worked their way through the granite walls, ceilings, and floors of the mines. The air was thick and smelled of sulfur, often to a nearly toxic level. Steam filled various tunnels as heavy moist air mixed with open fissures that led deep into underground rivers of magma. Tunnels led to rooms that led to tunnels and more rooms. An endless maze of slanted walkways connected the chambers much like an enormous ant nest.

Teaming with life, these mazes were filled with various species that had found a specialty which fit with their own skills and abilities. There were Altered Creatures who could cut away boulders with acid saliva, some were able to keep the air breathable and free of deadly gases, while others had claws strong enough to bore holes into rock walls. All of the Ov'Unday creatures seemed to have a clear purpose and a specialty perfect for the tasks they needed to perform.

The few that didn't labor in the mine were the Del'Unday, which included various dragon species for communication and lighting of tunnels, the dark armored Krupes who kept miners from moving too slowly, and a single Blothrud who barked orders at everyone.

Deep within the mines, Grewen picked up another large boulder out of the way and began carrying it toward the deposit area. Even though the rocks were very large, the task seemed to be perfect for his giant size and frame. His three thick fingers on each oversized hand, each with an extra joint, grabbed firmly on the rocks while his thumbs on each side of each hand balanced the load perfectly.

Grewen had spent the first half of the day walking down to the bottom of the pit and the second half helping move boulders while trying to find out who was in charge. He was not alone in these duties. There were several Mognins in the mine, all doing the same job. Most were slightly shorter than him, but still had all of right qualities to do the work.

Black-Tipped Silver Dragons nearly three-feet in height were perched behind flaming oil vats with their wings spread around the flames, reflecting and intensifying the light into the needed areas of the mines. With a flex of their muscles their glossy scales changed angles, causing the lights to flicker and notifying the miners it was time for a break.

During one of the breaks, Grewen approached a gathering of his fellow Mognins. It had been a while since he had been with his own kind. "Greetings. My name is Grewen."

The other Mognins all stood and politely bowed their heads. One stayed standing while the others sat back down to eat from a cart full of food that had been delivered. "Greetings Grewen, my name is Trewek. Would you join our pod for nourishment?"

"I've known several Mogs with that noble name. It would be a pleasure to join you," Grewen replied, sitting down with them to eat.

Mognins were known for three things; the size of their body which was taller than any other Altered Creature, their unbelievable strength, and their constant appetite which caused them to appear to always be eating. Wherever you find happy Mognins you will inevitably find plenty of food. Not just any food, for in spite of their size, they normally didn't eat meat.

Grewen reached into the cart filled with melons, squash, nuts, and leafy greens. His handful of sustenance was then placed before him on a large thick rubbery leaf that he had draped across his lap while sitting cross-legged, just as the other Mognins had done. "How long have you been working this mine?"

Swallowing his mouthful of large green leaves, Trewek spoke up first. "Several have been here all their lives. A few of us were relocated to this mine after our other work camps had been shut down." Placing a handful of long grass in his mouth, he continued. "What work camp do you come from?"

"Work camp?" Grewen tossed another small melon into his mouth and took a single bite before swallowing it, as juices ran out the side of his mouth. "I come from no work camp."

The facial expressions across the other Mognins showed their questioning of his answer.

"So, if not from a work camp..." Trewek said in his normal thoughtful and calm tone. "...then where, dear friend, could you have come from?"

"My birthplace was along the Ki'Volney Lake. Since then, I have traveled across this land from the northeast desert valley to the southwest tropical forests as well as from the Dor'Avell Range to these fine Cuev'Laru Mountains."

"Cuev'Laru?" one Mognin questioned while several of them began talking softly to each other.

Raising his hand to silence the others, Trewek asked, "You were part of an Overlord's traveling party?"

"No," Grewen answered. "I traveled for friends and for self-assessment of my own faculties."

"You determine your own path?"

"Yes. Although there have been times when I was following orders, such as in the civil war when I worked for Ambrosius." Grewen thought back to those times for a few seconds before making eye contact again.

"War." Trewek said softly, as the others shook their heads sadly. "We have seen this. It brings death and vengeful thoughts that corrupt the soul. Forever the desire to feel the need for a pound of flesh to ease the pain another has inflicted upon us. I do not believe these should be the ways of the Mognin."

Grewen nodded. "Even with that said, it was my choice to support his efforts. I have accepted full responsibility for the external harm I've done to others and the internal harm I inflicted upon myself. It took several years of searching the lands to once again find inner peace."

"To travel your own path must be difficult without a leader to provide plans and direction. How did you come by these traits?"

"From where I grew up, I was taught that all species have the right to be free and to seek out their own destiny."

"Would it not be dangerous to venture out without knowing that it's safe?"

"It is, but it is the cost of freedom. We mitigate the risk by sharing and helping each other out in villages. Much like here in this mine, some are suitable for farming while others have talents for woodworking, or construction, or other services needed to add to the community. The difference is that we select our endeavors."

The Mognins sat in awe of the ideas flourishing from the newcomer's mouth, as he filled it with food between sentences. Trewek finally injected his thoughts. "The Overlord would not allow such freedom. We have seen his response to this idea. War for independence and death for disobedience are related subjects."

"What war have you seen?" Grewen asked.

"There was a revolution in the mines several years ago. Their leader spoke of freedom, much like you. An army was formed to attack and destroy the Overlord before they even knew a revolution was starting. However, there was a weak thread in their cloak of darkness, and the Overlord staged a preemptive attack of his own. The revolutionaries were killed for such thoughts and acts, leaving us with less than half of our original workers." Trewek placed another large leaf into his mouth and chewed on it while talking. "Freedom must come to us in a different form if we shall succeed in obtaining it. Surely there is a peaceful way."

The silver dragons flickered the lights and all of the species stood up from their meals to return to work. Each had collected into groups of similar eating habits and usually with the same species type.

Setting the food he hadn't eaten back into the cart, Grewen turned and walked with Trewek back into the passage they had been working in. "May I ask, who is the Overlord? I have yet to see anyone standing out as the primary leader."

"The Overlord comes and goes without warning. You may think we are alone one moment only to find him standing among us the next. We never know when he will visit us from his home within the city of Pwellus Dementa', which houses all of the Overlords."

"There is more than one?"

"Yes. When we started, several of them would take turns inspecting our progress. Now only the one Overlord arrives on a periodic basis to provide new orders to the Blothrud, Savroc, who is constantly traveling up and down on the pit's platform to relay orders in the mines and in the city. He keeps things in order on a daily basis."

"I noticed a Blothrud on my way in. Perhaps it was him."

"He's the only one of his species at this work camp. Just stay out of his way. He has no patience with our types. His only interest is carrying out the Overlord's orders and keeping us working."

Grewen scrunched up his brown leathery forehead. "What exactly is it we are mining for? What is so important to allocate such resources for?"

"The Keystone is the final piece in a dam which will protect us. Once found and placed, our water will be fresh and skies will be generous to our needs for thousands of generations. The Overlord's paradise will be completed."

"What does the Keystone look like?"

"We don't truly know. They tell us that we will know what it is once we see it. It will be unique from the rest of the rocks we are removing."

Chapter 15
Protect Me from Myself

After a day of flying over the city and the surrounding mountain region, no farms nor towns were found. Avanda sat upon Chug, perched upon a peak above the city, gazing out over the southern valley at the forest and the Govi Glade. All was quiet below. "There's no life or motion in the glade any longer," she said softly, holding tight to her book which continued to crack and break off into small pieces. "Just like there is no life in Vesik anymore."

Pheosco sat before her on the larger dragon's neck taking in the warmth of the sun on his body. "It does not define you, Avanda. You are powerful without it."

"I was much more powerful with it."

"True." He growled at the thought of Thorik stealing it. "It is my fault. He took it from me while I held it for you. I am to blame."

The cool mountain air blew her colorful hair out of her face before it gently wafted behind her in the breeze. She calmly breathed in and then slowly exhaled with closed eyes. "I'm vulnerable again."

"We are all vulnerable. However, I am in your debt for your loss. I will always be here to protect you."

"I've heard that before from Thorik. But that just doesn't work out."

"I pledge myself to protect you."

She adjusted her position upon the large brown dragon as she thought deeply. "From what? From all others? From nature? From myself? How can anyone protect me from everything?"

"I will do whatever is needed," Pheosco said with a slight bow of his head.

"Ralph..."

"Pheosco," he quickly corrected before she continued.

"I'm beginning to think Thorik may have been right in taking Vesik away. Yet, I'm still furious with him for doing it. And yet, how can I hate him for doing something to me that he did out of love?" She sighed at her own words. "How can you protect me from my own insanity? What path do I travel?"

Pheosco sat idle as he thought about the question. "I find the best plan is to just select a path and then fly with it."

"I wish it was that easy. I've said things to Thorik that I now regret. He'll never forget my words of anger."

"He may not forget, but he may forgive."

"Will that be enough?"

"If not, then it will be his loss."

"But I do not wish to lose him. No matter how angry I've been with him, I've always loved him." A tear ran down her cheek and the cool wind caused her to shiver from the moist path in which it trailed. "I'm afraid."

"Of what?" Pheosco's head smoothly turned to scan the area for potential danger.

"That my desire to be completely safe from anyone wishing me harm will cost me all those who wish to protect me." She looked deeply into the yellow eyes of the small green dragon. "Can you protect me from that?"

After a moment of gazing back at her, his thin leathery eyelids blinked before turning away. The muscles in his thin long neck tensed as he struggled to give her an honest answer. Each tiny scale across his body shifted from the flexing of tendons underneath. "As Lord Rummon once said, 'Joy and life travel the same path as pain and death. To avoid one set of these is only accomplished by avoiding both sets.' What you ask is not something I can protect you from."

Silence followed as they both looked over the peaceful wooded valley. The scenic calmness below them was nearly hypnotic as the wind made various patterns in the canopy of treetops and the open grass fields. It continued this way for several relaxing moments, until an earth-shattering crack from down within the city broke their sense of serenity.

A section of one of the cliff-faces near the market had slid down, destroying the homes and structures below it. Locals screamed in horror and ran from the devastation, many of them not making it out in time and becoming buried in the rockslide.

A cloud of dust shot down the streets, encasing the residents with a layer of light gray filth. Blinded, they were unable to see and prepare for a smaller second thin slice of the mountainside to break free and fall onto a nearby set of buildings. Alarm bells began to ring from the turrets near the egress and echoed across the city.

Chaos reigned near the city's marketplace, due to the two rockslides only a few blocks away. Without warning, the calm environment had become a hub of commotion. Coated with gray residue and blood, some ran from the area or dragged loved ones to safety. Others rushed toward the fallen rocks in order to start removing the rubble and freeing any survivors.

"Go!" Avanda put her book away and grabbed onto Chug with clinched fists, as the brown dragon leaped from the peak and began to dive down to the scene of destruction. His speed increased so quickly that her legs trailed her body on their decent.

Pheosco flew next to her, his wings in tight and neck stretched out before him as the streets rushed toward them. Arching his body, he swooped into the dust cloud and out of view, hoping that Chug was going to follow him.

Snapping his wings out to his sides, Chug abruptly stopped on the street. The sudden halt caused Avanda to be knocked off, rolling into the dusty haze.

Gathering her senses while lying on the stone pathway, she had been separated from both dragons and was now on her own. The ground near her was littered with broken goods and wall fragments. It was then that she noticed the light gray dust that surrounded her began to turn dark from one specific direction. This was the very same direction that new screams of pain were coming from.

Before she could stand, one of the local elders ran out of the dust cloud toward her. Yelling, he bolted from the dark region and tripped over her. Falling, he clutched his arm and chest, which were dark gray and overly thin as though all of the flesh and muscles had dried up and were grasping onto the remaining bones. He quickly screamed at Avanda to help him before the injuries to his chest took his life, falling forward on top of her.

Unsure what had just happened, Avanda looked back at the darker section of the dust cloud which continued to deepen, allowing less light to pass through. The darkest section appeared to move within the haze as though it emanated from a person walking out from the rockslide destruction.

Broken clay pots near her feet began to lose their cohesion and crumble apart. Splinters of wood turned gray and shrunk into a charcoal looking state. Everything along the street near the darkness began to lose its luster and vitality as the evil passed by her location.

"Lord Bredgin." Crackling of fear lingered in Avanda's voice.

The movement of the darkness stopped.

Frozen with fear, she tried not to make any noise. Even the sound of her own heartbeat caused her concern as she held her breath to prevent any chance he would hear her.

Stones within the street cracked and items that laid upon them turned to colorless ashes that were blown away by the air currents.

Wishing to pull her feet and legs away from the nearing darkness, she feared the movement would give away her location. Instead she allowed her boots and clothes to slowly turn from deep leathery browns and colorful fabrics to dingy pale shades of gray. Her feet and legs began to ache and burn beneath their protective coverings.

She would have to move in order to save her lower limbs, and so she did. In doing so, the rustling of her and the debris on the street caused more of a noise than she had planned.

Alerted to her location, Lord Bredgin leaped forward. The darkness that surrounded him made it impossible for others to see, let alone survive. However, his E'rudite powers were not only strong enough to create the deathly darkness, but also to live and see within it.

Looking down at his prey, he was disappointed at what he found. A local elderly man was slowly dissolving away from Lord Bredgin's powers. Flesh quickly dried up and flaked off the bones that became brittle and gray. He had hoped to find a Num from his past.

Running through the dust cloud, Avanda would see Krupes arriving to the scene of the destruction, being led by a large red Blothrud. Racing with everything she could in order to escape the E'rudite, she avoided getting in the way of the Krupes. Turning to look back to see if Bredgin was chasing her, she ran into a human who grabbed her tight enough to prevent her from getting away. Kicking and screaming only caused the man to be more forceful, pushing her onto the ground and pressing his body on top of hers.

Her worse nightmare had come true as she visualized the rape she nearly sustained by Lucian back in Southwind. She was once again in a situation that she feared most as she attempted to kick and scratch her assailant.

"Stop it, Avanda!"

It took a moment to register his voice and that he had said her name, but she eventually realized that she knew this person. "Ericc?"

"Yes," he replied sternly. He showed no signs of being happy to see her. "Where is Thorik?"

"Thorik? Is that what this is all about? Are you all after him? Is Lord Bredgin here to find Thorik as well?"

"Not if I can find him first."

Chapter 16
Hunting Thorik

Thorik heard the rockslide from across the city as it echoed within its tall walls that surrounded the city's perimeter. The reverberation shook every path and wall as loose hanging items and décor fell from shelves and windows in homes and shops. There had been a temporary calm after the first two before they were followed by a series of explosions in a different part of the city.

Stopping at a street corner to determine which way to head next, Thorik could see the locals running for their lives in every direction. Nowhere seemed to be safe. He had managed to escape the guards at the front entrance over an hour ago only to be now caught up in an attack upon the city.

Panting from the sprint up the street, he spotted Gansler with one hand in the air, trying to calm everyone down and the other hand held his cane trying to keep his balance. It was difficult to slow anyone as the city's emergency bells were ringing in the distance, alerting everyone to immediately return to their homes until they stopped chiming.

Dodging the frantic locals running toward him, Thorik kept moving against the flow of traffic. "Gansler! I'm going to find out what caused the blasts. You need to return home."

Nearby, a large explosion in a nearby structure rocked the area and sent debris into every street. Reducing the building to rubble, a violent flame swept over the items remaining inside.

Creatures of all sorts ran from the devastation while Thorik charged toward it.

Gansler was the only one unruffled by the events. "Don't panic! Sovereign Gansler is here to resolve this." His unsuccessful attempts to shake their hands caused him to eventually be knocked over by the mad exit of locals.

Continuing to run against the crowd's flow, Thorik reached the newly destroyed structure, only to hear screaming from within the burning building.

Never thinking twice about it, he lunged forward through the flames toward the cries for help. Past the rubble and the fire into the back room, he found a small child trapped under a fallen shelving unit. "Hang on! You're going to be safe!" he yelled over the sound of the fire as smoke began filling the room. Lifting the edge of the unit, he yelled, "Climb out!" which the child did and then bolted out of the room without having to be ordered to do so.

By the time Thorik released his grip and turned to follow the lad, the doorway collapsed and fire sprang forth, blocking the Num's exit. Racing across the old wooden beams, the flames gathered fuel from everything it touched.

Thorik was trapped. His throat and lungs began to burn and his breaths became a struggle to gather the air needed. The visibility worsened and it hurt to keep his eyes open. He would be dead in a matter of moments.

"He's after you, you know," came a voice from within the murky room.

"Who's there?" Thorik coughed from the smoke in his lungs after every breath.

Stepping closer, a figure of a tall thin man could barely be seen. "He wants you to never be born. It would be to his benefit, but not to mine. You still have a task to perform that I need. So we must ensure he does not succeed. Use the Freedom Runestone. It will inhibit the powers of an E'rudite."

"We need to escape this fire! Can you help me?" Thorik choked and fell to his knees from the thick smoke that now occupied the entire room.

"Yes I can," said the stranger. Showing no signs of breathing issues, he placed a hand upon Thorik's shoulder. "Beware of him, Thorik Dain of Farbank. He is the one you must fear, not me. I would kill him myself if he was not of my bloodline."

Thorik continued on his hands and knees, gasping for air. He could see the faint view of white boots and the bottom of a white cloak before him.

"There now, you are safe from this fire. But you must still hide from him. His efforts to prevent your existence will kill all of us. You must not let him succeed."

The burning of Thorik's eyes and lungs began to subside, as though the air was clean and fresh. Looking about, he knew this not to be true, and yet it was causing him no harm. Not understanding what had happened, he turned to tell the stranger of his recovery only to find the man was no longer there.

Flames coated the walls and ceiling, wicking their way down onto the floorboards. Thorik still didn't see a way out without being burned. However, he noticed that he no longer felt the intense heat he had before.

Stepping closer to the fire, he reached out, only to find that his fingers did not burn. He was immune to flames and apparently the smoke as well. Still cautious, he tested his hand in the fire a few more times, but as the rafters began giving way, he took the plunge before it was too late and ran into the flames all the way through the building and eventually out into the now empty street.

Once there, he came to a complete stop and patted out the flames. He may have become fire resistant but his clothes were not. As he saved his garments, he turned to see Ambrosius standing just down the street.

"Thorik!" Ambrosius shouted. His voice was filled with anger and energy. Placing his wooden quarterstaff in both hands, he lifted up his arms toward the Num and screamed a war cry unlike anything the Num had ever heard before.

A wave of energy rushed forth from the E'rudite down the street, disrupting the sun's light along its route while it rolled like a wave just feet above the ground.

Agile, even for a Num, Thorik ducked and rolled out of the path of the intense power wave.

The visible disturbance continued past him until it struck another man, this one dressed in all white. Bald and bony, his solid white eyes didn't flicker as the forceful wave struck him. If not for the man's long white beard and robes blowing uncontrollably, it wouldn't have even appeared to have hit him. This was the man who had just saved Thorik.

The Num popped back up onto his feet and spun around to see himself standing directly between the brothers of war; Ambrosius and Darkmere. Twins and heirs to the throne of the Dovenar Kingdom, they nearly destroyed everything in their civil war against one another, and now Thorik stood in the center of them.

A sudden crack appeared at Darkmere's feet and darted down the street toward Ambrosius at the speed of sound, passing under Thorik's feet. Leaping to the side with his swiftness was not enough to get him to safety before the crack snapped open into a deep chasm. Catching Thorik by surprise, his leap to safety was less than successful. Grasping the side of the newly formed rift in the street, Thorik began lifting his body back up to the street.

Ambrosius waved one arm from his side to his front, causing a large section of wall from the destroyed structure to fling out directly toward the Num.

Unable to get up and out of the way fast enough, Thorik fell back down in the chasm to avoid being hit. He then dangled by his fingers from the side until he could attempt to climb out once again.

Darkmere watched as the flying chunk of wall just missed the Num and then roll directly at himself. He instantly changed his body from flesh and bone into a solid metal statue, causing the incoming wall to shatter upon impact. Before the wall debris even hit the ground, Darkmere changed the breathable air before him into a blue fiery inferno, reaching out over Thorik's head and out to Ambrosius.

Reaching forward, Ambrosius used his powers to deflect the colored flames from reaching him. But the fire didn't subside. Instead, it continued to increase, surrounding Ambrosius and causing the E'rudite to completely encapsulate himself.

It was at this time that Darkmere's street chasm ruptured even further, nearly shaking Thorik from his hanging position and widening under Ambrosius' feet.

Now in a defensive posture, Ambrosius not only shielded himself from the ongoing intense flames, but he was also levitating himself above the open chasm. And if that wasn't enough, a dark shadow moved down the street from behind him.

Cloaked in what appeared to be an area void of all light, Darkmere's son walked toward Ambrosius. Lord Bredgin's bald tattooed head pulled forward from the darkness that shrouded his body. His light gray skin showed no signs of flesh tones even in the sunlight. Trailing a wave of darkness behind him, such as a comet leaves a tail of itself, the stones in the road cracked under his feet where he stepped.

Unknowingly, Ambrosius was trapped between Darkmere and his son. Not only could he not reach Thorik, but he couldn't even see him through the flames lapping at his invisible defense.

Testing the flames with his hand first, Thorik pulled himself up and out of the chasm. Once he realized he was still immune to fire, he ran to the far side of the street and into an alley. He turned to witness the battle unfold. Darkmere continued to open the chasm and increase the flames, but it was obvious that he couldn't see beyond the point where his blue fire sprayed out in every direction after hitting his brother's protective barrier.

Stepping to the edge of the chasm and up to Ambrosius' shield, Lord Bredgin's darkness cloaked his body. Even the flames that coated his uncle could not survive within Bredgin's dark veil. It was as though there was no air for the fire to use in order to exist.

Placing his hands on the invisible shield, Bredgin began to force his darkness through. Each fingertip released a very thin stream of darkness, which pushed through the barrier and moved toward his victim like ten poisonous snakes.

Releasing his shield would cause Ambrosius instant death from either the flames or the approaching dark death. And if not that, he would fall into the chasm to his demise. His mortality was about to be tested.

Thin streams of darkness began to rap around his arms and neck, turning his skin gray and causing it to crack and flake off. The pain was like no other he had ever felt as he attempted to concentrate on his invisible shield's strength.

Lord Bredgin pressed his face up against the shield and gave the elder man a hideous smile of crazed love for pain before reaching his thin strings of darkness up to his uncle's face and into his nose and eyes.

Ambrosius screamed like he had never screamed before. The overwhelming anguish of the torture was more than he could bear. He had nothing more to give.

Over the roar of the fire, even Thorik could hear the E'rudite's last scream in horror. Thorik couldn't help Ambrosius, even if the old man hadn't been trying to kill him. "Nooooo!" he screamed back at his old friend.

Lord Bredgin's head snapped toward Thorik, giving the Num a look that would haunt his dreams for the rest of his life. It was just enough of a distraction to let Bredgin's attack waver.

Ambrosius released his shield and instantly refocused his energy on pushing himself down into the chasm, causing Darkmere's powerful blue flame to hit his son with full force.

Knocked back a dozen yards, Bredgin rolled to a stop before the darkness surrounded him once again.

Thorik and Darkmere had seen that Ambrosius had fallen.

"Run!" Darkmere yelled to Thorik. "Hide before it's too late!"

Hesitating, the Num wasn't used to taking orders from Darkmere.

In a blink of an eye, Ericc appeared next to the tall thin man in white, and immediately knocked the man down to the ground with a body block. From there, he looked up to see a dark haze down the street on the far side of a deep chasm.

"He fell in!" Thorik yelled from the alleyway without even thinking. His longtime friendship with Ambrosius still caused his instincts to want to help.

Looking down into the chasm, Ericc could see his father lying on a ledge. He instantly disappeared from view, only to reappear kneeling with Ambrosius on the street near Thorik.

Obviously injured, the elder E'rudite opened his eyes and saw the Num who was stepping out of the shadows. "Ericc, grab him!" Ambrosius shouted.

Thorik backed up in fear from such a statement from one he just helped save.

Standing, Ericc approached. "Enough hiding, Thorik! We need this to end!"

By this time, Lord Bredgin was back on his feet and moving toward them, while his father shook off the unexpected body block.

Thorik turned and began to run down the alley, only to find Ericc blocking his path.

"No more running. We need to finish this!" Ericc yelled as he approached to grab the Num by the shoulder. And just before he did, he saw the darkness of Bredgin and the blue flames from Darkmere rush toward his father. Ericc instantly vanished from the alley and appeared next to his father. And just like that the two of them had vanished.

Bredgin reached the location from where they had disappeared. They were gone. In addition, the alley was now empty as well. He had missed his target.

Reaching out with his powers, darkness fell upon a city block, causing everything within its reach to crumble into dust and ashes.

Chapter 17
Gansler's Evening Duties

Thorik's Log:
Ambrosius, his son Ericc, Darkmere, and his son Bredgin have arrived in Dolor. They're all after me for something I may have done or an action I will take in my future. Either way, I'm not safe out in public. Fortunately, the E'rudites don't seem to be a threat to the locals as long as the residents stay out of their way. Apparently I'm the catalyst for their tempers and violent conduct which lays waste to all those in their path. It's clear my actions are more important than even I assumed. It's odd that they don't rip this city apart looking for me. Perhaps there is something they are avoiding as well. Even with that said, I think it's best for everyone if I stay off the streets. However, I'd feel better if I knew where Avanda was. She has yet to return home. If it was not for the threat on my life, I'd be out looking for her.

Night had fallen on the city of Dolor and the ringing of the bells had ended. Even though the alarm had stopped, the curfew ensured no citizens would have been out of their homes. Most had heard the rockslide near the market. Many knew of the battle of magic that was fought in the streets. However, all residents believed that the Overlord would resolve and protect them from any future harm. It was not the first time that disasters such as cave-ins and rockslides had occurred. Clean up crews would be appointed and life would return to normal, as arduous and dull lives at they were.

Savroc raised his Blothrud muzzle in the air and sniffed the odors that lingered in the cracked street where the E'rudite battle had taken place. His Krupe troops searched for signs of what had taken place while he had been distracted by the destruction near the egress. "Assign a few dozen miners to start reconstruction on each of the damaged sites first thing in the morning." Glaring at the wide chasm down the center of the street and demolition to the surrounding buildings, he growled. "I will alert our master that we have some uninvited guests."

Several blocks away and after hours of searching the empty streets while hiding from the E'rudites, patrolling Krupes and a nasty looking Blothrud, Avanda peered out from an alley. "I don't see anyone. Let's go, Ralph."

"Pheosco," the green dragon replied under his breath. "If the E'rudites can't find Thorik, what makes you think we can?"

She rested her back against a cold gray stone wall and sighed. "I don't know. But I have to keep looking."

"Why? You're better off without him."

"Not long ago, I would have agreed with you. But the more time I spend without Vesik's influence, the more I find myself thinking clearly. Even though I feel more vulnerable without Vesik's powers, I also feel more self-assured in my own abilities. As much as I struggle to say it, Thorik may have saved my life by removing my dependence on her."

Pheosco recoiled his neck and tilted his head in question. "Then why do you continue to cling to her?"

Glancing down at the book tucked in tight under one arm, she seemed confused and struggled to give him an answer. "I don't know why I'm still holding on. Even in her death, my inner core craves her in spite of my mind's better judgment." Gently inserting the brittle book into her pack she hesitated only once before closing the top. "Even placing her out of sight and out of my touch seems difficult." Her hands shook for a moment as she held them in front of her, empty of Vesik.

Leaning out into the street for a clear view of their surroundings, Pheosco saw no signs of life. "It's been too long and Chug has not reported back in from Gansler's home. I was concerned about sending him there to see if Thorik had made his way back. Either he's lost, been attacked, or most likely found some food and has forgotten to return to us. We have to assume he's not returning. What is our next move?"

"It would appear that all the E'rudites are hunting Thorik, so…" She paused as a figure hobbled through the darkness and into view. "What is he doing out here after curfew?"

"Risking his life, much like we are." Pheosco's eyes continued to dart back and forth for any potential dangers.

Avanda checked the street once again for danger. "Let's follow him to see what he's up to."

Striking his cane upon the stone with a crisp snap each and every time he stepped, the Num coming down the street was none other than Gansler.

Curious as to what exactly he did after dark, Avanda and Pheosco kept their distance as they followed Gansler down various streets and through a short maze of alleyways to a pale and bland home built onto the side of a mammoth limestone rock which housed a dozen homes; all with gray wooden doors and small dirty windows. Then again, all homes in Dolor were bland stone blocks or wood frames and built up against the large rocks that reached high into the air. No homes were unique other than perhaps their shape and size. None had numbers or names to distinguish one from another, nor did the streets for that matter.

Pheosco perched on a roof while Avanda rushed forward before hiding behind a pile of trash in the alley. They both kept a trained eye upon the Num's moves.

Stopping at the doorway, Gansler paused and suddenly appeared nervous. His hand reached up three times before he made a fist and used it to knock on the door.

A few moments went by and Gansler nearly used the delay as an excuse to leave. He turned to walk back the way he came.

Avanda slapped her back against the wall, knowing she would easily be caught if he walked past her.

The door that Gansler had knocked on, however, opened before he could leave the front step.

Standing in the open doorway was Ren. His head hung low like a wilted flower but from beneath his shoulder length hair his glare at Gansler was firm as an oak. "It's about time."

Mist rolled down the mountain walls and the sides of the homes and then across Gansler's feet as he nodded in agreement and waited to be invited in. The chilled tension in the air should have made the mist freeze as he struggled to look Ren in the eyes. "I'm sorry," is all that Gansler could squeeze out.

"My wife can't take this anymore. It's happening more frequently."

"I know."

"Do you, Gansler? Do you know how it affects us? My children can't sleep. They have night terrors every single night and wake up screaming in horror. I don't recall the last time I felt safe in my own home. I always feel like I'm being watched, never knowing when it will happen again."

"I'm sorry."

"Sure you are, now that we have to pay the price of your actions. But you were so stubborn back then that you wouldn't listen to us. Do you recall me coming to you? I begged you to leave my son alone!"

"He wanted to-"

"I don't care!" By this point his voice was echoing down the alley from his shouting. "I asked you as a friend to leave him out of it. But you couldn't do this for me or my wife or my other children. You had to take him with you so that you could fulfill your destiny. Instead, you left us all with an eternity of pain and suffering."

"I'm truly sorry this happened."

"I know! You're always sorry…now. You're a pitiful worthless man who pretends to be someone he's not while apologizing for the decisions you made for others without our consent."

Gansler took the abuse and waited to be invited in.

Ren shook his head at the man outside his door for a few minutes while his anger subsided enough to speak without shouting. "Get in here. No reason to delay our anguish any longer than we have to."

Gansler waited for Ren to step back into the home before he followed the man in and then closed the door behind him.

Avanda jumped up in the alley and ran down the rest of the way to the home's window in order to see what was happening inside. Her heart raced as she risked the chance of getting caught. However, curiosity had always coaxed her into taking larger risks, and she felt compelled to find out what Gansler was really up to.

Recognizing Ren from the market when they first entered the city, she peered through the dirty windows. She could see Ren's family huddled together in one corner. They all had dark rings under their eyes and worn looks upon their faces. She had seen this look enough times from people who were overly tired and exhausted. A teenage boy and a preteen girl clutched to their parents while waiting for the problem to be resolved.

The room was not well lit or well furnished. It was just enough to exist with no luxuries beyond the tools to cook and clean as well basic furniture of wooden shelving, chairs and a table.

Gansler walked into the center of the room before stopping and unsheathing his sword. Raising it up in the air, with the hilt upward, he called out. "Hear me now. I am responsible for your death." A gem in the base of the hilt began to glow bright, to which Gansler covered it with a cloth to only allow a fraction of the light escape. "Tublen? Are you there?"

The poorly constructed window and frame allowed Avanda to easily hear his voice inside.

"Tublen, it's me, Gansler."

"*General?*" a distant sounding voice responded from within the room.

"Yes, it's General Gansler. Where are you?"

"*I'm here, at home. I can't find my family, sir.*" The disembodied voice sounded nervous and scared. "*I've looked everywhere. They've either left me or been captured and killed by the Overlord.*"

"They are here, son. They want to see you."

"*You're not listening!*" The tone began to rise and sounded similar to Ren's voice when he became angry. "*I've already looked. They've been taken!*"

Items in the room began to fly off of shelves and across the room. Chairs lifted off the floor only to be smashed back down into pieces. Cookware and knives were pulled from their drawers and were thrown in various directions from an unseen force. "*I'll kill him for taking my family!*"

Ren attempted to shield his family from the objects coming their way.

Gansler dodged a few items and was hit with a few others. "Tublen! Stop! Listen to me. Your family is safe. I've brought them here for you."

The house calmed for the moment.

"*You did? Where are they?*"

"Yes. I did. I'll show you them in a few moments. But to do so I need you to do something for me."

An immediate response was filled with emotions. *"Where are they? I can't see them?"*

"Tublen! This is General Gansler. Are you still under my command?" Gansler's voice was firm and commanding, unlike his normal tone.

All went quiet again until the voice spoke again. *"Yes, General. I am at your command."*

A sigh of relief escaped from Gansler's lips. "Excellent. I have one last mission for you."

"Yes, sir."

"I want you to pick up an object and walk into the center of the room, holding it out in front of you." Lowering the sword, he waited for one of the objects in the room to move.

The family and Gansler glanced around the room, looking for something moving on its own.

"Look, father," one of the children stated, pointing to a wood carving that had lifted off the floor. Ren quickly placed a hand over his daughter's mouth to prevent her from saying anything more.

"Sis? Is that you?" The voice became excited and the object began to lower. "Where are you?"

Gansler spoke up quickly. "Yes. They are on their way. We need to hurry and finish this task before they arrive."

"But-"

"I need you to carry out my last order. Do you hear me?"

The wooden carving of a man lifted back up. *"Yes, sir."*

Once the object had stopped in the center of the room, Gansler waved the family over. "Tublen, I need you to close your eyes and hold the statue perfectly still out in front of you."

Each of the family members stepped up to the floating statue and one by one placed a hand on it. Ren's wife was the last and her hand shook the most.

"With your eyes still closed, I want you to think of your family. Envision them standing in this very room, each one standing here in the center of the room with you and each one placing a hand on the statue you are holding before you." Gansler looked to Ren to see if he and his family were ready.

There was a mixed response. His wife began to shake her head no while he nodded yes to Gansler.

"Do you have this vision in your head yet?"

"*Yes.*"

"Excellent. Now I want you to listen very closely with your eyes still shut while you continue this thought. You will start to hear them call to you." With that, he nodded to Ren.

Ren opened his mouth, but looked for approval one last time from his family. He didn't receive it. He spoke anyway. "Son? Are you there?"

"*Father?*"

"Yes, it's me."

"*Where is Mother?*"

"She's here." He motioned his head for her to talk, but she refused. "She's so excited to see you. So are your brother and sister."

"*Mother? Are you there?*"

She refused to answer as tears ran down her face.

"*I'm so sorry, Mother. I didn't mean to disappoint you. Please don't stay angry at me.*"

"I'm not angry," she said softly under her breath before glaring an evil look at Gansler for making her go through this.

"*You promised that you would never leave. I've been so lonely living at home by myself. And the hauntings keep me up. Things move on their own and I hear footsteps. The house has been taken over by the dead.*"

"Come back to us now." Ren's voice cracked as he fought off the emotions.

"*Come back?*"

Gansler stepped closer. "Yes. Can you see your family in your head? They are all in front of you. Each of them wants you to return."

"*Yes, I can see something slowly appearing.*"

"Good. Now slowly open your eyes. But do not move and do not let go of your statue."

Slowly a faint ghostly image began to appear in the center of the room. Its bones became more opaque, and semitransparent muscles began to form upon them. It was a young man with similar body frame as Ren. Within his now solid skull, two eyes came into view as the apparition turned his head to Ren. "Father?"

"Yes, Son. It's me."

"*Where is everyone else?*"

Ren nodded at his children who appeared fearful of their older brother as his ghostly image slowly materialized out of nothing. With a second nod from their father, they both asked Tublen to come home.

As each one asked him to return home, Tublen's internal organs and muscles became less transparent and more solid, but no skin had begun to form. It was obvious that he was also able to see them once the request was made. In spite of his lipless smile when he was able to see his family, he was still uneasy. "Mother? I still can't see you."

Gansler motioned for her to ask.

"I can't do this. Not again!" She screamed as she collapsed to her knees and cried uncontrollably.

"*Mother!*" As his muscles finished forming, the family could see deep rips in his body and decayed sections that had turned black with dark green puss dripping from them.

Gansler interjected and took control. Preventing Ren from breaking his hold of the statue to comfort his wife, he called out. "Your mother is fine. She is just so pleased to see that you are here. It will take a moment for her to get control over her faculties."

"You bastard!" she cursed Gansler under her breath while eyeing him with hatred.

"Here she comes," he called out to Tublen before turning back to his mother. "The other option is worse. Don't do this to him." He then helped her to her feet.

Pulling away from Gansler, she straightened herself up and slowly moved her hand to the statue. Once there, she closed her eyes and said, "Please come home, dear. I miss you terribly."

It was with that statement that the young man gazed upon his mother while his skin filled in, exposing extensive injuries and infected segments on the side of his skull and across his torso and legs. The ghostly apparition was gone and her flesh and blood son now stood before them. He was dreadful to gaze upon, but he was home. He was safe. He could see them and they could see him. It was the end of a process that was causing everyone to fear every minute in their own home.

Tublen grinned with ripped lips at the sight before him of his loving family staring back at him. "I've missed you all so much. You have no idea how much I love you."

Without warning, a long blade entered through Tublen's back and ripped out from his chest. Blood splattered across his family's faces as they all continued to hold the statue.

Tublen looked down at the sharp blade poking out of his body and looked up at his mother. "Why, mother? Why?"

The look of betrayal on her son's face crushed his mother's heart, causing her to turn away from her son as he fell to his death on the floor. Blood quickly pooled around the lifeless body. Ren pulled the statue out of his children's hands and threw it at Gansler before hugging his children who were now crying.

"Why?" she screamed. "Why does he always look at me and ask that question?"

Once the gem on the hilt stopped glowing, Gansler bent down and pulled his sword back out of the young man. He then began to clean the blade on his way out of the room. "I truly am sorry," he said to Ren's wife.

"Get out!" she yelled hysterically while throwing items from the floor at him as he made his way to the front door.

Letting himself out, Gansler closed the door behind him and fell to his knees in the alley and began crying. The stress had finally got to him.

"You killed him." A voice said just feet away.

Gansler swiveled to his feet and pulled his sword out in front of him, stopping less than a finger's thickness from his potential victim's throat.

Without moving, Avanda looked at Gansler with a new perspective.

Chapter 18

A Murderer's Confession

Gansler slumped his shoulders inward and his forehead down, emotionally drained from killing a good young man in front of his family. And a good family they were. Ren had been one of Gansler's best friends until the upheaval against the Overlord. Since then they rarely talked.

Avanda stood over him with her arms crossed and Pheosco at her side. "Is this what you do at night when you help your fellow neighbors? You bring their dead family members back to life and then kill them?"

"Yes. That is exactly what I do. I am an evil man performing hideous acts. I should be put to death." There was no sarcasm in his voice. He was absolutely serious, which conflicted with his normal insanely happy demeanor.

"But why? Why would you do this in the first place?"

"I have no choice."

Pheosco hissed at the comment. "That's an excuse. We always have a choice, and this one seems pretty easy to make."

"You would think so. But it is my punishment from the Overlord for attempting to free our people."

"Punishment?" Avanda asked.

"Yes. I recruited hundreds to join me in our effort to break free of our confines and to live a life we chose instead of mining for the Overlord for the rest of our lives. The majority of those who joined me were young men with no children of their own. Parents of these young men pleaded with me to not allow them to join my crusade, including Ren and his wife. They were so afraid that I was going to get their son killed, which I inevitably did by losing our battle for freedom. But that was just the beginning."

Gansler paused for a moment and shook his head before continuing. "The Overlord wanted to make sure no one would forget the cost of attempting to overthrow him, so he used his powers to send the soldier's spirits back to their homes to remind these families of what they had lost. Slowly emerging back in their homes, these souls would roam aimlessly within them in an effort to find their family. While in spirit forms they don't have the ability to see anyone of the living. Because of this, they would often panic when their family moved items or made noises. To them, we are the ghosts in the home they are trapped in and they often fight back by yelling and making a mess of things."

Glancing back in the window of Ren's home, Avanda thought about it for a moment. "So they are the ghosts that make noises to us, while we are the ghosts that make noises to them. All of them living in the same location but unable to see each other?"

Pheosco shook his body and changed the angles of his scales by flexing the muscles under them. "I don't believe it."

Gansler gained his composure and stood up straight. "And yet she is correct. It can be frightening and possibly dangerous to allow them to continue existing as spirits." Turning away, he began the walk home.

"They can't co-exist?" she asked. "There is no way to communicate across this chasm between the living and dead?" Avanda quickly caught up to him on the empty street while Pheosco flew ahead to scout for danger.

"We've tried. It has only agitated the dead and caused the hauntings to increase."

"So you bring them back into this world, the world of the living, to end the hauntings."

"Yes."

"Why don't the families just leave?"

"Leave? To where? This is a work camp, not a free city. We have designated locations to live. We can't just pack up and move should we choose. Plus, only the families have the emotional tie needed to coax the dead into this world. If we don't, the fallen will continue to get angrier and create more damage as time goes on. Remember, these are young men that still think they are fighting a battle for freedom but are now trapped in a small empty haunted house."

"I understand, but once you bring the dead soldiers back to life wouldn't this issue be resolved?"

"No. They must be terminated immediately. Once they are among the living, they are driven to continue to fight. We've attempted to let them live, but it always ended with catastrophic results. Their punishment for joining my forces is to not only remind their families of the dead family members in order to prevent future outbreaks, but also to punish the young men with an overpowering urge to fight. Within days after returning from the dead, they would begin killing their own families and anyone else they meet. They are driven to kill."

"Surely not."

"It is true. They do not sleep. Instead, they roam aimlessly looking for potential victims. If a family does not call upon me, they are sentencing their own family to a cruel and brutal death. The obvious better option is to kill them and send them back to the dead where they remain until returning to their home once more. I've even had to do this with my children as well. In fact, we recently just performed this on our son while Thorik was sleeping downstairs."

"I'm sorry that you must endure this, but why must it be *you* who performs this?"

A solemn chuckle was released as he thought about his answer. "This is my sentence for leading the rebellion against the Overlord. I must be the one to murder these poor souls, young men that followed me into battle and trusted me with their lives. And now the irony is that I must kill them all, not just once, but over and over again while looking into the faces of their family members."

"Can't they do this without you?"

"They can bring them back to life without me, but killing them only immediately places them back into a ghostly form with an attitude much worse than before. For them to forget the encounter and get vanquished from the home for months on time, it takes my hand on this specific sword, given to me by the Overlord for this purpose. Once I raise this sword and call to them, the gem in the hilt awakens and guides them to us. Apparently its light can be seen from the spirit realm."

"Then why did you cover it with a cloth?"

"If I didn't, this sword's light would be wakening every spirit in the city. Every household would be suddenly filled with awoken undead warriors, drawn to this light in search of their battle orders. You saw what damage a single spirit can do. The chaos would be devastating if they were all released at the same time."

Avanda tried to understand the full scope of his story and how it affected this city and those that lived within it. "The residents of this city must hate you."

He nodded slightly. "Many do. Some pity me while others just pacify me with kindness in order to make sure that I am quick to respond to their needs when a loved one returns home from the war again."

"How do you handle it?"

"I don't. I wouldn't be able to block it out, if it weren't for Narra. She helps me not think of such things or have such feelings."

Chapter 19
Tales of the Mountain King

Perched high upon a building, Pheosco watched for dangers with his trained eyes. The only nearby movement was the two Nums below. Nodding to them that the coast was clear, he moved on to scout ahead once again.

Slowly sneaking their way through the back alleys to avoid the E'rudites or Krupes, Avanda and Gansler eventually arrived back in the cul-de-sac. Still surrounded with moss and fungi covered wooden trash stacked up against the homes, Chug had found his way home and was chewing on several large decomposing timbers. A large hole in the upper floor for one of the other homes exposed where the wooden beam was collected from. Resting up against the massive dragon was Thorik, as he watched the stars hover overhead.

"Thorik!" Avanda yelled, racing from Gansler's side. Several quick steps crossed the distance to him before she grabbed him and squeezed him with all her might as she started to cry.

Gansler grinned at the scene while limping with his cane over to one of the many piles of wooden debris to reorganize them.

"Avanda?" Thorik placed his hands around her and patted her back. "Are you okay?"

"You fool!" she said with a sniff before pulling back to look at him. "Where have you been? We thought you were dead."

"I've been here, keeping out of sight of the E'rudites."

"So, you're not hurt?"

"No, I'm fine."

"You mean you kept me worried and you've been uninjured all this time?"

Thorik still smiled from seeing her alive and well. "Apparently. Why? What did you think happened to me?"

"I thought you were dead! I saw Lord Bredgin and Ericc here in the city. They're after you!" Wiping her tears, she looked at him with more serious eyes. "What have you done this time?"

"Done? Nothing…aside from existing. Bredgin wants me dead before Ambrosius and Ericc prevent my birth…which in a sense causes me to be dead as well."

"So you now have three E'rudites here in this city to deal with?"

Thorik squinted his eyes and rolled his head before answering. "Darkmere is here as well. But I don't think he's a threat."

Stepping back from the Num, she wiped her eyes one more time before placing her hands on her hips.

"I'll figure a way out of this. I always do." Thorik stepped closer to her, hoping to recapture their embrace before the feeling was completely lost.

Avanda stepped back at the exact same moment. Apparently the feeling had been lost. "So you have four E'rudites trying to kill you?"

"Actually, Darkmere is trying to help me."

A single eyebrow rose, questioning his comment.

"No, really. I was in a burning building with rafters falling in around me and smoke filling my lungs. He gave me the ability to walk out unharmed and escape the fire. I didn't feel any pain."

Stepping back toward him, she tilted her head and pondered his story.

A warm feeling fell over him as he anticipated another long hug from the woman he loved. "Ouch!" he yelped from her pinching his arm.

"No pain? Really? Darkmere is now your friend and now you have supernatural powers? Thorik, just because I don't have Vesik any longer doesn't mean I need a hero to take care of me. I understand my desire to be safe is unrealistic, but don't make up stories to give me a false sense of security."

"What? No! I'm not!"

"I just need to know you're not going to give up on me, even when I'm struggling. No games or stories to make me feel better. I need to know the truth."

"Truth. Got it."

"I don't have the powers I used to have with Vesik, but I have my own brand of magic that has served us pretty well before I found her."

"Yes. Brand of magic," he repeated, trying to be as supportive as he could.

"So we need to work together. No more distance between us. I need you as much as you need me. We are a team, the best team ever. We can achieve anything we want...even without Vesik.

"Team. Yes."

"Stop talking so much and kiss me." Pulling him tight up against her, she wrapped her arms around him and kissed him firmly on the lips.

Inside the home, Brimmelle raised his arms to add to the excitement of the story he was telling Narra, as they sat next to the fireplace. "Then the Mountain King singlehandedly fought off a horde of Blothruds. Altered Creatures came from every direction in their attempt to stop our fearless King in his quest to free the Nums from the evil Notarians. His weapon had broken and he only had his bare hands to defend himself as blood ran down from open wounds across his body."

Narra shook from the idea of such a bloody battle. "How did he survive?"

"That Num had more strength and valor in his little finger than most armies have collectively. With every swipe of his fists he would knock half a dozen creatures up into the air and out of the battle."

Holding Revi tight to her chest, she tried to envision the scene. "He defeated them all?"

"Yes. All had been defeated or escaped...except for a vile demon of a Red Dragon by the name of Rummon. Superior in size to any creature that has ever walked this earth, it blocked out the sun when it descended from the sky onto the Mountain King. A battle unparalleled in history ensued and the Mountain King held his own against the demon along the White Summit mountainside. However, as the King prepared to strike his final blow, he allowed the dragon one last request."

"A last request? But why?"

"The Mountain King's valor and honor was greater than we will ever know. We may never be able to understand his ways."

"What was the Rummon's last request?"

"The demon asked to bow to the Polenum that was able to defeat him. It was final show of respect."

"Was he allowed to do so?"

"Yes, the Mountain King granted him this one last honorable request, only to be tricked by the dragon and attacked by a quick claw slapping him into a cave. Before the King could gain his bearings, the dragon swiped his mighty tail upon the glacier, causing an avalanche to trap the King inside the mountain forever."

"All was lost?"

"No, all was not lost. True, the dragon escaped with his life, along with many of the other Altered Creatures, but so few of them survived that they couldn't cause any more harm to the Nums and humans. The Mountain King had successfully removed the slavery masters and their Altered Creature armies, allowing us to live in freedom."

An unexpected clapping came from the other side of the room. Thorik and Avanda had arrived with Gansler and had been listening to the story as well. "Well told, Uncle. That's the most energetic version I have ever heard you give."

Brimmelle's eyebrow's lowered. "It's inappropriate to tease a Fir."

"Not at all, Fir Brimmelle. I'm absolutely honest. I can recall when I used to struggle to stay awake through your monotone voice and lack of hand gestures. I much prefer this version."

The elder Num cordially helped Narra out of her chair. "I'll tell you more about the Mountain King and his writings when we have a less vocal audience."

"Please don't let me interrupt," Thorik said.

"It's all right," she replied. "I need to make some tea for my husband before he goes to bed."

Gansler stepped into the room with his sword in its sheath and a sack in his hand, hearing her statement. "Not tonight, dear."

Startled, she turned toward him. "Dear, you know you need your tea to relax you otherwise you'll struggle to sleep."

"Perhaps I should struggle a bit more than I have been." It was obvious there was a lot on his mind and tension in his rigid body.

The gaze in her eyes quickly caused his shoulders to soften. "Gansler, we've had this discussion before. I'll make you some tea and then we'll get a good night's sleep. If you want to talk more about this in the morning, then we can…in private."

Gansler's eyelids fell halfway and he handed her his items. "Yes, dear."

Narra led Gansler into the kitchen.

Brimmelle followed closely behind. He was less than discreet about wanting more of her attention. Whether it was because she listened to his stories or if was something more, he followed her around most of the day while reciting verses from the Runestone scrolls that had been lost long ago during a Thrasher attack soon after leaving Farbank. Fortunately Brimmelle had a perfect memory and he could recite them as though he was reading them for his first time. The feel of the paper, the smell of the day, and the music in the background all rushed in as he replayed the moments when he initially read the scrolls. It was almost less of a memory and more of reliving the moments.

Silence fell upon the main chamber after the three Nums had left Thorik and Avanda alone.

After a moment of quiet, he guided her to the floor in front of the fireplace and asked, "Would you miss me?"

"What?"

"If Ambrosius finds me and prevents me from ever existing…would you miss me?"

"That's what you were thinking about when I arrived, isn't it?"

"If I was never born I wouldn't have stolen Vesik from you. That would play a factor."

"I wouldn't have ever received Vesik if it wasn't for you, so no it wouldn't."

"You wouldn't have left Farbank and your parents."

"True, but I would have lived my life always wishing I had journeyed over the mountains instead of ever actually doing it."

"Well?" he added.

"Well what?" she asked, avoiding his obvious question.

"I would miss you."

She smiled. "If you weren't born you wouldn't have missed anything."

Thorik waited patiently for a real answer.

"Okay. Yes, I would miss you." Taking a moment to give the question some thought, she continued. "I would have missed the opportunity of daydreaming about you during your weekly

Runestone teachings back in Farbank, when I was younger. I would have missed the way you make me feel when you reach out and touch my hand. I would miss knowing what it feels like to be in love with my best friend."

Thorik closed his eyes and thought for a moment, before reaching out and softly touching her hand. "I would miss that last one most of all."

A long quiet moment gave him courage to look up and gaze into her eyes.

Leaning forward, he reached around her back to pull her toward him. Closing his eyes, he tilted his head and pressed his lips upon hers. He was amazed at how soft and supple they were, and how every nerve ending on his lips suddenly felt a hundred times more sensitive. The world seemed to disappear and the only thing his body could register was the sensation of her lips upon his.

"What, in the name of the Mountain King, is going on here?" Brimmelle announced while walking into the room with Narra. His lazy day of teaching Narra the virtues of the Mountain King and how his teachings have helped create a civil society was suddenly uprooted by the scene of Thorik kissing Avanda. Embarrassed by the scene, he glanced over his shoulder at Narra who was pleasantly smiling at the two Nums.

Jumping to his feet, Thorik could feel his skin go flush from his head to his toes. The overwhelming feeling of embarrassment of being caught by his uncle made him feel like the child he once was, back when he was a spiritual Sec for Fir Brimmelle.

Avanda, on the other hand, appeared defiant to Brimmelle's rude interruption of such a magical moment. Her eyes squared off with Brimmelle's as her eyebrows pulled down toward her nose.

Sipping a cup of tea, Gansler entered the room and could feel the tension from everyone within it. Continuing his sip, he turned and quickly made his way out the front door to enjoy the company of Chug, closing the door firmly behind him.

Brimmelle eventually relinquished the stare down with Avanda and turned to an easier target, Thorik. "You would tarnish the purity of Avanda with your lust?"

"Purity?" Thorik responded, before realizing how it sounded. Turning to Avanda, he began to explain, "Not that you're not pure, it's just that-"

"And to display your carnal cravings," Brimmelle continued over the top of Thorik, "in public for all to see is beyond my understanding."

"Carnal cravings?" Thorik's initial sense of guilt quickly changed to defending his actions. This was an action he always had troubles doing with the man who had raised him after his parents died. Brimmelle had saved Thorik's life more than once and had used it against him to keep him under control.

"And to nearly rape her in public to satisfy your voyeur fantasies? You should be ashamed of yourself!"

"Rape? Voyeur? Public? We were in an empty room of a house! We kissed! That's all we did. And it was a great kiss until you showed up. I've been waiting my whole life for this kiss and then you messed it up with your higher than thou attitude."

Flabbergasted at Thorik's response, Brimmelle tensed up his back and puffed up his chest. "How *dare* you speak to me in such a manner! I am Fir Brimmelle Riddlewood the Seventh of Farbank, the teacher of the Mountain King's words, the leader of our villagers, the saver of your life, and your elder. You are never to speak to your superior in such a disrespectful way. Have you lost your mind?"

"Perhaps I have." Thorik calmed his voice down without losing the strength within it. "I respect your position as our spiritual leader and your vast knowledge of the Mountain King's words. There is no one that can match your memory of the King's teachings. I appreciate what you did for me when I was younger, but I have repaid that debt long ago and I can sleep well knowing this."

Thorik stood up straight and stepped closer to his uncle, looking him straight in the eyes before speaking again. "But as a mentor and superior, you are greatly mistaken. Your actions do not display the words you speak from the scrolls. You use the King's phrases that do your bidding and conveniently ignore the ones that would prevent you from getting what you want."

"Well, I never-"

"And as far as being my superior," Thorik interrupted his uncle. "No one is my superior. I might still have a lot to learn from others and I surely do not feel I'm superior to them, but I will never again accept, or even believe, that anyone is superior to me."

Brimmelle was dumbfounded at the words and the tone of his nephew's speech. Unsure what to say, his mouth moved in order to start various words but his mind struggled to determine which ones to use. "Love should develop prior to any physical relations," he finally blurted out.

Thorik shook his head at him. "It did, Uncle. Where have you been?" Turning to look back at Avanda, he smiled. "Love has been blooming for a long time. I have been just avoiding it in order to live up to the unrealistic standards you expect of me, and to prevent myself from becoming weak to its power. How did I not see that love would actually make me stronger?"

Before Avanda could respond to him, Gansler rushed in through the front door, yelling to all that would listen. "He's back! They found it! It's over!"

Hearing his voice, Narra stepped over to her husband to calm him down.

"It's been found!" Gansler's body was shaking with excitement as he danced his way through the room, grabbed Narra, and twirled her around in the air.

Avanda glanced back and forth from Thorik to Brimmelle. "What's happened?" Slight shrugs from the other Nums let her know that they were just as in the dark about his words.

"Slow down," Narra said, while he picked her up off the floor with an enormous hug.

"They'll leave now. There's no reason for them to stay." Setting Narra down, he stepped back and started pacing the room like a madman. "So much to do, you know. They're all counting on me."

Avanda was just too curious not to ask the obvious question. "What has happened?"

Narra straightened her dress. Her slight smile and casual behavior appeared that she had been through this before. "They must have lit the liege lantern. My husband reacts like this every time the Overlord visits."

The Nums watched the crazed man rifle through chests and cabinets in a frenzied search. Placing several rolled up papers under one arm, he tossed the majority of the documents over his shoulder into the center of the room. In addition, he carefully grabbed a silver inkwell and long fountain pen.

It was quickly followed up with Thorik asking, "What are you looking for? Perhaps we can help."

"I'm not helping," Brimmelle grumbled, still upset with Thorik.

"No one asked you to," Thorik said, walking away from his uncle and next to Gansler. "Are you looking for a specific document?"

Snapping his body toward the Num, Gansler grabbed Thorik with his free hand. "Did you find it?"

"No. I don't even know what it is."

"Then how do you know I'm looking for it?"

"Just a guess, seeing you have a lot of documents already collected."

"Well, it should be here someplace."

Thorik glanced down into a chest full of papers and picked up a few to inspect. "I can help if you let me know what to look for."

"The Consuming Addendum, of course. Did you think I would leave out that part of our agreement?"

"No. Absolutely not," Thorik said, playing along with Gansler to keep the man in good spirits. "We definitely want to make sure the consuming continues."

Dropping all of his papers on the floor, Gansler's eyes went wide. Staring at Thorik, his fists began to shake and he began to distort his face with anger.

"Gansler!" Narra ran over and jumped between the two. "He doesn't understand. They aren't from around here. Thorik doesn't know what he's talking about."

Brimmelle gave a slight grin and softly mumbled, "Agreed."

With wild eyes, Gansler appeared ready to attack the Num and very well might have if it hadn't been for Narra. "He said he supports the consuming!"

Lowering her voice, Narra attempted to calm the situation. "I know. But it might mean something different to him."

Nodding his head, Thorik attempted to correct his mistake. "Yes. That's correct. From where I come from, consuming means to eat and digest for nourishment."

Gansler's arms flailed about in an attempt to strike the Num. "See! He knows exactly what it means. He approves of this hideous act. Get out of my house! Leave my city! I don't need your kind here."

Narra struggled to keep him from attacking Thorik as she grasped her husband around the waist while addressing Thorik. "You should go outside! It will take him some time to calm down, especially if you stay."

Thorik slowly backed away from them. "I'm sorry. I was just trying to help."

She nodded back. "You two need to leave. I will handle this. Avanda, please go in the kitchen and pour Gansler some more tea. It helps relax him."

Avanda nodded and left as the two male Nums backed away from the crazed man while he continued to yell at them for their barbaric beliefs.

"Nicely done, Thorik," Brimmelle grumbled as they left. "I was just trying to help," he said in his imitation of Thorik's voice.

Thorik ignored the comment.

"But once again, you didn't help. Now you've learned absolutely nothing about what's going on in this city."

Once outside, Thorik closed the front door to ensure Gansler couldn't overhear them. "I'm not so sure that's true, Uncle."

"And why is that?"

Holding up one of the papers he had grabbed from the chest, Thorik noted the name of the document. "The Consuming Addendum," he read out loud. "It might be our way out. Let me explain..."

Chapter 20
Insane Plans

A bsolutely not!" Brimmelle turned his head and wanted nothing more to do with the idea. Standing on the far side of the courtyard in front of Gansler's home, he had no plans on entertaining Thorik's escape plan. "It's too dangerous. I would rather live here in this city the rest of my life than to take such a risk."

"You very well may end up dying from hard labor in those mines if we don't escape. And so far this is our best option."

"I'm not working in the mines. I'll find something else to do here."

"Such as? Are you planning on becoming their Fir and start a new following?"

"That's not a bad idea. They could use some guidance."

Thorik glanced up at a new light he hadn't seen before. A large lantern hung high above the entrance to the mines on the far side of the city, giving off a bright white glow. It must have been the light that Narra mentioned. "You can't do that here. If the Overlord finds out that there is a belief system, other than following his own orders, they will end your Fir reign as well as your life.

"You don't know that."

"Open your eyes. These citizens have been beaten. They've given up. They may not have shackles, but they are slaves nonetheless. Any individual growth or entertainment has been stripped from them."

Grabbing an old piece of wood from one of the many piles in the courtyard, Brimmelle toyed with the idea of what it once was used for. "It's not that bad here. I don't see anyone starving. The system they have seems to work. There are no rich and poor like we saw in the Dovenar Kingdom. Everyone here is equal, even the Altered Creatures."

"That's not true. There are those who work directly for the Overlord. They do not live among the rest. They eat better food and are treated better."

"Thorik, you're always going to have some of that in any society. The key is for us to make sure we're in that group."

"What's wrong with living like one of the commoners? Not good enough for you?"

"I didn't say that." Brimmelle tossed the item back on the pile with the rest of the wooden fragments.

"No, but you're fine with any system where you are on the upper tier."

"You don't understand the way it works, Thorik. Most people need someone to tell them what to do and they're fine with this as long as they have food, water, and a place to live. These people have all of these needs met for them. The only thing they are missing is the understanding of the Mountain King's words. What's wrong with me knowing my potential to help guide others?"

"Nothing," Thorik said, shaking his head. "We just disagree. I believe everyone should rise to their own level based on their actions. You believe that a minority should rule the majority who are forced to be equal regardless of their contribution."

"That's a little simplified, but accurate. I see nothing wrong with this. There is always a leader among equals. I have experience in this."

Thorik shook his head. "If there are no benefits or rewards for better actions than better actions will become extinct. Even the Mountain King's scrolls speak of this...."

"Sounds as if I am interrupting a deep conversation," Avanda commented. She had walked around the sleeping brown dragon and through the courtyard while overhearing the last few statements. "Gansler is calming down. However, we had best give him some more time to himself. You really got him going."

"Sorry about that." Thorik's gaze didn't leave Brimmelle. He was still bothered by his uncle's beliefs and an awkward silence continued for a bit.

"So," Avanda eventually said. "Did I miss something?"

Brimmelle scoffed at the comment. "Only that Thorik and I disagree on something, which shouldn't be a shock to you."

"Oh, pray tell, what this time?"

"Go on Thorik, tell her your great escape plan."

Avanda's face brightened up slightly and the tone of her soul-markings lightened a shade. "Well?"

Thorik showed her the document he had picked out of the chest.

"You stole the document he was looking for?"

"No. I had a half-dozen papers in my hand when he went crazy. I was so shocked that I just walked out with them. It wasn't until I was out the doorway until I noticed what I had."

"And what does his document on 'eating' have to do with an escape plan?"

"It's 'consuming' not 'eating'."

"Thanks for correcting me," she said sarcastically.

Thorik immediately knew that it was stupid for him to have made the comment. "This Consumption Addendum is Gansler's attempt to stop the feeding of the Dolor citizens to Bakalor."

"What?"

"Apparently, when Bakalor is in need of nourishment, the weak and frail are rounded up to be fed to the demon. It also appears that those who attempt to cultivate new ideas about running the city or upset the current order are also on the list for consumption."

"That's awful. But what does that have to do with our escape from the city? If anything it would discourage us from trying anything."

Brimmelle smiled and waited for Thorik to explain his plan. "Go on, Thorik. Tell her."

"My idea was that we get caught planning to do something wrong and then get placed on the list."

"Are you insane?"

"Thank you!" Brimmelle stated with his hands out to his sides.

"Just wait. Let me finish," Thorik pleaded. "We've seen the path they travel to get to Bakalor's cave so we know what we're up against."

"Yes. A Demon!"

"Yes, but I think I can talk him into not eating us."

"Really?" Her body language was less than impressed.

"Yes. He's hated me for so long-"

"That's a good angle to start with," Brimmelle interrupted.

Thorik continued, "But he doesn't know me any longer. He's been reborn. This time I think we can free him. You see, he's a slave. By freeing him, he will save us."

There was a long pause by everyone.

"And…" Avanda stated. "Is that the whole plan?"

"Well, I still need to work out exactly how I would free him and what I'll say to him. But, I'm sure I'll come up with something."

She was less than impressed. "Thorik Dain of Farbank, you have lost all sense of logic. There is no reasoning with Bakalor, and there sure is no way for us to defeat him. I don't wish to stay here any longer then you, but we can wait until the time is right and we can leave without having to take on the demon of the underworld."

"For how long are we willing to wait? A week? A month? A decade? I've hated slavery ever since the first time I saw Altered Creatures being chained up as slaves in the north Woodlen city of Pyrth. The idea heats a fire within me that I struggle to control when watching such injustices. But to become a slave myself…I don't believe I can live in such a manner."

"I'm not asking for decades, only for days or perhaps a week."

"What makes you think it will be such a short time?"

"Gansler said it's been found. So it's just a matter of time now." Avanda cupped her hand and held it under a piece of hollowed out wood that had been funneling water down through a maze of paths which Gansler had created until it eventually reached the street.

"What's been found? By who? And how do we really know that it will end slavery?"

Sipping the water from her hands, she then wiped them on her clothes. "They found what the Overlord has been looking for. The search for the Keystone is over."

Thorik shook his head. "Didn't you hear Narra? She said he does this every time they light that lantern. It's a signal that the Overlord has arrived."

Looking up at the new light high above the city, she smiled. "Yes, she did. But this time is different. He said the light is normally yellow. This time it's white, signaling the search is over."

"We can't trust him," Brimmelle argued. "He's lost his mind. You can't have a serious conversation with him. He's fortunate to have Narra to take care of him."

"He's not crazy. He's just struggling to cope with his past."
Avanda paused before continuing. "I think we've all been guilty of
that from time to time."

Thorik nodding in agreement.

"I haven't," Brimmelle said with his square chin lifted
slightly.

"Avanda, I hope you're right, but we need to find out for
sure. At daybreak, I'll take Gansler to the mines to find out the
truth."

"And if you find out he's right?" she asked.

"If we find out that the Overlord is going to leave with his
treasure and allow the citizens to live here in a freedom, I will still
need to lead the E'rudites away from here in order to save the city.
So, no matter the outcome, we need to leave this city to reduce their
risk."

"Don't you mean that you need to leave," Brimmelle noted.
"We do not. You can't even travel the streets without being seen and
attacked by E'rudites. You're the only one bringing danger upon us."

Thorik's eyes moved toward Avanda. "That's true. You
would be able to live here in peace. For some reason, that I have yet
to understand, all the E'rudites have left the city alone ever since
their initial attack on me. I can't believe they gave up, so we have to
assume they'll come back for me. I will have to leave to save the
city."

Reaching out, she held both of his hands. "I'm not at peace
without you." Leaning forward, she cupped the back of his head with
her hand and pulled him forward for a long kiss.

Brimmelle was stunned and Avanda knew it, which is why
she made sure it lasted until he left the courtyard and returned to the
house.

Laughing at his displeasure, they held each other and grinned.

"Thank you for saving me from myself," she said softly.

"I will never give up on you," he replied.

Chapter 21
The Blothrud, Savroc

Separating from the other Mognins, Grewen grabbed another large granite block from the wall and slowly carried it through the tall tunnels before stacking it in a distant room. His trips back and forth continued just as they had the last time he was there and just as his Mognin brothers were doing. It seemed unstructured and yet every creature had a task perfectly designed for them so it all worked in an effective and efficient fashion. Finding the Keystone could take years or even a lifetime, or it could be found any minute. It was truly the luck of the draw.

Cut with acid on most sides and ready to be removed, Grewen snapped yet another block of stone from the wall like he had done so many times before. This time, however, when he stepped back from the wall he bumped into someone passing by.

Shifting the weight of the block, to prevent his momentum backward, he shuffled his feet to stay balanced. Unfortunately Mognins, including Grewen, were not very agile and the few stumbling dance steps ended in him falling and dropping the large block.

Landing with a hard thud, he was just thankful that no one was hurt.

"Watch were you're going, Fesh!" growled the creature Grewen had bumped into.

Rolling to his side in order to stand back up, Grewen saw a muscular creature standing only a head shorter than a Mognin. With a dragon face, broad sculpted human chest, hairy wolf legs, and blades extending across his shoulders and back of his arms, it was obvious that this was the Blothrud, Savroc.

"This isn't a rest cycle. Get on your feet!" Savroc's red skin glistened from his sweat pouring down his body.

"I apologize." Grewen instinctively reached out to receive assistance back up to his feet.

Slapping Grewen's hand away, the blades on the back of his hand ripped through the Mognin's thick flesh. "Don't you ever raise your hand to me!"

"I'm sorry. I must have been thinking of another Blothrud. One with better manners."

"Manners? To a Fesh?" Savroc reached down and grabbed the sides of Grewen's chest. His sharp nails dug into the Mognin's skin while his jagged blades pierced the underside of Grewen's arms.

Grewen had been shot with flaming arrows and stabbed with multiple blades during his life, but he didn't recall if he had ever felt such debilitating pain before. In addition, the placement if the Blothruds nails hit nerves that nearly caused paralysis. It was obvious that this Blothrud knew exactly where Mognin's were vulnerable.

With his victim subdued, Savroc used his amazing strength to lift the giant Mognin up off the floor and slowly into the air. Once Grewen's feet dangled a few inches from the ground, Savroc pushed him backward, slamming him into a rock wall. "And who is this Blothrud that has manners for a Mognin?"

Dazed and in pain, Grewen answered as instructed. "Santorray."

Pulling the Mognin back from the wall, he slammed him back against it a few more times. "You lie!"

Before allowing Grewen a chance to recover or respond to the comment, Savroc heaved his own body backward, pulling the Mognin with him. Utilizing his velocity, he swiveled around before releasing Grewen across the hall into the far wall.

Crashing hard against the mine's wall, Grewen's body not only cracked the rocks it was made of, but he crashed through the rocks into an unknown cavern before rolling to a stop inside.

Hot wind rushed past Grewen and out of the newly made hole, practically burning the hairs on his body. Various toxins wafted out into the mine and down the hall.

Savroc stepped over to the hole in the wall and coughed a few times as the air cleared before waving one of the dragons over.

Clutching the oil vat's central hook in its claws, the dragon flew over to the opening in order to shine a light into the newly found chamber beyond.

Filled with large crystals, the room bounced the vat's light around the room like a hall of mirrors, brightening it up as though a switch had been turned on. Angled in every direction, thin spires of quartz pierced the walls and floors as well as each other.

The wind died off and odors subsided as Grewen sat up to see where he had landed. Surrounded by the amazing view, he gazed at the large room with wonderment. In the back of the cavern was one single crystal larger than all the rest. Thicker than Grewen was tall, the length was easily a few dozen yards. Prisms of light refracted from the clear monolith, casting colors across the room. This was something special. This was unique. This was the Keystone the Overlord had been searching for.

Savroc nodded at the sight before addressing Grewen. "Stand up, Mognin. We have work to do."

The miners quickly started excavating the rest of the wall. It needed to be large enough to remove the colossal sized crystal within the new chamber.

As dozens of creatures all performed their special talents at removing the stone wall, others worked rapidly at creating a wooden litter to carry the Keystone. The frame was designed to appear like a giant ladder, roughly seven yards wide and thirty yards long. Each rung of the ladder extended on each side for the Mognins to use as poles to carry upon their shoulders.

Removing the crystal would be a difficult task. However, placing it upon the mighty framework and carrying it up the ramp of the pit was a challenge all of its own.

Helping remove rocks from the wall, Grewen stopped for a moment to heal his wounds from the confrontation that led to him being thrown through a wall. Within earshot, he listened to the Blothrud bark orders and organize the miner's efforts.

Savroc was cruel and demanding and yet very effective in accomplishing his tasks. Turning to a lead Krupe, he gave further instructions. "Once it's loaded on the platform, I will leave to inform the Overlord. Bring the Keystone up the ramp, through the city, and out the egress. Those not needed in transporting the crystal are expendable and will be terminated."

Chapter 22
True Colors

The soft sound of a spoon stirring within a cup was just enough to pull Thorik from his slumber. The unconscious thoughts of E'rudites chasing him blended in with the realities of a dark room as the red ashes clung to life within the base of the fireplace.

Again, the sounds caught his ears. A single metal utensil was being used in the kitchen by someone who couldn't sleep and Thorik's natural curiosity had kicked in long before he was able to coax his tired body into standing up and playing along. However, his mind won over his exhausted muscles which moved him up and across the room before entering the kitchen.

"Can't sleep?" he asked Narra.

She glanced up from the table upon hearing his voice. "No." Her normal pleasant tone was soft and serious. "Did I wake you?"

He considered telling her the truth. "No. I was between nightmares anyway."

"Can I get you something to sip on?" Scooting her chair back, she began to stand.

"No. I'm fine. Relax and enjoy your drink."

Nodding, she thanked him and sat back down. "I'm actually glad you are awake."

Yawning, he wiped his eyes and couldn't think of one good reason not to be sleeping as he slumped down in a chair across from her. "And why is that?"

Taking a nice long sip she hesitated before answering. "Because I need your help."

"Help?" Struggling to kick the last of the sleepy cobwebs out of his mind, he firmly blinked a few times and sat up a little more at attention. "Absolutely. What can I do for you?"

"Stop Gansler from taking those documents to the Overlord."

The air about them suddenly felt different; more tense and less conversational. There was no doubt in Thorik's mind that the way she stated her request it was more of an order. "I...I don't understand. Why would I stop him?"

"Do you understand who Gansler is?"

Thorik straightened up and considered his words carefully. His perception of the pleasant nurturing housewife quickly was being modified to a woman who was in complete control of her life and those around her. "He said he was the leader of a rebellious force that freed the city from slavery."

"Do you believe that?"

"No, ma'am. He strikes me as a good-hearted colorful man who often lives in his own world."

"He is my husband…and one of the wisest men you will ever meet."

"I meant no offense, Narra."

"He was the father of my children."

He looked down at her pregnant stomach and nodded. "Was?"

"We had three children."

Thorik was suddenly lost and waited to hear more.

"We had a daughter and then two boys. They were everything to me. My life was fulfilled as I watched them grow from babies to their first steps and then to their first days at the mine. My husband was one of the foremen in the mine and was paid handsomely for insuring the workers kept very busy. We had many things of value such as this large home, but more importantly we were rich with love and memories."

Taking a sip of her drink she slowly continued to explain. "Watching our children grow up as miners gave us a new perspective of the unfortunate and brutal state that most were living in. Eventually Gansler became frustrated with the miner's working conditions and the lack of respect to all creatures. He argued with the leaders in the mines and protested against their ways. Our time together grew thin as he spent time writing and negotiating agreements and new rules for all of us to live by. Unfortunately, his stacks of proposed documents were never reviewed by the Overlord, causing Gansler to finally launch the battle that would end our lives."

"End your lives?"

"Gansler led the charge to rise up against the Overlord, only to have his army killed, including our two sons."

Thorik looked down at his feet as he struggled to look into her eyes. "And your daughter?"

"She was knocked down into the pit during the battle while attempting to save one of her brothers."

"So, did the Overlord cause Gansler to go crazy to pay for his actions?"

"No. Worse. He allowed him to stay fully sane in order to keep all of his memories intact so he would never forget what he had done. His punishment was to remember and to face those who also remembered."

Perplexed, Thorik had to ask the obvious question. "Then why does he not act like a man in pain?"

She sipped on her drink and gave a slight nod, understanding his confusion. "Do you know the wood he brings home with him?"

"Yes."

Her voice continued to stay calm, soft and in control. "The soft wood in these parts tend to grow moss and fungi on them when exposed to the constant hot steam vents."

"I've noticed."

"When used properly, the fungi can be used to...let's say calm the nerves."

It only took but a moment for Thorik to understand. "The tea you give him?"

She nodded prior to taking another sip. "Not the black tea I drink, but the brown tea he has with meals. In fact, you had some of this on your first night here. It had no ill effects on you, I presume."

With mixed emotions, he wasn't sure how to react. "You're keeping him intoxicated in order to keep him happy? How can you do this and say you love him and your children?"

"It is because of them that I do this. Have you not seen him? He enjoys his work. He comes home in a good mood and plays with Revi. He is a loving father and husband. We are becoming a happy family again."

"I can't believe you are doing this to him."

"*For* him. And for us. We are rebuilding what we lost. We have Revi and will soon have our second child back. Once we have one more, our family will be whole again."

Thorik stood up from the table. "Are you hearing your own words? You're trying to recreate a family that no longer exists."

"Yes." Her voice continued to come across softly through a slight pleasant smile. "And I wish to keep it that way. Which comes to the favor I need from you."

"I don't understand. You apparently have this all figured out."

"Yes. I did. Until you arrived and started giving him hope again. Now that the Overlord is back, he actually thinks he can win our freedom again with his meaningless contracts and new rules for society. His concepts for living are wise words. Unfortunately, they cannot work in our city, regardless of how much you may entice him to believe."

"Are you blaming me?"

"I'm asking you to stop giving him hope that we can be free. It is pointless. We can be happy without any change. He's happy with how things are. And I nearly have our family back. Why would we risk this?"

"You can't rebuild your past and pretend nothing has happened. You can't take away his drive for your freedom."

"I can and I have."

"But it's not real."

"It's real enough for me and my children. He owes me my life back. He owes me my children back. I want our life back to normal. I want him to go to work and then to come home and play with the kids. I don't care if that means we are free or not."

Thorik was shocked at the entire idea and didn't know how to continue.

Setting her cup down, she reached across the table with both hands and softly held his. "Is it so wrong to want peace? To desire a husband and father who is good to us and spends time with us? I'm not willing to risk losing this again."

"But what if Gansler is willing to?"

"He had his chance and we paid the ultimate price and lost everything. This time it's my decision."

Thorik slowly pulled his hands out of the comfort of her palms. "We're talking about more than you and your wishes. This affects the entire city."

Leaning back, she picked her cup up again. "A city that you do not belong in, where the residents have given you the cold shoulder. This is not your city, nor your people. Don't push your beliefs on us because you feel your moral values are better than ours. We have done fine without you. We didn't invite you here and we surely didn't ask for your help."

Swallowing hard, her words hurt because he knew them to be true. And yet he was still conflicted about what he should do.

Taking the last sip of her drink, she sighed at the flavorful blend of her black tea. "Well, I think I will see if I can get a little more sleep before everyone gets up for the day." Using the table and back of the chair, she began lifting her pregnant body out of the chair.

Thorik instinctively jumped up and helped her out of the chair.

"I've lost one family, Thorik. Don't allow him to cause me to lose another," she said, upon standing up, before turning and walking out of the kitchen and up the stairs.

Half dazed by the conversation, Thorik stumbled back into the great room and placed a fresh log on the hot coals before sitting in his chair. There he sat and stared into the lapping flames as he pondered his place and his actions. Who was he to decide these people's fate?

Chapter 23
The Keystone

Thorik's Log:
The city has been far too quiet as of late. As much as I would like to, I can't believe the E'rudites have given up on finding me. Regardless, I'm going to travel out into the streets today in an attempt to understand what exactly is going on in this city. My simple disguise should help me blend in from prying eyes. I can't lie, I'm nervous.

S overeign Gansler," he announced, shaking hands with various citizens while heading toward the mines with Thorik disguised with a gray cloak that covered his entire body. A slight bounce in Gansler's limp added to his enthusiasm in spite of the lifeless response he received back from the local citizens as the two worked their way through busy streets filled with emotionless faces and lowered eyelids.

Keeping his head down to avoid being identified, Thorik's arms were filled with rolled up documents which kept trying to fall out from the rest as he struggled to keep up with Gansler. "I think we would have been more helpful if we went to the market for Narra."

"She will be fine. Especially with the assistance of your friends to help haul back whatever she ends up purchasing. I have more important things to do."

"What exactly are we going to do?"

"We? Oh dear, no. It is I that will be doing all the talking. I've been waiting for this moment for many years. I knew this day would eventually come."

The sea of gray clothed residents passed them by without notice or concern as the two Nums strolled down the main walkways. If word of their freedom had reached the locals, it hadn't had any effect on their demeanor.

Nearing the mine's entrance, the long line to enter the long spiral march down into the massive hole had come to a halt. There was no one going down or coming up from the opposite spiral path within the large pit that led to the mine below.

The two enormous doors were closed, as usual, but were now manned by Krupes, as they prepared to open them. They had cleared out the area in front of the doors and had started clearing out the residents down the large streets that led from the mine to the center of the city before turning toward the city's market place and egress.

Ignoring the obvious changes, Gansler walked past the Krupes as though he was on a mission. However, his attempt to enter his normal side door was unsuccessful for no one answered the door, regardless of how loud he knocked on it. "I don't understand. I've always been able to get in. I'm-"

"You're Sovereign Gansler. Yes, I know." Thorik picked up one of the rolled up documents that he had dropped near his feet. He glanced at the man's leg which was crippled beyond medical help. He was lucky to be alive with such little disfigurement after orchestrating a coup against his Overlord. Still conflicted about his chat with Narra several hours earlier, he wondered if he was doing the right thing by helping Gansler, who was feeling the high of his fungi tea. "Perhaps this isn't such a good idea. There is obviously something else going on here today and they most likely won't have time to give you an audience with the Overlord. We can try again tomorrow."

"Nonsense! Are you suggesting we give up on our freedom?"

Biting his lip, he had to be honest. "No. But perhaps we should go a few days without any tea and clear our heads before making such decisions."

"No tea?"

"Yes. It's good to fast a few days with only drinking water before making critical choices that have such wide affects."

By this point, the locals were lining both sides of the main street with anticipation of seeing what would come out of the massive doors and down the streets of their city. What had all their years of effort been for?

Unable to cross the street without pushing the crowded parade audience out of the way, Thorik found them standing on the wrong side of the street to make their way back home. And before he was able to determine another plan, he lost control of their situation.

The massive doors began to open as Krupes pulled from the outside and others pushed from the inside, swinging both doors open to reveal two rows of Mognins carrying their payload. The ten to thirteen foot tall Mognins looked small in comparison to the gigantic crystal they all struggled to keep up in the air.

Resting on a framework, with long bars along the sides for the Mognin's to hold and rest upon their broad shoulders, the crystal narrowly fit through the doorway and out into the city. Light reflected and refracted at varying depths within the clear quartz, displaying layers of crystallizations deep inside and showering the street and the crowd with moving prisms of dancing lights.

Mognin after Mognin walked out of the doorway, causing the locals to doubt if there was any end to the crystal they transported. Straight out into the street, the last few Mognins stood over forty yards behind those in the front.

Krupes pushed the citizens back to clear a way for the moving of the treasure. There were no suggestions or easing the crowd back, instead the bulky black-armored creatures swung their swords and maces about as though they were cutting through a deep jungle with a machete.

The locals scattered and ran for their lives as others were chopped down for simply being too slow.

Blood filled the streets where the Mognins walked, coating their feet red, as a sadness was apparent upon their faces for the massacre. One of the soft-spoken giants stopped prior to stepping on the blood and was knocked out of line by the power of the rest of their movement.

Two of the Krupes moved toward him in order to push the Mognin nearly twice their size back into formation to help carry the load.

"Grewen?" Thorik asked himself, recognizing the one member who let go of the framework. "Grewen!" he yelled from the crowd, once he believed his eyes. Pushing his cloak back, he exposed his face to the Mognin.

Holding the two Krupes at bay, with one hand on each of them, Grewen turned his head. "Thorik! It's good to see you as well, little man."

"You found the stone. It's over. The city can now be free," Thorik shouted as he ran out to greet him.

One of the Krupes who controlled the crowd, quickly moved to push the Num back with the swinging of a large mace, but not before Grewen was able step forward and grab the weapon from his hand in mid swing. "That's not needed," said the Mognin.

By this point, Grewen had one Krupe held off with his left hand, another on the ground under one of his oversized feet, and then the third one now reaching up for his weapon. If that wasn't astounding enough, he paid the three captives little interest as he continued his conversation with his friend, Thorik. "Deleth has given the Krupes and Mognins instructions. Yes, his mission here is over and he will no longer need this mine. But there is more, Thorik."

The Num didn't like the sound of his friend's voice. "Shouldn't that be a good thing for the citizens? Are they moving them all to another mine or work camp?"

"No. He plans to seal the exit and melt the glacier, flooding the city."

Thorik attempted to turn a positive spin on the news. "Surely the flooding will take place after they allow the citizens to leave."

Grewen's eyes lowered as he shook his head. However, the Mognin didn't have time to reply even if he wanted to, as two more Krupes arrived and restrained him from holding back the first three. He was then pushed and prodded back into line to grab the framework's bar and assist the other Mognins in their carrying of the crystal out of the city.

Meanwhile, Thorik was grabbed by a Krupe and tossed back into the crowd, landing hard onto the street. There was no rolling to his feet and running back to save his friend this time, as the crowd pushed and shoved each other in order to get a good look at the enormous crystal while stepping on Thorik's hands and back.

"You are a clumsy fellow, aren't you?" Gansler gladly helped Thorik to his feet. "No wonder they have you cleaning streets instead of working the mines."

"Gansler, I need you to be serious right now. We can't allow that crystal to leave this city. How can we stop it?"

Placing his finger to his nose, Gansler tapped it twice and winked at the Num. "I see your game. I can figure out your riddle, you just wait and see."

Frustrated, Thorik searched about for various ideas.

"I know!" Gansler expressed with glee and raised his cane in the air. "We could hide it."

"Hide that gigantic city block long crystal? Are you serious? Where would you hide such a thing?"

Glancing in his pocket, he quickly realized that was no good. "Too obvious." Lifting a loose stone with his foot, he considered hiding it there for a moment before dismissing it. "Maybe we could hide it in my coat closet. No, I lose so much in there; we may never find it again." He then laughed at a few more ideas too silly for even him to suggest. "I know! We could hide it in the mine!"

"How much tea did you drink this morning? They just took it out of the mine."

"Yes! It would be the last place they would look."

"But it's filled with…" glancing over at the open doors, Thorik could see the mine was completely empty. "…nothing. What a wonderfully crazy plan."

"It is my city, and I didn't get to be sovereign just by my charm." His normal foolish smile came across as a look of complete insanity.

"Obviously."

"So, now all we need to do is sneak the crystal back into the mine and close the doors." While he talked, Gansler lifted his cane and pushed with all his might against one of the massive doors. He continued to lean and push and slam his shoulder against it, but the door never quivered. "Once I get it started I'm sure its own momentum will carry it the rest of the way."

"Great. So I have a week to get the crystal back inside before you have the door closed," Thorik said with obvious sarcasm.

Groaning due to the effort he was using to push the door, his response was stressed. "No…You better…make it…two weeks."

"We don't have time for this." Glaring down the wide main street toward the center of the city, Thorik then glanced down another street that led to the city's egress. "They are forced to take the long path because those are the only streets wide enough for their load. We can cut at an angle and reach the market to alert the locals so we're ready to fight off the Krupes and redirect the Mognins carrying the crystal."

"I'll be right with you. I think I'm starting to feel some momentum."

There was none to be seen. "Stop this foolishness, we need to…"

Before Thorik could finish his sentence he could feel the hairs on the back of his neck rise, alerting him that something was very wrong. Turning around, he witnessed a dark mass moving down the street toward him. Less of a shadow, it was more like a hole cut into space. Surrounding the man-shaped mass was an aura of darkness that bent and devoured light that strayed too close. Lord Bredgin had found Thorik.

Before the Thorik could react, Ambrosius and Ericc appeared on the opposite street. He had fallen in the trap he was hoping to avoid. "Hurry!" Thorik yelled to his friend. Grabbing his sack of Runestones, he reached inside for a specific one.

Pushing the massive door with all his might, Gansler called back over his shoulder. "A little help would be appreciated."

A wave of energy launched from Ambrosius and rolled down the street at waist height, knocking anything in its way down in its path. Carts exploded, poles snapped, walls buckled, and crates were crushed or tossed in the air. Lanterns snapped from their confines and shattered against structures, lighting them on fire. The nearly invisible wave carried debris in its wake as it rushed toward Thorik.

Accidently dropping his cane, Gansler bent down to pick it up just as the wave hit the massive door, slamming it shut, but missing the Num. "I knew I had some momentum built up," he said proudly.

Crashing upon Thorik's position, Ambrosius' energy hit against him as an ocean wave slaps against a rock outcropping. Rolling around his position, it reformed and continued down its path toward Bredgin. Grasping the Freedom Runestone with both hands, Thorik shook from the blast of power like a chime after being struck.

Extending his own powers forward, Bredgin neutralized most of the wave's impact, taming it down to the point where it was nothing more than a strong breeze by the time it struck. In doing so, Bredgin had stepped beyond the barrier of a total void of light back into a viewable dark gray form of man who continued his mission toward Thorik.

The Num now stood in yet another street in the city set ablaze and being turned to rubble. It was war zone created by the hands of the E'rudites, much like several other locations.

"I can't keep doing this," Thorik mumbled. "My being here continues to compromise the city and right now it's preventing me from saving it."

Wiping his brow, Gansler leaned up against his now closed door. "This one is closed. That one is yours."

"Run to the market and tell everyone that they must prevent the Keystone from leaving the city. If they don't, we will all be killed."

"Seems a little dramatic and pushy, doesn't it? How about if I suggest they slow the crystal's removal to delay issues?" Nodding, he was pleased with the rewrite of his speech.

"No! Tell them they will die if that crystal leaves!" Thorik yelled, as he protected himself from a tighter band of energy from Ambrosius which nearly knocked him off his feet in spite of using the Runestone for protection.

Throwing one of his hands up in the air, Gansler gave in and started walking down the street of burning buildings and battle debris, totally ignoring the destruction on the street next to him. As he approached Ambrosius and his son, he reached out and shook Ericc's hand. "Sovereign Gansler. Welcome to my city."

Ericc was temporarily mystified at the action and took a double glance as the odd Num continued limping down the street without a care in the world.

The E'rudites continued to move forward and closed in on Thorik as powers were used back and forth while the Num focused as much energy as he could on the Runestone to protect himself. Darkness ate away at the invisible barrier created by his Runestone as though it was acid eating at his skin. Powerful blasts of focused energy warped the barrier at various points, nearly breaking through. It would not be long before they would break in.

Ericc materialized just outside of Thorik's Runestone shield and jumped in to grab him. The barrier only protected against E'rudite powers and not the natural environment, so Ericc's tackle was successful as the two rolled out from between Ambrosius and Bredgin. However, they hadn't rolled far enough to be safe now that Thorik had lost concentration and his Runestone had stopped working. So Ericc quickly transported them down the street and out of the line of fire.

Thinking quickly, Thorik kicked free and ran for freedom, only to find Ericc materializing a few yards in front of him.

"You can't outrun me," Ericc said frankly.

Looking for options to evade Ericc, Thorik leaped into one of the burning buildings. He had taken a gamble that whatever Darkmere had performed to protect him from fire would still be effective. Fortunately for him, it was as he moved about inside the burning building without any issues.

Ericc, on the other hand was not resistant to fire, and could not follow. Even if he could, he didn't have the luxury of time to do so. Darkmere had appeared on the street behind Ambrosius. His priority was quickly changed from the capture of Thorik to the saving of his father.

Powers of all four E'rudites clashed in the center of the street. Thunder roared and flames sprung to life as wave after wave of their powers collided, merged, and rebound from one another. The noise was deafening. The vibrations shook everything within city. The pulsing of bright lights and pure darkness prevented any onlookers from staring.

Without any notice, everything stopped. Silence flooded the battleground and movement slowed to a fraction of its pace.

This was especially surprising to the E'rudites who had not discontinued their attacks. And yet none of their powers were effective any longer as they froze as statues in mid motion.

Standing in the center of the street, between all of the E'rudites, was Deleth with a confused look upon his face. "I know not of who created you. Return to Pwellus Dementa' and travel here no more. You have been warned." With a flick of a finger, all four E'rudites vanished.

Noise rushed in following their disappearance, as to catch up on itself before all was back to normal.

Savroc walked up the street and bowed to the Overlord, Deleth. "I smell these men. They are the same that caused the prior destructions. I should have killed them for you, my master."

"No. They might be the handiwork of Feshlan. He struggles to control his creations."

"Is it worth preparing in case they return?"

"No. We should be gone before they can return. If not, I'll resolve this by returning them to the elements they were generated from. You have more important orders to carry out."

With a slight shift with Deleth's hand a large portal appeared in the street. Like a swirling watery doorway leading into a room that didn't exist on the street, Deleth led Savroc into it. Once through, the portal spun itself out of existence and they had all but vanished from the street.

Thorik had witnessed the scene from within the burning building. Still uneasy about simply stepping out into the vacant street, he raced through the buildings, which were all connected, Thorik eventually exited them in a back alley, out of sight of his attackers, before starting toward the market. He had once again escaped the E'rudites, but he knew his battle was not over. It had only been delayed.

Chapter 24

Death Awaits Us

Gansler introduced himself to the locals in the market. "Sovereign Gansler," he said with a smile while shaking their hands. "You should be aware that the Overlord plans to kill all of us once the Keystone is removed from the city. Have a nice day." Leaving a trail of bewildered citizens, he worked his way through the entire market.

Common for tight-knit communities, rumors and gossip seem to be the fastest mode of transmitting information. Dolor was no exception. Word spread quickly about the Overlord defeating the E'rudites, putting everyone at ease. Gansler's story about the Overlord's plan to wipe out the city was less likely and quickly overlooked.

Meanwhile, on the opposite side of the market, Thorik worked his way past the reconstruction of the area hit by the rockslide. This path had slowed him down greatly, but eventually he found his way down a few smaller streets before bolting into the busy main street. Creatures of every sort slowly bumped into one another as they moved from one shop to another. It was clear that they all felt there wouldn't be any future devastation.

Polenums were far from the tallest of the creatures in the city, and in fact were on the shorter side, so Thorik's ability to see very far was limited. His quick thinking led him up the outside wall of one of the buildings so he could stand on the roof and survey the entire marketplace.

Hundreds of heads and shoulders filled his view in a palette of gray shaded clothing. His friends' whereabouts were anything but obvious. Knowing that Avanda and Narra left for the market, he hoped to find someone other than Gansler to help him. Unfortunately, he didn't see them. They could be in a shop, or perhaps had already gone back home, or they may not have even arrived yet. He could be completely wasting his time while he could be helping Gansler gather support.

It was then when he caught a movement out of the ordinary. Several stacked barrels fell over and a few of the locals were pushed to the side. There was something very wide and large walking at the far end and eventually he saw what he was looking for, a wagging brown tail and a ruffling of giant wings from Chug's back. They were here.

Down off the roof and through the maze of legs and torsos, Thorik jumped, skipped, and dove his way to the last location he saw the dragon. Once there he looked and listened for clues to which way they went. It wasn't long before a stack of crates could be heard crashing down. And within seconds, Thorik arrived at the scene.

Chug was busy eating crates of various melons and red pitayas, crate and all. The pitaya's dark red magenta insides coated the dragon's face and most of Avanda's arms as she attempted to pull his head out of the shop before there was nothing left inside it.

"Chug!" Thorik yelled, to help the situation.

The dragon froze in mid bite before turning to see where the voice came from. Once he noticed Thorik, he backed out of the shop and gave Thorik a long lick across his face.

Wiping the strawberry-raspberry tasting fruit off his face, Thorik scratched behind his friend's ear to keep him calm. "Avanda! Come here quick!"

She stopped apologizing to the shop owner and came to see what the emergency was, cleaning her arms and hands off along the way.

"They found the Keystone and are on their way here with it."

Avanda wiped off the remaining pitaya residue on Thorik's face from Chug's lick. "So Gansler was right. It's over. These people don't need to mine any longer. They can be free."

"You're half right. They aren't needed any longer." He then pointed up at the glacier surrounding the mountain opening to the city. "See all that? Once Deleth has his crystal out of the city, he plans to close off the exit and melt the ice to flood the city, killing the citizens."

"Thorik, we can't let him do that."

"Do what?" Narra asked as she approached with Revi clinging to her side.

Thorik pulled his lips in tight. He knew she would not like what he had to say. "You need to go back home, Narra. This area is no place for you, Revi or your unborn child."

"Why would the market not be safe?" Her words were clear and confrontational.

"Gansler and I are about to save these citizens from certain death by the Overlord. We need to unite before it's too late. You have to leave!"

"I'm not going anywhere. I asked you to do me a favor and this is how you support me? You help him launch another rebellion?"

Avanda was clearly in the dark. "What are you talking about? What favor? What rebellion?"

Narra's eyes tighten upon Thorik. "Gansler has done this before. He attempted to overthrow the Overlord and we all have paid the price for it. Now that things are almost back to normal, Thorik has taken it upon himself to seduce my husband with talk of freedom. He has chosen a path to get us all killed instead of talking my husband out of it, like I had asked."

"Thorik? How could you?" Avanda's hands were on her hips as she stood disappointed in him.

Chug could feel the tension of the stares from the two women and lowered his head to stay out of trouble.

Raising his hands to defend himself, Thorik held his palms toward them. "We don't have time for this. I wanted to talk Gansler out of this, but we talked to Grewen. He found out the truth and told us that Deleth doesn't want these people to contaminate his world, so he means to kill them all once he leaves with that stone."

"I don't believe it," Narra argued. "I've heard stories like this before. It's always best to stay away from conflicts and wait them out."

Screeching from above, Pheosco came flying in and landing hard on Chug's head with no apologies. "You might all want to know that Gansler is going to get himself killed."

Narra's eyes opened with terror. "What are talking about?"

"He's at the city's egress and he's got a crowd listening to his plans to stop the Overlord. It won't be long before the Krupes put a permanent stop to it."

"Out of my way!" Narra yelled after handing Revi to Avanda.

"No! You need to go home where it's safe." Thorik replied.

Stopping long enough to get her point across, she looked him square in the eyes. "I am not leaving my husband. I've worked too hard to get him back. Don't you understand that?" She then turned and started pushing her way forward.

Thorik knew she wouldn't make it through the crowded street in time, especially in her condition. "Chug! Take Narra to Gansler!"

Upon his order, Chug made a few quick strides forward, knocking several citizens off their feet along the way, and then hunched forward to allow Narra to easily climb up onto him.

She hesitated. She had never been on a dragon or high in the air. What if she fell? What if the ride hurt her unborn child? "Can you get us there quickly without flying?"

Chug nodded and smiled, pleased to do whatever was asked of him.

It was not graceful by any stretch of the imagination, but she made it up onto Chug's back and he took off like an arrow down the street, leaving a flume of hideous smelling brown vapors behind him. A howl exploded from his mouth, warning all in front of him to beware of the dangers of staying in his path. Only once was the threat not heated, and Chug spread his wings just long enough to lift off and land on the far side of a few Gathlers who couldn't move out of the way fast enough.

Reaching the far side of the market, they could see the egress from the city. Gansler had climbed his way up into one of the turrets that rose above both sides of the tunnel.

A crowd had gathered below him as he attempted to get their support. It would only be a matter of time before a Krupe would make his way up the inside stairwell and capture him.

Chug came to a stop, causing Narra to fall forward and then off to the side of the brown dragon.

Landing on her feet, she grabbed her stomach. She was in pain, but she needed to stop her husband before it was too late. Stepping away from Chug, she started working through the crowd.

Thorik and Avanda eventually caught up to the brown dragon, and looked up at Gansler and the gathering of locals below. They could see Narra near the front of the crowd, yelling up to him.

By this time, Pheosco had stopped circling and had landed on Chug's back. "Like I said, he's going to get himself killed," the green dragon spat out.

"Not if we can help it," Thorik replied, stepping forward toward the entrance.

Avanda stopped him. "It's here," She said softly, pointing in the opposite direction of the exit tunnel.

Heading toward them, in the distance, Mognins carried the giant crystal down the main street, directly toward the egress.

Thorik knew he had to do something quickly. "Avanda, try to slow them down while I talk to the crowd." Without waiting for a response, he headed for the front of the crowd and then climbed up the turret on the opposite side of the egress. Once there, he could see Avanda, Chug, and Pheosco heading toward the Krupes who led the crystal.

Addressing the crowd, he needed them to stop mocking Gansler as a crazy old fool in order to get them to take the issue seriously. "You need to listen to us. Your lives are about to change!"

The response he received from the crowd was a mixture of denials. Most of them had spent their entire life in the city without any changes. It was too difficult of an idea to accept.

Thorik looked down at Narra, who was visibly upset at Thorik for encouraging this line of thinking. "Your world has been about working the mines, correct?" he asked the crowd, receiving various nods of agreement. "What would you do if there was no more mining?"

Confused looks stared up at Thorik and then at each other, until Narra spoke up. "There has always been a mine and there always will be."

Raising his hands to calm the chatter in agreement with Narra, Thorik finally was able to speak again. "But if at some point in the future the mine closed, what would you do?"

Mumbling throughout the crowd discussed the option without anyone willing to speak up. A general shaking of heads at the concept was still the majority.

"If it closed and you didn't mine, would the food stop?" Thorik asked.

Several shaking of heads changed to nodding.

"The Overlord only provides food for those who work in the mines. If the mine closed and you no longer worked, he would stop paying you with food. So, you'd have to farm your own." Thorik waited for the concept to sink in. "How many of you know how to farm?"

Searching the crowd, Thorik didn't see anyone raise their hand, until he caught a glimpse of Gansler's arm raised to answer the question. "So, if you don't mine and you don't get fed and you can't feed yourselves, then you become a burden to the Overlord." Again, he waited for it to sink in before continuing. "And if we are all a burden to him, then he does not need us and he will close this egress and fill our city in with ice from above us. We will be gone and forgotten as though we never existed."

It was obvious that he had the crowd by now as tempers started to show and the noise from below increased.

"But we haven't stopped mining!" Narra yelled to the group, calming them down. "We mine, we are fed, we have families, we live on. Our system works. Only if we disrupt this cycle will we live out Thorik's scenario. There is no reason to believe anything will change if we simply continue to do our jobs."

The crowd cheered her words praised her thoughts. Without question, she had won this round. Even Gansler cheered for her from his turret.

Thorik took in a deep breath and waited for the excitement to die down enough to be heard again. "The future you are trying to hide from is now! And it is right behind you!" Pointing down the street, he listened to the gasping of the crowd as they gazed upon the giant crystal being carried by the Mognins. "This is what you've all been mining for. If this crystal leaves the city, my scenario becomes true. The mine is now officially closed. Within days you will be out of food. You will die from starvation or by the Overlord's hands. To do nothing right now at this moment is to sentence you and your loved ones to death!"

A roar of anger filled the street below him. The visual of the incredible crystal along with his words had hit a cord and forced them into a survival mode.

Sensing he had them at his call, Thorik took the opportunity to execute the actions needed and take command. "Fight the Krupes! Lead the Mognin's back into the city and we will hide the crystal! As long as we have the Keystone, the Overlord needs this city to exist."

Cheering, the crowd charged toward the Krupes guarding the crystal, while others attacked the Krupes protecting the egress. It was a chaotic mob of a scene below the turrets, except for one pregnant Num who glared at Thorik with anger in her eyes. She knew this would be the end of her plans. Her life had just changed without her approval.

The flat black armored Krupes swung their weapons, injuring and killing those attacking them until the sheer numbers overwhelmed them. Their fight to their death was over within minutes. The city's tenants had taken control.

Thorik made his way down the turret, back to the street below, he could feel the heavy glare from Narra upon him. "I'm trying to save you and your family," he explained to her.

"I didn't ask you to." Her words were bitter and body language was tight.

"But it's the right thing to do for our city."

"It's not your city!" Narra shouted.

Thorik hesitated. "I'm just trying to make things better."

"You haven't so far and you won't in the future. You have just set in motion actions that will change everything. Are you going to be here when those actions have consequences or are you going to avoid them by moving on with your travels?"

Stunned by the question, Thorik hadn't ever planned on staying with this community.

The glazed expression to her question provided the answer. "That's what I thought."

Chapter 25

Hiding in Plain Sight

Thorik and Avanda led the horde of locals and the Mognins, who carried the giant crystal, through the streets. "We can't hide the Keystone for long before waves of Krupes start attacking," he said to himself.

"What's your plan?" Avanda asked.

"I don't know yet."

"Thorik, you started this without having a plan?"

"I didn't really have the time. I knew we had to prevent it from being removed in order to buy us more time." Looking back over his shoulder, they were followed by Pheosco perched upon Chug, with Gansler, Narra, and Revi nearby. Behind them, he could see the amount of trust the locals had put in him. "We're doing the right thing."

Avanda looked over her shoulder as well and then back to Thorik. "Are you trying to convince me or yourself?"

"I couldn't sit idle and watch them all be killed."

"So why are you struggling with your decision so much?"

"Because...She's right."

"Who?"

"Narra. I've been pushing my ways upon them ever since I arrived. And once this is done, we're planning on leaving."

Avanda smiled at the comment. "I think your ego has grown to the size of the Keystone."

"What?"

"Thorik Dain, do you honestly believe that you talked all these people into changing their core values in the short time we've been here?"

Shrugging his shoulders, it was obvious to him that he had.

"Well, let me be the one to deflate your ego for you," she said with a laugh. "You did what you felt was right and if these people weren't ready to hear your message your words would have fallen on deaf ears."

Feeling sheepish, he replied, "I had to have made some impact."

She could see his bruised self-worth by his expression and in his walk. "However, because you were there and had the courage to say what you did, you were able to push them past their own fears to fight for their lives." Watching him straighten up in his walk, she laughed. "You are so easy to read."

"What?"

"It's okay. I kind of love that about you." Giving him a quick kiss, she reached out and held his hand as they paraded down the main street. "So, what do we do when Deleth comes looking for his crystal? You know we can't fight him off, right?"

"I know. We'll all die a bloody death if we attempt to battle him."

"So we're trapped?"

"Yes. But there's always a way out of every problem. I just need to figure it out."

"Careful, your ego is growing again."

Looking into her eyes, he smiled. "Sorry. *We* just need to figure it out."

"Yes, but not now."

"Why's that?"

"Because we have other issues at the moment." She nodded her head toward the side street where they could see in the distance several dozen Krupes marching toward them with weapons drawn.

Thorik glanced back and forth from the Krupes to the crowd of locals who were festive in their recent success. "I was hoping we had more time to plan."

"Sometimes there isn't time." She then turned around to face the citizens. "Krupes!" she yelled back. "Set the Keystone down! Everyone who can fight needs to come to the front!"

Nodding his head, he agreed. "That's what I was about to say."

"You're a terrible liar, Thorik," she replied.

"We should hold our ground and let them come to us."

"I don't like being defensive when we can take an offensive posture."

Thorik agreed that it was definitely her normal posture. "How about if we compromise and do both?"

"Agreed," she answered before calling over her shoulder. "Ralph?"

"Pheosco," the green dragon corrected, as usual. Lifting off of Chug, he began flying above her.

"I want you and Chug to make a rear attack moments before the Krupes clash with us. That will cause them to be disorientated and provide us with a small advantage."

"You'll need all the advantages you can get," Pheosco replied. "You have a mob fighting properly armed soldiers. Fortunately we have the amazing Thorik Dain of Farbank on our side." Rolling his eyes, Pheosco turned and lifted off toward Chug. "I'm not sure if that is an advantage to us or to them. Get in the air, my large friend, we have work to do."

Pulling out his sack of Runestones, several of Gansler's documents fell out onto the street. Picking them up, he stuffed them back into his tattered pack. "Everyone's trust in me is so very invigorating."

"Ralphs just being facetious. The time to worry is when he stops making jokes about you. Then you know he doesn't like you. And that's not good."

By the time the Krupes arrived at the end of the street, the locals had created a semi-circle at the junction. However, the army of soldiers never slowed their strong forward pace with their weapons ready for battle.

Dragons screamed from above and behind the Krupes just before the first blood was spilled. By the time the back few rows had turned around Chug had already crashed his own heavy body into several of the soldiers, crushing them and breaking their bones.

Pheosco buzzed past the army, near the front, in order to distract them from swinging their weapons at the civilians. Chaos had started and it was now time for Avanda and Thorik to attack.

Raising one arm up in the air, Avanda slapped her other hand on her forearm, crushing various magical components. A mist swirled from her arms in a tight spiral, waiting for her command. "Murk Heiveil Opsu!" And with that the mist from each arm sailed across the street and gathered around two of the Krupe's helmets, blinding their vision and making them easy targets.

Thorik stepped forward directly into the army of Krupes. Focused on a Runestone, it caused all near him to become lightheaded and fall to the ground. By the time they began to stand again, the locals where attacking them.

Gansler raised his cane in the air and charged into the mix, slapping his wooden stick up against the Krupes disabled by Thorik and Avanda.

Narra screamed in vain for her husband to return. He was in the thick of it. Her worst nightmare had returned. He had once again gone to war.

Taking Revi behind the Keystone, Narra covered her daughter's eyes from the bloodshed. She couldn't bear to have Revi see her father's death.

The giant Mognins and Gathlers stepped in to assist the humans and Polenums. However, the Ov'Unday refused to cause harm to others, but they were willing to do their part. Utilizing their massive size, they were able to work together to grab Krupes, tie them up, and then set them aside out of the battle where they couldn't cause anyone any injuries.

The battle raged and echoed down the streets. Blood was spilled and death came to those on both sides. Losses were taken, but mostly to the Krupes who had underestimated the citizens.

"Victory is ours!" Avanda announced. Success seemed to be obvious with minimal injuries to their citizens.

It was that very moment when a powerful unexpected wave of energy knocked everyone down to the ground and tossed the dragons up over the buildings. Krupes, humans, and Nums all fell from the unnatural influence. Even the mighty Ov'Unday were tossed to the side and knocked off their feet from this unexpected blast. Ambrosius was back and appeared to be ready for battle.

As expected, when one E'rudite appeared another soon followed. Lord Bredgin had arrived to complete his mission as well. Releasing a thin layer of his dark forces in a wide radius down the street, every living being that existed in its path was struggled to survive. Skin dried and cracked, joints ached, and muscles shook in violent seizures. Every creature in the area battled to stay alive.

A second blast of Ambrosius' energy snapped down the street, blowing the darkness away, as well as most of the fallen, as though a giant invisible broom swept across the way. Bodies flew through the air, landing against walls and the Keystone, while others rolled up into piles. Loose weapons and debris shot through the air piercing objects and citizens in its path.

Thorik had grabbed his Freedom Runestone and focused on it instead of the pain that screamed from every part of his body. Knowing the E'rudites were there for him, he was putting everyone at risk and needed to leave in order to save them, so he ran from the battle, hoping they would follow.

The E'rudites trailed after Thorik as they used their powers against each other along the way, destroying buildings and everything else on their way.

By the time Avanda looked up, Thorik and the E'rudites were out of sight. However, the people of Dolor were still there, broken and hurt, but they were there. "Ralph?" she yelled up into the air, causing her lungs to hurt from the action. Every nerve of her body was active with pains she couldn't even describe. Her toes to her fingers were stiff and difficult to move and her back cracked and shook in spasms as she stood. Even her vision was blurry as she searched the sky for her friend.

There was no reply from her call so she tried again. "Ralph?" Again, no answer. Prior to another attempt, Chug struggled to flap his way over the buildings. Rips in his wings made it difficult to fly while a deep cut in his upper body bled down his thick leg as well as his large body. A coating of fresh blood caked his brown underbody as he carried the green dragon in his clutches.

Landing with only two legs, Chug accidently flopped on his side. Pulling in his injured leg, the large brown dragon protected his small companion from being crushed upon impact. Once at a full stop, he reached out his claw toward Avanda to show her the little dragon's condition.

Avanda shook off her own pain long enough to race over to save the green dragon from Chug's claws. Gently pulling him up to her chest, she rocked him slightly as she inspected the rips in his wings, a broken leg, and a single puncture to his chest. "Ralph? Are you still with us?"

The dragon stayed limp within her arms. No movement indicated signs of death or at the very least unconsciousness.

"Ralph," she said again, hoping to wake him. "Ralph!" she yelled as she started to panic as the reality of his death was suddenly rushing up to her. "Don't you dare leave me! I need you too much. Wake up! Wake up, Pheosco! Please wake up!" Crying at the scene in her hands she didn't know how to accept the reality before her.

"Pheosco," came a soft spoken slurred voice slowly rolling from the green dragon's mouth.

"Yes. That's right. Pheosco." Stunned and ecstatic that he was alive, she calmed her movements once she noticed the shuffling of her excitement was causing him discomfort. "Pheosco. You're alive. Stay with me, Pheosco." She felt using his real name was helping pull him back to from potential death. "I'll never call you Ralph again, I promise. Just don't leave me. I can't lose anyone else. I need you."

Small eyes slowly opened halfway on the green dragon's head as he gently nodded his approval to her comment. "Pheosco is bound to Avanda." Taking a few deep breaths, he continued. "I am not leaving any time soon."

Pleased to hear the words, she held him tight with pleasure as his blood ran from the gouge in his chest. Gently laying him down, she began tending to the wound. "I need to cast a spell to help heal you. Do you trust me, Ral...Pheosco?"

"With my life."

Slowly the citizens began to recoup from the devastation, caused by the E'rudite's powers, as they began helping each other mend wounds and wrap splints to broken bones.

Exhausted, Thorik had once again escaped from the E'rudites. In spite of his own fatigue, he raced back into the street where he had left his companions. To his dismay, the damage was far worse than he recalled.

The locals were still recovering and mourning those they had lost. The majority of the injuries were not from the Krupes, but instead from those who were hunting Thorik.

Consoling those in pain as he made his way past them, Thorik stopped and tried to help several citizens before he reached the Keystone and saw the back of a familiar Num. "Avanda, are you injured?"

Turning, she was cut and was crying. She grieved not for herself, but for a fallen friend. "Oh, Thorik, what have we done?"

Past Avanda, Thorik could see Narra, kneeling next to her husband who remained lifeless. A deep head laceration had been caused by his fall from the blast. For the first time, he looked upon the man as the husband and father that he was, instead of the crazy friend who introduced himself as Sovereign Gansler. Narra's husband and Revi's father had been killed during the battle.

"You took him from me," Narra said to Thorik upon his approach. "I asked you not to go down this path. I begged you not to take him from me. All I wanted was to be left in peace with my family, and you couldn't allow that to happen."

Thorik was stunned and in disbelief of his own eyes. "I meant no harm. I was trying to save you...both of you...all of you."

"I told you this would happen if you interfered, and you did it anyway."

"It wasn't me. It was the E'rudites. I had no control."

"You knew they were after you and you led them straight to us!"

"I didn't...I...I did," Thorik said, correcting himself. "It wasn't on purpose, but you're correct. I led them here, and we can expect them to return as long as I'm here with you. The only way I can prevent this from happening again is to leave."

"And I told you that you would leave us once you started this mess."

"Yes, again, you spoke the truth and I didn't listen. I now need to leave you and the city."

Avanda stepped up to Thorik. "You're not serious, are you? You asked these people to steal the Keystone and now you're leaving them to be slaughtered by the Krupes?"

"Every minute I'm here, I'm putting everyone at risk of being slaughtered by E'rudites. They stand a greater chance of survival against the Krupe soldiers. I have to leave to draw the larger threat away. It's the right thing to do."

"You're going to fight the E'rudites on your own? I think not. You're not going anywhere without me."

"Not this time." Thorik's words were firm and final.

"Why? Because I'm not powerful enough, now that I don't have Vesik?"

"Even with Vesik, we could never take them on. This cannot be won by us fighting them. We need someone more powerful than us." He thought for a moment. "We need someone more powerful than them."

"Who is more powerful than an E'rudite?"

"Deleth."

Blinking a few times, Avanda couldn't believe her ears. "Are you insane?"

"Most likely, but it's my only option at this point. I am going to ask Deleth for his support to stop the E'rudites from destroying his city and land. In return, we will stop our rebellion and give back the Keystone."

"What makes you think you can persuade him?"

"I've been through worse. I've dealt with the Myth'Unday, the Oracle Ovlan, the demons Ergrauth and Bakalor, and the great red dragon Lord Rummon. If anyone can convince him, surely it would be me. Besides, what's my other option?"

"Stay here and we fight our way past the Krupes and out of the city."

"That is an excellent plan which very well may work with the right leadership as long as I am not with you attracting E'rudites. Therefore, you must lead them out to safety while I distract Deleth and hopefully eliminate our other threats."

It took a moment for her realize Thorik was serious. "Me? I'm not a leader. I am no one. That is your forte."

"Avanda, you are the bravest Num I have ever met. Nothing has ever stood in your way when you have made up your mind to obtain it. Leading others starts by believing in yourself, and I know no one that can stand up to you in that ability."

"We will need more than the few weapons held by miners to execute an escape. I don't have the power of Vesik any longer to put us in the advantage."

"You had the ability to create spells long before you had Vesik and you still retain those talents. More importantly, you are extremely resourceful and creative. If all else fails, head to the mines."

"The mines?"

"Yes. As crazy as this sounds, Gansler had the right idea all along. I guess he was sharper than what I gave him credit for. If you hide it behind the doors of the mine's entrance, you can always threaten to push it down into the pit if he doesn't allow these people to be set free."

Avanda shook her head. "Thorik, I'm not you. I can't do this."

Pulling a thin blue crystal from his pouch, he gently set it in her hand. It was a symbol of his trust and love for her, found when they both fought for their lives in the underworld, Della Estovia. "I trust no one more than I do you. You can do this."

Tears began to run down her face again. "Will I ever see you again?"

Grinning, he nodded. "All you need to do is lead these miners past a few hundred Krupes and all I need to do is stop four E'rudites. Sounds to me like we'll be meeting in the Govi Glade by morning."

Embracing him with both arms, she took in his scent one last time. "I love you, Thorik Dain of Farbank."

"And I love you," he whispered in her ear as he held her tight, wishing he never had to release her.

The long silent hug was interrupted by a deep voice. "We had best be on our way before you are tracked back here again," Grewen said.

Ending his embrace, Thorik held Avanda's hand as he turned to look up at the Mognin. "I think we need you here."

"I disagree, little man. You know I, like my brothers, am not going to fight the Krupes. However, I do know Ambrosius even better than you and I have met Deleth before. Perhaps I can help you accomplish your undertaking."

"You understand that I'm going to ask him to fight your longtime friend, Ambrosius."

"I do. But perhaps Deleth can stop him without having to fight or injure him."

Thorik smiled. "I would like to see that very much. Thank you. I accept your offer."

"Then we should be on our way before they bring the battle back here."

"Agreed," he told the Mognin before turning back to Avanda. "It's time for me to leave. I know you'll do great. You always have. You always will."

"This is goodbye, isn't it?"

"Even if I must search the catacombs of Della Estovia, we will see each other again."

And with that, Thorik and Grewen turned and walked away.

Chapter 26
Avanda Steps Up

Slowly, gently, Narra released her dead husband back down to the ground, placing her hand upon his face one last time to feel his skin against hers. With a tender motherly touch, she pulled Revi from Gansler and embraced her daughter. The two cried in each other's arms as Narra rocked them back and forth.

Avanda placed a soft hand upon Narra's shoulder to console her.

Shuddering at the touch, Narra pulled away. Bitter and angry over his death, she lashed out at Avanda. "This is all your fault. Yours and Thorik's. We lived in peace until you came."

Tears ran down Avanda's cheeks and off her chin at the scene before her. "We meant no harm. We surely didn't want anyone to die."

"And yet here my husband lies along with dozens more. How many more must you kill as you justify your own ways upon us?" Pulling Revi in tight, she didn't want her to see her mother's anger. "I wish none of you had come here. Fir Brimmelle is the only healthy-minded one among you."

"Brimmelle? He's still at your home. He has no idea what is happening in the city. We have to warn him." Searching for options, she quickly realized what needed to be done. "I'll return shortly!" Wiping her face, she turned to Pheosco who was still recovering from his wounds. "Stay here with Narra and Revi." Before the green dragon could argue, she jumped on Chug and they started down the street.

With a puncture in his upper front leg and chest, the brown dragon limped along until he was able to use his long wingspan to lift them from ground. Once airborne, Chug was in his element, in spite of his torn wings. Within a few moments they were out of the street and over the buildings.

Swooping over the gray homes, Avanda and Chug could see smoke from numerous buildings on fire as well as many small groups of Krupes combing the streets, killing all the citizens they ran into.

Returning to the cul-de-sac Avanda could see the front door of Narra's home had been broken into and Gansler's stacks of wooden items had been crushed and scattered about. The silence in the courtyard was deafening as her senses were heightened with fear of the unknown before her. "Wait here," she told the brown dragon as Chug attempted to set down easily.

Chug was not known for his soft landings. The tattered wings and injuries in his rib cage did not improve his normal technique.

Leaping off Chug, as he collided with the front steps upon landing, Avanda flew through the front doors and caught her bearings halfway into the great room. A view she had hoped not to see teased her around the doorway to the kitchen as blood ran its course across the floor. "Fir Brimmelle?" she asked, not truly expecting an answer and if one had been given she would have jumped out of her skin.

Lacking the better judgment to be overly cautious at the scene of a potential murder, she recklessly lunged forward as her legs attempted to keep up with her across the room and to the blood stained doorway floor.

On the kitchen floor laid a body with blood pouring from open gashes across his back. Death had arrived prior to her return. Fortunately it was in the form of a Krupe.

"Fir Brimmelle?" she yelled out, hoping he was still alive somewhere in the home. Not hearing a response, she darted out into the great room and called out to him again.

"He was trying to kill me," said a voice from a side room. Brimmelle had collapsed on the floor and was leaning against the wall.

Excited to hear his voice, she dashed over and helped him stand.

Covered with the Krupe's blood and a large cut on his own leg, he clutched Gansler's long sword with a shaking hand. "What has happened? Why did that creature come in to kill me?"

"They don't need the city any longer now that they shut down the mine, so they are killing everyone."

His hands continued to shake from the rear attack he had made on the Krupe. Fear had controlled his actions to save his own life by taking another. "Why wouldn't they just take what they found and leave us be?"

"We've stolen the Keystone from them and we're are going to fight our way out of the city."

"I don't understand." He limped outside and sat down on the top step, still struggling with his own actions. "What do you plan to do with the Keystone?"

Removing the sword from his hand, she held it across her lap. "Nothing. It serves no purpose to us. We just can't allow it to leave before we do."

Shaking his head, he attempted to understand what was at play. "Was the attack on me a result of these actions? Has the fighting started everywhere? Are there any deaths?"

"Yes to all your questions. Some have been killed, including Gansler."

"This is Thorik's doing, isn't it?" Tenseness and anger took control of his fear.

"It was his idea to take the Keystone, but you don't understand."

Brimmelle was furious that Thorik had once again destroyed a place that he had seen as peaceful. Raising his chest with a deep breath, he gave off a loud sigh. "We must give back this Keystone and ask for forgiveness. With any luck, we can return some of these lives to normal."

"There is no turning back. The world is changing whether we wish it to or not."

"It doesn't have to change. We can keep it the way it's always been, just like in Farbank."

"As much as I loved Farbank, we were living a lie. The entire world around us was changing and we were pretending it wasn't."

"I wasn't pretending. I was shielding you and the others from such changes. It can be done again."

"No, it can't. We've seen the reality outside our borders. We can't turn a blind eye and hope it never arrives, only to have it hit us so hard we can't handle it. These people deserve better than that. They deserve to be free and to understand the benefits and dangers of such."

"I am the Fir here, not you."

"Your status as a Fir has no bearing here. Besides, even if we give the Keystone back, they will still slaughter us." Setting the sword down on the steps, she stood up and helped him start limping his way to Chug so they could return to the others.

"You don't know that. Thorik's words are not of those of the Mountain King. He is just a Num, a Num who makes more mistakes that most of us."

Rolling her eyes, she replied half under her breath. "I'm sure the Mountain King made his share of mistakes."

"Don't talk of him in such tone. He was more than an average Num. He was superior to us in so many ways. He is a symbol of our heritage and our beliefs. We could only dream of living up to a fraction of his wisdom."

"Perhaps. But unless you can conjure some of that wisdom to save us we are going to have to battle our way out of here." Helping him up on top of the brown dragon, she asked, "What wise words did he have for surviving an unbeatable enemy?"

"He said, 'In times of battle, learn what not to do and what can be achieved from the survivors as well as the dead.'" Brimmelle's perfect memory could allow him to quote every scroll word for word. It was a skill he was proud of.

The words caught her attention more than she had expected and Avanda repeated the Mountain King's words several times to herself. "Fir Brimmelle, you're a genius."

"I'm aware of that," he replied, proudly straightening his dirty ripped shirt.

Before she could respond, Chug gave off a loud and ominous roar, knocking the Fir off his back and onto the street.

Avanda immediately spotted several Krupes turning the corner and entering the cul-de-sac as the brown dragon made such a commotion that the instincts of most creatures would cause them to run for their lives.

The Krupes instincts were obviously impaired as they continued forward with weapons drawn.

Avanda's natural instincts were working just fine. However, instead of jumping on the dragon to escape the approaching danger, she bolted for the front steps.

Slapping his tail against Gansler's wooden masterpiece in the courtyard, Chug had turned from his normal playful self to a massive destructive force, biting and clawing his enemies with the strength and weight that few creatures had. But even with his natural abilities, he couldn't block them all as a few of them were able to move around the dragon.

"Chug! Retreat!" Avanda yelled from the front steps, "Fly Brimmelle to safety and then return for me!"

With a sudden burst of strength from his legs, the dragon leaped upward, spread out his long wings, and grabbed Brimmelle just as the Krupes had swung their swords at him. Lifting him into the air, Chug needed to circle the open area to gain the altitude he needed to clear the buildings. In doing so, he gave the Krupes the opportunity to throw their spears at them. One of which pierced Chug's leg as he breached the cul-de-sac's confines, spinning him out of control over the rooftops.

Three of the Krupes moved back down the street to find where Chug had crash landed while the remaining two Krupes moved toward Avanda.

Concern for Chug and Brimmelle was quickly replaced with her own wellbeing as she grabbed Gansler's sword from the steps and ran into the house and then up the staircase. There she stopped and spun around while grabbing a few spell components from her purse.

Stomping their way into the home to kill the Num, the Krupes heard her soft voice chanting rhythmic words from upstairs. Immediately they started up toward her as the old wooden steps creaked from their weight.

Frustrated at the time it took to complete the spell she had rushed it too fast the first time and had to start a second time, causing the Krupes to be within arm's reach before her spell was activated and she tossed the beads onto the staircase.

Within a blink of an eye, step after step became frozen as ice formed upon them and up the sidewall as well as the entire length of the stair's railing, bleeding onto the floor on both levels.

The lead Krupe nearly slipped, but caught himself before taking the final step up on the second floor landing.

Avanda stepped back slowly. She could turn and run into one of the bedrooms, but it would only delay their attack on her by a few minutes. The moment of truth was upon her as she speculated if she could save herself without the help of Vesik. Doubt crept back into her thoughts as she questioned her own abilities. Emotions flooded her judgment and she started to panic. Her hand moved her pack where she felt the book crack from her touch. Even if she had wanted it, it was no longer an option. In a way, it was the excuse she needed to not give in to the yearning to feel its touch.

As the lead Krupe pulled his sword back to swing toward her, Avanda started a second spell with hopes that she could finish it in time. Unfortunately, she wasn't able to complete it as his sword swung through the air toward her.

Her muscles locked up in fear.

A loud crack erupted from the frozen staircase and floor which the lead Krupe stood upon. Shattered from the weight, the brittle flooring collapsed, sending both Krupes tumbling back down to the first floor. Frozen particles flew through the air, across the room, and even out the front door. It was a victory for the Num. However, it was short lived as the enemy slowly stood back up and pulled out their heavy maces. Swinging them over their heads, they started punching holes in the ceiling and through the floor of the second story near Avanda.

Snapping out of her uncertainty, Avanda ran into Narra's bedroom to avoid the floor from collapsing from underneath her feet. Searching the bedroom for anything that could help, she realized she already had her best option in hand, Gansler's long sword.

Large chunks of the upstairs flooring were quickly knocked out and enough debris had fallen to allow one of the Krupes to climb his way back up to the second level. Once there, he charged his way into the room to find the Num, blowing out the headboard and part of the wall due to his size.

Hiding behind the door, she waited until he had passed before she raced out of the room to make an escape back downstairs, only to find the other Krupe halfway up a pile of broken flooring as he climbed to the second floor. She turned back to find herself between the two.

Before the one in the room turned around to see her, she leaped onto the bed and then sprang up into the air, landing her strike with the long sword deep into his back.

Shocked by the unexpected attack, the Krupe stood motionless for a moment before falling forward, bringing Avanda along for the ride. This had been the second time in the past hour that the sword had been used this way. First by Brimmelle, and now by

Avanda. It wasn't a noble attack, but the rear attacks had kept them both alive.

Gathering her wits, she stood up and pulled the sword out of the dead Krupe. Avanda quickly moved over to the open front window with the sword in hand, glancing down at the courtyard below. "I should be able to make that," she said, trying to convince herself that the statement was true, even though it was more likely she would break a leg or arm in her attempt.

Entering the room, the second black armored Krupe said nothing, as usual, and simply pulled out his sword in order to slay her. He stood twice her height and easily outweighed her by a factor of four. He would reach her long before she could collect the components for another spell. He had the upper hand and the battle seemed to be nearly finished.

It was then that she decided that she had nothing to lose, so she leaped out the window.

A leap of faith is nothing more than playing the odds that somehow, someway, everything will work out regardless of what logic would tell someone. It's often a recipe for disaster for many. When someone leaps off a cliff into a shallow pool of water and rocks, faith is usually not enough to save them. So is true when Polenums leap out of second story windows onto a hard stone street. Normally, typically, it should end in disaster. However, faith and fortune was on her side this time.

Chug swooped into the cul-de-sac as Avanda jumped out of the window to escape the attacking Krupe. Covering the brown dragon's face and claws, blood flung off onto the buildings as he passed them by. Catching her in mid fall, he clung to her tightly as he banked his flight around the circle and back up over the roofs where they were safe from her attackers.

Over several homes and then down into a street, Chug's wings grazed the buildings on both sides as he came in for his rough landing. Dropping her on the street, he then tumbled down the street to a stop. Wounded and in great pain from the earlier attack by the Krupes, his endurance was being tested with every effort he made to regain his footing.

Rolling across the street and into a cart, a hard crack into a wall eventually stopped her momentum. The impact of the landing had jolted her spell components and Gansler's sword from her hand. Her items were scattered across the stone path, but appeared to be unbroken.

Two Krupes lay slaughtered in the street from deep bite and claw marks after a battle with a brown dragon. Chug had torn them to shreds, littering the street with their organs.

Brimmelle raced over to see if Avanda was injured. He had been dropped off by Chug earlier, after the dragon's first escape from the cul-de-sac.

Climbing back to her feet, Avanda stumbled a few times before gathering her composure. "I'm fine, Brimmelle." Pushing his hands away, after he helped her stand up straight, she quickly started collecting her gear. "And I now know what we must do to free these people. All of these people."

Chapter 27
Thorik Confronts Deleth

Leaning over a map, Deleth instructed the Blothrud, Savroc, as to the route to take the Keystone. "I have the barge waiting at this point along the Cucurrian River. After Keystone is loaded, follow the river downstream, out into the lake, and then to this island. Once installed, it will hold the ocean barrier secure for thousands of years. I have important business in the Temple of Surod to deal with first and will rendezvous with you on the island to perform the Keystone's installation."

"Understood, my master," Savroc replied. "Is there anything that needs to be salvaged prior to destroying the city?"

"No. I've notified Ovlan to stop shipping supplies from Pwellus Dementa. This city's undertaking has been accomplished and is not required further. Take what you wish and dispose of the rest."

Savroc nodded before turning and leaving the room.

Reviewing his maps and calculations, Deleth had only begun making some notes before being interrupted by Savroc once more. "Master, there is an issue with the Keystone."

Raising one eyebrow at the thought, his dark semi-transparent face tightened. His skull could vaguely be seen underneath the liquefied tissue layers. "Issue?"

"Yes, Master. I have just been informed that protestors have taken it and are hiding it within the city."

Continuing to look at his map, Deleth was visibly disappointed. "They've hidden a crystal the size of a city street in an environment they cannot escape from? How is this possible?"

"I have also been informed that a dozen soldiers were sent out but failed to retrieve it. However, we have captured the leaders of the protestors."

"Bring them in. this won't take long."

Nodding, Savroc stepped out into the hall and waved the Krupe guards in, along with their prisoners. Turning back to his master, he asked, "Shall I personally take charge of this problem?"

"Yes. Utilize all of my soldiers. An army of Krupes should easily defeat whatever rudimentary force they have piecemealed together."

"It won't help," a new voice said with confidence.

Pulling up from his notes, Deleth could see a Mognin and Polenum being escorted across his chamber by Savroc and a few Krupes. The small Num had been the one doing the talking.

Leading them to Deleth, the Blothrud stopped and introduced his prisoners. "My master, these two were captured near the market. They said they know where the Keystone is hidden."

Thorik shook his head at the misleading wording. "We put up no fight. We came here freely in order to present to you an offer that will end this conflict."

Vaguely amused, Deleth grinned. "And what, pray tell, does a Mognin and a Polenum have to offer me?"

"I am Thorik Dain of Farbank," the Num said. "I am responsible for taking your Keystone." Hiding his fears from the dark Oracle was a struggle with each and every word in his attempt to show confidence and command of the situation.

Deleth showed little interest as he looked back down at his notes. "Impressive pedigree. Should your name mean something to me?"

Thorik's shoulders were pulled back and his chin slightly raised to hide his nervousness. It was his time to use all that he had learned over the years to deal with an Oracle so powerful. Deleth's sheer thought could kill the Num in an instant. "I have been instrumental in preventing the flooding of the Dovenar Kingdom and the sacrifice of Ericc Dovenar. I have helped destroy mighty cities as well as massive armies. I have championed beasts and dragons to serve my needs. I am not to be toyed with. And now I am responsible for taking your Keystone."

Totally ignoring the Num's speech, Deleth never looked up from his map and notes.

The loud beat of Num's heart slapped against his chest as his deathly fear of being in the presence of the Dark Oracle competed with the control of his emotions he had learned over his years. "I know that once that crystal leaves the city, you mean to kill all that live within those walls," Thorik said, standing firm and poised. "And I also know that we have the ability to keep it from you and hold off your soldiers. I have proven to be successful in such missions. We also have a plan to destroy it if you are unwilling to negotiate. Surely you don't want to lose such a powerful crystal. I doubt there is another like it anywhere in the world." His cards had been played. He felt comfortable that he had the upper hand. The Oracle would never risk them destroying a crystal he had spent decades to find.

Mildly amused, Deleth made eye contact with the Num and played along. "I see. You're holding my crystal hostage for freedom of the Dolor citizens, I would presume. Consider the matter resolved."

Thorik peered up at Grewen. His plan was going well so far. In fact, it was going much easier than he had even hoped. His shoulders rolled forward and he relaxed his posture. "Thank you. It is appreciated," he said, unsure how to ask for more.

Deleth returned his attention to his notes and maps. "Unfortunately that spoiled your alternative reason for being here."

Glancing back and forth from Deleth and Grewen, Thorik could tell they didn't have the advantage he thought he did. "Alternative?"

"Don't be coy with me. Those E'rudites have been tearing up the countryside and the city in search of you. I did some checking after sending them to Pwellus Dementa' only to find that they are not our creations. In fact, they are not from this time."

Thorik cleared his throat. "You know about them?"

"I do. I also know you're not from this time either." Glaring at the Num, he squinted his eyes. "Disruption of time is punishable by death."

Realizing his secrets had been revealed, Thorik came clean. "Deleth, I need your help. I fell through a sphere in the Govi Glade and into your time. Now I'm being hunted by these men of great power. I am not here on purpose."

Cold in tone, Deleth spoke softly and clearly. "What you fail to understand is that I honestly don't care about your stories of valor or the challenges that face you. I have a world to create and having someone from another time being here is dangerous to my plans."

"We'd gladly go back if you could help eliminate those who threaten us. They do not belong in your time either. These men have destroyed kingdoms and are dangerous to your world as well as mine."

Looking away from the Num and to the Savroc, Deleth continued. "Have the guards take these two to Bakalor for a dinner. I'll deal with these E'rudites later when they return. I want you to prepare our soldiers for a full scale annihilation of the all Dolor citizens to regain my Keystone."

"Deleth! We can help each other!" Thorik announced as a Krupe grabbed him from behind.

"I don't require your assistance." Unlike the Num's voice, Deleth's was calm and collected even though his body language showed he was annoyed.

Being dragged from the room, Thorik shouted back, "Do what you will with us, but you promised to set them free!"

Calmly, quietly, Deleth's voice could be heard clearly down the hallway. "I promised nothing. I told you to consider the matter resolved, and it is resolved. I don't need them any longer. They are now simply a drain on resources."

Satisfied with his plans, Deleth turned around toward the back of the room. Utilizing his powers, a portal opened up within the wall, showing a bridge leading to a temple built into the side of a dark mountain. The bone colored temple was in the shape of a large skeleton's torso, arms, and head. Stepping through the portal, the wall reappeared behind him as it had prior to his opening of it. No sign of the Overlord or the hole in space was visible.

Pushed down the hall, Thorik tripped twice in his efforts to get back on his feet while the Krupe continued to shove the Num.

Rounding a few corners, Thorik eventually realized that he was not going to get another audience with Deleth and he needed to accept it.

"That didn't quite go as planned," Grewen mentioned to the Num as they were both pushed down a large corridor, away from Deleth's chambers. "What's our next step?"

"I thought it was going to work, so I hadn't come up with a backup plan."

"Apparently this wasn't the time to start that practice."

Chapter 28
Leadership Arrives

A trail of blood leading down the street followed Avanda and Chug as Brimmelle nursed his leg while riding the injured dragon. They had fought their way through the streets, back to the Keystone and the citizens who held it hostage. They were not greeted as heroes or as enemy. They were not greeted at all. In fact, few noticed them approach at all.

Leaderless, they were each tending to the wounds of others in need. It was a time to heal and a time to cry for their lost love ones. It was as if an explosion had not only ripped apart this street intersection and those within it, but had also torn out any remaining internal longing for something better.

Avanda could see in their eyes the lack of desire to fight back and to salvage and save those that they still could. "How do I fight our way out of this city with an army who has no interest in escaping or risking any more lives?"

Brimmelle shook his head at her comment. "You can't." Spotting Narra, he slowly lowered himself off of Chug to make his way to her, limping slowly as he nursed his leg.

"I will fight for you," said a voice near Avanda.

Turning, she saw a battle worn little green dragon. "You and who else?"

"Chug will join in. He's a bit of an oaf, but his heart is in the right place."

She smiled and nodded her head. "Two tattered dragons and an apprentice spell caster without her spell book. We'll make an amazing team."

"They'll have celebrated fables about our heroic battle to free this city."

"Sure they will. They'll have songs and everything. Do we have to die in the battle to become legendary?" Scanning the survivors, she tried to assess what she truly had to work with. "I've never had to do this, Pheosco. Thorik has always taken on these responsibilities."

"Not alone. You were always there at his side, just as I am with you now."

Smiling ever so slightly, she appreciated his words and kneeled near him. "Thorik had to pull everyone together to work as a united front. All I had to do was open Vesik and perform." Her thoughts drifted back to having the security of Vesik being only a moment away to keep her safe. Just the thoughts of utilizing her book of magic gave her a sudden rush of pleasure.

"Were you never there for him prior to Vesik?"

"What? Of course I was."

"Then he succeeded because of you, not Vesik."

Half nodding, she agreed. "True, but he didn't succeed just because of me."

"Thorik succeeded because he was smart enough to utilize your talents as well as the talents of many others. He is a natural leader, even if it makes me ill just thinking about a Num leading dragons. However, Thorik knows when you're ready to meet a challenge. He loves you, Avanda. He would not set you up to fail. He truly believes you have the ability to lead these people out of the city."

Tilting her head, she eyed him for a moment. "Do I get the feeling you're starting to like Thorik?"

"Leaning toward respect, not like. His moral compass is pointing a few degrees off for my liking." Ruffling his wings for a moment, he gave her a meaningful look. "Truth is, he's willing to let go of things that prevent him from moving forward with life. A challenge you have struggled with."

His comment caused Avanda to place a hand on the outside of her pack. She could feel Vesik crack with every touch. "That's what this is all about, isn't it? I'm no different than these citizens. We're all hanging on to our safety so tight that we are missing the freedom and joy that life has to offer." Standing back up, she pulled her thoughts together. "Where's Narra? She is key to our plan of escape."

Curious as to what the plan was, Pheosco led her to Narra and Revi who were still grieving over the loss of Gansler.

"Narra, it is time." Avanda's voice was clear and firm.

Holding her pregnant stomach as she cried, Narra looked up with vacant eyes. "Haven't you done enough?"

"No I haven't. Neither of us has done enough. We have to face our greatest fear and let go of the security we once had. It's time to change."

Shocked, Narra didn't know how to respond.

"Are you willing to do what it takes to ensure your children are happy?"

"I always have. Are you questioning that?"

"I'm questioning your desire to make sure they live a life worth living. What are you willing to do for their future?"

"I don't know what you're asking. I've just lost my husband, the father and provider for my children. What more can I give?"

"Everything!" Avanda shouted loud enough for everyone to hear. "We must be willing to give up everything we have in order to free ourselves. Our sins and thoughts of the past have weighed us down for too long. It is time we let go and start over."

The citizens were silent as she stepped up onto an overturned wagon so more could hear her words. "You did not ask to be slaves, and you felt guilty because you never asked for freedom out of fear of losing what comforts you did have. Then when Gansler led a battle to free you, you felt guilty for not supporting him and turned it into blame against him for worse living conditions and the unnatural return of your children who participated in his war effort. It was a constant reminder, providing constant shame and fear of change."

Staring into their eyes, she knew she had their attention. "You're all holding onto that little bit of security of knowing where your next meal is at and where you will sleep tonight. You're afraid of how it could be worse if you said, 'No more!' and then left this city. Sometimes you have to let go. This is one of those times. We have nothing else to lose...except your children's future."

"But we've lost this battle before!" Narra yelled up to her.

"NO!" Avanda yelled back, pointing directly at Narra before pointing it out to the crowd. "The reason you lost last time is you were fighting the wrong enemies. You were fighting the Krupes when you should have been fighting your own fear of the unknown. With thousands of citizens in this city, there is no way they could have prevented you from leaving. They even left the egress open and you never even attempted to leave. The curfew to protect you was a hoax to keep you off the streets. You never challenged them. Your fear is your enemy, not the Overlord and the Krupes."

Narra stood up with the help of Brimmelle. "What do you expect us to do? Even if we get past our fears, they have weapons and trained soldiers."

Eyeing the crowd, Avanda grinned. "Once we agree on the goal of leaving this city, how we leave becomes easy, as long as we don't put limits on what we're willing to do to achieve it."

Brimmelle didn't like the sound of that. "Limits? There have to be limits!"

Narra grabbed Revi's hand as the crowd started getting loud with their own discussion on her statement. "What more can we give?"

Avanda stood up tall for all to hear. "I may ask you to do things that don't seem right. In fact, they will seem extremely wrong. But I promise you, if we are convicted to ensure our escape, we will prevail."

The crowd erupted with questions and cheers as they moved in toward her to hear the plan.

Chapter 29
Bakalor's Liar

With hands tied together behind their backs Thorik and Grewen were led up the windy thin path to the entrance of Bakalor. Straightening his weathered backpack, he considered his options. There were two fully armored Krupes with spears and swords behind them and one in front. The odds of escaping were not in their favor.

Glancing back at the tall Mognin, well over twice his height, Thorik replied, "I'm sorry I got you into this."

The fresh cool mountain air breeze felt good on Grewen's body. "If I recall, I invited myself."

Thorik could hear the inflection of a smile on the Mognin's face as he spoke. "You did at that, and I'm glad to have you at my side during my last moments."

"The mighty Thorik Dain of Farbank has finally given up?" The Mognin's smile faded. "That's not the Num I know."

"I stood up to Deleth and he tossed me aside as though I was but an insect."

"And you expected him to bow to you?"

"No. Of course not. But I've worked so hard to get here. My soul-markings finally came in. I've won battles. I've saved lives. I've fallen in love. I finally feel I have the courage to stand up to anyone and I think I've earned the right to do so. And yet, after all that I've been through, he feeds me to his pet."

Grewen chuckled at the thought. "Thorik, Deleth is practically a god. I'm still impressed you were able to get an audience with him, seeing that we can't actually offer him anything he can't obtain without us." Grinning at the foolhardy attempt, he continued. "Besides, even if he wasn't so powerful, Deleth doesn't know your story, nor would he care about it if he did. You failed to enchant him with who you were because you were relying on him caring about what you've done in your past. It simply doesn't work that way."

"What are you talking about? I did no such thing."

"You were overconfident that he would even have a conversation with you. You can't rest on your laurels. Each challenge is a new opportunity to determine your future. Your fate is in your hands."

"I have to prove myself every day for the rest of my life?"

"That's part of your problem. You shouldn't have to prove anything to anyone. You just need to be someone who does the right thing every day. Don't point to your history to get what you want right now or tomorrow. Use what you learned from your past to make today better."

Thorik shrugged. "Somehow when my soul-markings came in I thought it would be easier to get respect. It's as though I'm the only one that noticed them."

"That's because you're the only one who sees them as being important. Everyone else pays more attention to your current actions than what you look like or what you feel they should remember about you."

"Do my past and current actions mean nothing tomorrow? How do I ensure I will affect the future properly?"

Grewen grinned at the small Num. "Of course they do. You change forthcoming events with each decision you make. Your concern should not be how you will affect the future. Instead, it should be what actions will you take today that leads to a better tomorrow."

Thorik nodded in agreement. "A lesson too late to learn...as we walk to our deaths."

"It's never too late to learn and grow, little man."

"Seeing that I haven't learned enough on how to fight a rock demon twice your height, I think I can safely say it's a bit late for me to learn to feel good about myself."

"Is violence our only option?"

"How else? He plans to take over the entire world and eats creatures like us for strength to do so. He cares not about our plight."

"There are many ways to fight for a cause without having to use violence. You can refuse to help in actions you oppose, or create a peaceful protest if you must, or simply leave and avoid the conflict. You could always attempt to find a balance with your adversary, such as what I have done in the past."

"That worked phenomenally well for us with Deleth." Thorik's voice was a little more sarcastic than he had planned. "I'm sorry. I'm not having the best of days, seeing that my friends are about to be murdered by Krupes and we're about to be eaten by Bakalor."

"It is a choice you make when you allow events around you to affect your attitude."

"Are you telling me that you're not the least bit nervous about walking up to meet our end?"

"Nervous? No. What possible good would come of this?" Turning from the mountain, the Mognin smiled. "Gaze upon the beautiful landscapes. So few ever have the opportunity to soak in such sights."

"Only those that are headed to their death."

"I understand that you are afraid, but by doing so you limit your thoughts and your creative ability to determine options."

Thorik chuckled. "Then you must be filled with plenty of options. I'd like to hear a few before we arrive at our destination."

"Perhaps we can reason with this creature."

"Reason with Bakalor? He's a demon. He was created by Deleth for the single purpose of destroying others and gaining power. I've dealt with him before and narrowly escaped with my life."

"Excellent. I knew this would help you."

Thorik looked over his shoulder at the grinning Mognin. "How is this excellent?"

"With a clear head, you have expressed that he has needs. All we need to do now is see if we can provide some of these needs in exchange for what we want."

"I believe him eating us will provide him with his needs. This negotiation seems a little one-sided."

"Look beyond that. How can we help him?"

"Why would we help him? Again, he wants to eat us and our friends, and take over the world."

"A good mediator can always find a way to obtain the needs of others in order to compromise and work together on a common goal."

"Are you proposing that I suggest a tastier meal for him in order for us to be set free?"

"Enjoy the process of enlightened reflection and creativity, my little friend, and your journey will take you to places you never thought were possible."

"Enlightened? I know, we'll just ask Bakalor if he wants to help us free the citizens he's been eating for nourishment in a battle against his maker, Deleth, who continues to give him strength and new powers." Again, the sarcasm was thick, but it was meant to be this time.

The Mognin nodded in agreement. "Do you believe you can do that?"

Laughing at the Mognin's inability to realize he was joking, Thorik began to reply, but then stopped to think about it. "You know, I don't think I can do that, but I might be able to do something similar."

The two continued to talk about the Num's plan as they finished the rocky trail to the entrance to the mountain, which led to Bakalor's cavern. The vertically sliced pieces of mountain rested against one another and the gaps between them still had bridges to cross from one to another. Most were old and strained under the Mognin's weight. A few were new, as they got closer to the actual mountain cave entrance. It appeared to Thorik as though the bridges and support beams had been rebuilt since his last visit from Bakalor's chamber.

Walking into the cavern tunnel, it became dark and difficult to see. Step by step, Thorik envisioned various scenarios in his head, trying to determine which would play out best. This continued until they reached a large open cavern filled with green light from burning oils that dripped off of a massive rock creature which stood twice the height of Grewen.

The floor grates had been repaired but still showed signs of damage from Thorik's prior escape. Lava still flowed into the short walled nursery, but no child was present.

Stretching his rock body, the demon pulled tight on the chain attached to his ankle while reaching out with one hand as far as he could toward a distant wall.

There, in a crack, was a lanky elderly human, hiding just out of reach from the thick giant finger which was trying to nudge the man out into the open. Seeing the Mognin and the Num enter, the man waved for help. In doing so, he moved just enough to allow

Bakalor to press his massive finger against the man's arm, trapping it firmly against the rock wall.

Bakalor kept the pressure firmly on the arm and slowly dragged the man out of hiding, tearing layers of human flesh against the abrasive rock wall. Once the demon pulled his frail body into the room, he scooped up the man into his enormous flaming hand.

The man screamed from the fiery blaze surrounding him and pleaded for the Mognin and Num to help him.

"Wait!" Thorik yelled to stop the killing. "You don't want to burn him to death, do you?"

"Thorik Dain of Farbank?" Bakalor said with surprise, turning slowly to see if it was true.

The Num was pleased the demon remembered. "If I recall, you prefer to eat your meals alive, not lifeless."

Smiling, the demon mentally commanded the flames in his hand to damper, causing his fist to go into a state of paralysis without the power of the burning oil's light. "How do I deserve such fortune to see you again?"

Exhausted, the man struggled to free himself from the rock hand without any success.

Thorik nodded to reassure Grewen that he had a plan, but his eyes gave away the fact that the Num was unsure if it would work. "Hello, Bakalor. I've come back to make you an offer."

The demon rotated his large diamond eyes to see the three Krupes standing guard so the prisoners couldn't escape back out of the tunnel. "I see. And these Krupes are your private guards?" The eye that Pheosco had pushed out of the socket had been returned to its proper place, and his lids were half closed in order to keep any little dragons from flying in and pushing them out again.

"No. However, this was the only way I could obtain an audience with you."

The demon laughed. "So you came here on purpose? How brave of you." Squeezing his other stone fist tightly, producing extra oil to extrude from between his fingers, which caused the ill-colored green flames to explode around his fist. "I'm hungry, Num. Make your compelling proposal quick. What could you possibly offer me?"

Stepping closer to the prisoners, Bakalor reached the end of the magical chain Deleth had attached to his ankle to keep him from leaving. His distance from the center of the room was limited, but it was enough to allow him to reach the meals standing before him.

Before Thorik could react, the demon tossed the elderly human into his oversized mouth. Bakalor slowly closed his mouth, causing his victim a slow and painful death, to ensure that Thorik could see and hear the anguish that awaited him.

The sound of bones breaking and organs popping was intimidating enough to Thorik that he nearly lost his composure. Lengthy scraping sounds of human bones working down the demon's throat caused the Num's spine to twitch with fear.

"That was my appetizer. The Mognin will be my main course, and you my trouble-making friend will be my dessert if I don't like your offer."

Thorik crossed his arms over his chest in defiance. "The offer is off the table!"

Baffled, the demon wasn't sure how to react.

"Are you sure?" Grewen was puzzled as well.

"Yes. And it is a pity you will never find out what it was."

Bakalor's confusion turned to anger and the oil that allowed the rock joints to move doubled their flame output. "What? How dare you not tell me what I want to know!"

Thorik turned his back to the demon and lifted his head to show he couldn't be intimidated.

"I'll crush you!" Bakalor yelled.

"Then you're guaranteed never to find out."

Bakalor stomped his feet a few times in anger, causing recently repaired floor grates to snap in the same fraction locations, while rocks dropped from the ceiling. "Then I'll eat your friend here if you don't!"

Thorik turned back toward the demon and looked at him with all seriousness. "I will tell you only if you don't harm either one of us until you have made a decision on what I have to offer."

Stepping back, he processed the request. "So all I have to do is wait long enough for you to tell me before I eat both of you?"

"Yes, assuming you don't take my offer."

Impatient, he roared at the little Num. "Then get on with it and let me hear what you have in that puny little mind of yours!"

Thorik relaxed slightly, knowing he finally had the demon's full attention. "You are the most powerful being in our world, correct?"

Bakalor grinned. "I know of no other."

"What is the one thing holding you back from taking control and ruling us all?"

Struggling for a moment, he hadn't really asked himself that question. "Deleth?"

"No."

"No?"

Thorik looked about the room. "Deleth is not here, and yet here you are instead of being out there creating your empire. Why is that?"

"Because I can't leave this room, because of Deleth."

"No."

"No?" Bakalor was becoming agitated at being wrong twice now.

"You can't leave this room because of the chain Deleth has linked to you. All we need to do is break the chain."

"But he has special forces that prevent even I from breaking it." He shook his head at the idea. "This is idiotic. If I can't break them, a tiny Polenum surely can't." Stepping toward them he had made his decision. "I do not accept your offer."

"But I haven't made it yet."

Frustrated, Bakalor stopped in his tracks. "Then make it already!"

"I have a way to remove Deleth's special forces from the chain long enough for you to fracture a link and free yourself."

Thinking about the idea he pondered the idea for a few moments. "I don't believe you have this gift."

"What do you have to lose? If I try and I fail, then you eat us. If I'm successful then you go free to do as you please. But if you eat us now, you will forever wonder if you missed your chance to leave this prison of Deleth's making." Thorik felt he was close and needed to finish the deal quickly. "Besides, who knows if Deleth will ever allow you to leave? How many toes will you have to cut off before he demands you remove an arm or a leg? It appears that you are simply a specimen for him to experiment on. If he truly wished for you to rule the world, why would he hide you away and treat you with such disrespect?"

Three times the demon began to speak before he finally decided what to say. "And if you should achieve this unlikely task of freeing me, what are you expecting in return?"

Thorik smiled at the question. "First, I wish your services to do what you do best. I have a few individuals that are causing me great strife and I need you to get rid of them."

"You want me to eliminate your enemies?"

"I would imagine you would enjoy such a challenge."

"Always." Bakalor grinned. "And your second expectation?"

"Your promise to allow me time in order to lead others to safe distant lands if they do not wish to fight your unstoppable force. It will make your takeover faster, fewer lives will be lost in battles, and those who stay will be less likely to resist your throne."

"Let you leave my lands and empire?"

"Then do we have a deal?" Thorik waited for an answer and his doubt grew with each passing moment of silence.

A sinister grin crossed his face and eventually the demon started laughing from deep down. "Never have I had someone so small and powerless hold my attention so long. I will remember you, Thorik Dain of Farbank, for the rest of the days that my flames hold my life upon this earth."

Glancing up at the Mognin, the Num was obviously unsure if an agreement had been made.

Stepping back to the far side of the round room, Bakalor sized the two captives up. "Guards! Move the Num to the center of the grates. I have decided to eat my desert prior to the entrée, but prepare to bring me the other one as well. The little one won't take long."

"Bakalor, you're making a mistake," Thorik said as one of the Krupes grabbed him and pushed him to the center of the room near the center pole that held the end of the chain, while the other two pulled the Mognin up just behind the Num.

"I don't make mistakes," the demon said with a smile. "Cut their bindings. I want them to fight for their lives to get their blood boiling before I eat."

Thorik felt the Krupes blade shave against his skin as the ropes were cut. He had only a few moments left to change the demon's mind. "I'm willing to negotiate the terms!"

Before the Num had a chance to continue with his agreement, Bakalor lunged forward and grabbed the first Krupe by the neck with one hand and snapping his head clean off.

The other two Krupes never had time to react before the demon knocked them to the ground and crushed them both with his massive feet and weight.

Turning back to Thorik, he lifted the chain that held him to the pole in the center of the room. "It's only a pact if you can remove his powers. I'm still very hungry, so I would suggest you hurry before I change my mind."

Thorik nodded in agreement and quickly grabbed his sack of Runestones, pulling out the Freedom Runestone, "I hope Delcth's powers are similar to the E'rudites," he mumbled to himself before addressing the demon. "Pull the chain taut."

Walking to the edge of the grates, Bakalor leaned down and pulled the slack out of the metal restraint.

Stepping over to a link in the center of the chain, Thorik sat down, cross legged, with the link before him. The single link was nearly as long and thick as his arm which intimidated the Num for a moment as he wondered if Bakalor could break it even if Deleth's powers were removed. Setting the Runestone on the metal chain, he closed his eyes and began to concentrate on the stone, allowing it to guide his thoughts. Within moments, he could feel the tingling of energy run through his fingers, up one arm, across his chest, and then back down the other arm to complete the connection.

He could feel the difference in the air about him, the unnatural energy seemed to fade away, leaving a calmness surrounding him. Quietly, he spoke, as he attempted to keep his focus. "Now."

Bakalor began to pull on the chain, but he had no more success than he had had during prior attempts.

"Pull harder," Thorik said, never opening his eyes or raising his voice as he felt the chain move about from the tug of war the demon was having with the pole the other end of the chain was connected to. "I can feel the change. Keep going."

"This is nonsense," the demon said as he pulled with all his might.

Unimpressed, Grewen stepped over to see if any changes were occurring. As the chain shook from the intense pressure, the link next to Thorik began to bend and warp ever so slightly. "It's starting to work."

Gritting his rock teeth, Bakalor continued to pull with all his effort, only to see minor changes in the one link. At this rate, they would be at this for hours and would most likely only bend the link into an odd shape.

Just as the demon was about to give up he felt the chain pull back from the other direction. It was the Mognin. Grewen had grabbed the far end and was using the metal pole as leverage to pull in the opposite direction then Bakalor, whose feet were now bending the metal floor grates from the pressure. Within seconds of this new strategy, they were starting to see results. The metal began bending and cracking before their eyes.

Snapping, the chain flung both ways; half toward Bakalor and the other toward the Grewen, knocking them both off their feet from the release of tension. The demon was now free.

Bakalor stood back up and then leaned forward, so close to the Num that the flames from the demon's body were felt against his sensitive skin. "I will never forget the name Thorik Dain of Farbank."

"Glad to be of service." The Num returned the Runestone into the sack and placed the sack into the pack with another subtle ripping of fabric. "Now, I do hope you'll follow through on your side of our business."

"Business? I don't recall any business," he said with a laugh as he stretched with freedom, walking out of his chambers and down the tunnel that led outside. "However, I do recall an opportunity to give a thrashing to a few fools who would cause anxiety to a friend of mine…A follower of mine…yes, the first of thousands of my toady bootlickers." Laughing as he stomped down the tunnel in his escape from any more of Deleth's tests. "I will prove to all that I am the most powerful creature ever. I will be worshipped and feared!"

Grewen started to follow Thorik behind the enormous fiery rock demon. "Are you sure this was a good idea?"

"Not really. But if he can help resolve Ambrosius' relentless hunting of me, than I can return to Dolor and help defend the city."

Chapter 30
Taking a Stand

Stepping out into the street of the market place, near the egress to freedom, Avanda led the citizens of Dolor calmly out into the center of the empty intersection of multiple streets. Family after family followed her, holding hands. Polenum, humans, Mognins, Gathlers, and many other Ov'Unday stepped out to be seen in their peaceful walk to freedom.

Hundreds of Krupes had been unloading weapons and gear to prepare for a battle in order to recover the Keystone, which was not being presented by the locals. Stopping their tasks, they slowly turned and stared at the defenseless citizens.

Avanda stopped over halfway across.

The crowd behind her stopped as well. Their eyes were not filled with fear or even anger, nor did they position themselves for a battle. Instead, they all seemed to have a clear view before them as they continued to focus on the egress.

"We will be leaving now," Avanda notified the Krupes. "You may step aside, or we will have to remove you. This is your decision."

Faces covered by thick metal helmets, the Krupes stood ready for battle as they waited for orders from their leader. The dark flat black armor covered their entire bodies from head to toe. They stood like statues, waiting for the citizens to attack.

Avanda took a step forward, toward the egress. It was followed within a moment by all the Krupes stepping in toward her.

Shouting loud enough for all the citizens behind her to hear, she kept facing forward. "It's time!"

Each family had stayed together in small groups and were all holding onto a single item that they all were touching. Once they heard her call, they turned toward their family members and started calling for their lost loved ones which had died years ago in Gansler's first battle for freedom.

Narra and Revi stepped up behind Avanda and turned around to face the families that came to join them. The wife of the fallen general stood before them, preparing to execute something she hated to perform. Lifting up high over her head, she held Gansler's long sword. Attached to the hilt was the only hand that could summon the power to call the dead back to the living. A grey cloth wrapped tightly around Gansler's severed wrist which was tied firmly to the sword, causing the gem in the end to glow with full brightness.

The marketplace suddenly gave off an odd eerie vibration as voices from hundreds of families began calling the names of children and siblings. Faint wispy voices began calling back to them as they also held onto the item their family had selected. Soon voices from the dead filled the streets, humming in the ears of all the Krupes.

The Krupes did not move or respond. They stood their ground and waited for the citizens to approach in order to engage in battle.

Slowly materializing from gaseous states to bones and flesh and then skin, Gansler's defeated army retook their forms in full gear to finish what they had started.

Pulling out a few magical components, Avanda waited until most of the apparitions had fully formed before speaking. Perhaps 'fully formed' was an overstatement. Skin, muscles, and even organs hung loosely from their bodies while many parts were ravaged by disease, fungi, or rot. Many were missing eyes, hands, or even limbs. But in spite of their appearances, they were all prepared to fight to the end.

"One last battle, one last thrust, show your families who they can trust!" Using spells taught to her by her master, Bryus Grum, Avanda launched a series of dust balls out with a sling toward the Krupes.

Gansler's army turned from their families one last time to end the battle they never had a chance to start. As they rushed at the Krupes, Avanda activated her dust balls, sending up columns of red smoke which expanded in every direction. Within seconds the Krupes stood confused in a thick cloud as Gansler's army rushed in from every side.

Screams of pain were heard from both sides as weapons clashed and wagons were knocked over during the brawl.

Working on her next spell, Avanda stepped closer to the egress and focused her efforts directly between the turrets. Casting her spells without utilizing Vesik became liberating as she quickly recalled what her former master, Bryus Grum, had taught her.

Cupping her hands together she whistled through them, causing the spell components to flutter out the other side. The sound of her whistle amplified as it moved forward to the point of blasting open a hole in the red cloud and knocking out a few of the Krupes who were standing in the way.

Fighting continued on both sides of the egress which was now safe to enter.

Turning back to Narra, Avanda gave her instructions. "Lead them to freedom. I'll make sure none follow us."

With a nod, Narra handed Avanda the long sword and waved the others forward. "Thank you."

Brimmelle was one of the first to rush from the back as he quickly made his way to Narra to ensure she was helped through the tunnel. Overprotective of the pregnant Num, he nearly forgot about Revi, who ran over to hold her mother's other hand.

The battle continued within the magically created clouds as the citizens funneled through the center and into the egress tunnel. Avanda continued to send in spell after spell as Krupes attempted to escape the clouds of doom, while the escape of the locals was still in play.

Nearing the end of the escape, she noticed a band of Mognins standing firm. "Hurry!" she shouted.

The leader of the Mognin's stepped forward. "We will not leave you alone. We will leave when you leave. And we think it's time you leave."

Before she could reply, she noticed that once the noise from her last spell dissipated, there weren't any battle cries remaining. She had been so caught up in the excitement that she had been casting attack spells long after the battle had ended.

With one final spell, she chased the thick red clouds away to reveal the carnage left from the massacre. Krupe bodies were torn apart, still incased in their black armor as though limbs of crabs had been ripped from the bodies and scattered about.

Remains of Gansler's army were dispersed as well. None had survived, although none were expected to. Long overdue, their duties had been completed. They had successfully freed their families.

Pheosco climbed up Avanda's side and back for a good look over her shoulder at the results. "And you doubted yourself?"

Smiling, she finally let out a sigh of relief. "Actually, that was easier than I had imagined."

"What precisely did you anticipate?" said an unexpected voice. Standing between the turrets and directly in front of the egress, a tall red-skinned bulky Blothrud waited for an answer.

Fear crept into every part of Avanda's body. She had seen this Blothrud before and had been successful in avoiding him. "You're…"

"I'm Savroc and you are out of place, slaves."

Blothruds were the most vicious fighters of all the Altered Creatures and Avanda was well aware of this fact. The unexpected arrival of such a beast caused her to hesitate and become unsure of her abilities. "Stay back! We have your Keystone!" Her voice quivered as she attempted to delay any attack by him while she came up with a plan.

Growling at the sight of the dead Krupes, the Blothrud turned back to the citizens of Dolor. Stretching his fingers before making them into fists, he sized up his enemy. "I will personally kill each and every one of you in the most painful way possible."

This was no voiceless Krupe. This was a nine-foot tall blade covered muscular fighting machine with a temper that had just been ignited. His threats were more of a promise.

Avanda froze with fear. She had seen the devastation one of these creatures could create. She knew her skills were often aggressive, while she relied on Thorik to handle negotiations. Unfortunately, she was on her own, until she realized that she still had resources to pull from.

Turning to the Mognin leader, she nervously nodded for him to step forward. "If you are anything like my friend, Grewen, you can help remedy this conflict."

The Mognin stepped forward, just a step in front of Avanda. "Savroc, I am Trewek. You have fed us, clothed us, and sheltered us for our hard labor over the years. It was an arrangement we both lived with. Perhaps there is a new arrangement that could be created."

Savroc started forward as his eyes fixated on the Mognin as his first victim. "You have no leverage to barter with me. I will spare you the time to negotiate for a lost cause!"

Trewek, stayed calm and continued mediations as the Blothrud charged forward. "Your army is gone. You have no way to transport your prize. We will carry the Keystone for you to salvage your orders and please the Overlord."

Savroc reached the Mognin upon his last few words and the blades across the back of his forearm snapped up against Trewek's neck; ready to swipe a rough series of cuts across his throat. The tips of the blades dug just deep enough into the thick skin of the giant to draw blood before the Blothrud stopped his arm from going further. "What game are you playing, Fesh?"

"None, Savroc."

"How do you know of the need to move the Keystone to a barge and then downstream?"

"I do not know of anything more than it needs to be moved. A task we can perform. We will follow your lead as we have done for so many years. All we ask is that you allow the citizens not required to help with this mission to go free."

Still pressing his forearm up against the Mognin's neck, his lips rose and exposed his teeth while growling at the idea. "Slaves can't fend for themselves. They will die within a week."

"Then you have nothing to lose. They will die a long painful death, just as you had hoped they would."

After giving it some thought, he retracted his arm and released the Mognin. "I will strike out and kill anyone or all of you at the first sign of treachery or upheaval."

"Understood," Trewek said calmly. "We have an agreement."

Avanda was relieved that a deal had been struck and they would soon be free. However, she quickly changed her thoughts to wonder if Thorik had succeeded on his own journey to defeat the E'rudites. "Is there any chance you will be heading past the Govi Glade on the way to your barge?"

Savroc raised an arm to silence her. He didn't approve of slaves asking questions. "It's along the way. Start moving. No more questions!"

Chapter 31
Thorik Confronts E'rudites

The thick forest ended, exposing a refreshing open field with the occasional boulder or tree stump to break up the uniformity of waist high grass blowing in slight breezy swirls that seemed to waft out of nowhere. Tones of blue moonlight coated the various green blades of grass that changed shades based on their dance within the wind gusts.

Near the center of the clearing was a disruption from within the tall grass. Sparks of lightning began to spring forth, but were stopped within the confines of a large glass-like sphere rising from soil.

Thorik had returned to the Govi Glade to end the running once and for all.

A nervous sense of energy rushed through the Num as he explored the landscape for signs of the E'rudites who he assumed were still hunting for him. He wanted the hiding to be over. He wished it had never come to this point. He wanted to return to the city to save Avanda and his friends and his family. He wanted to do just about anything else than to start a battle with some of the most powerful beings in the world, especially seeing that these E'rudites wanted him dead or to have never been born.

What Thorik dreaded the most was the idea that he was willfully going to try to kill his mentor and dear friend, Ambrosius. Just the thought caused his stomach to tighten into a knot as a single tear ran down his face. He concluded that by the end of this battle one of them, if not both of them, would be dead. There was no turning back once he started this.

"The other option is to leave. Go someplace far away to avoid this conflict," the Mognin said, realizing the Num's conflict.

Thorik's lips thinned and he sniffed as he wiped away the tear. "No. I will not live the rest of my days running from this, living in fear of being caught, always watching over my shoulder, and placing anyone I love in constant danger." He thought about what he said for a moment and realized someone had done just that. "Ambrosius attempted this very strategy after the civil war. It earned him the slaying of his wife and having to let others raise his son. In a sense, he lost everything. I wish not to repeat this lesson he taught me."

"Let's get on with this." Bakalor had no patience and no fear as he stood behind them both. The oil lubricating his stone body parts gave off a low ill-green glow which casted shadows of the other two into the glade. Towering over both Grewen and Thorik, there was no hiding the fact that they had arrived. "I have a world to conquer."

His words caused great concern for Thorik, wondering if he was releasing this demon upon the world in return of his own safety. This exchange did not sit well in Thorik's mind. How could he do this to the future people of the world? How could he live with the ramifications? Would Bakalor live up to his agreement and allow Thorik a chance to lead some out of Terra Australis. The internal conflicts within the Num caused him to drift off into his own existence in an unwinnable tug-of-war.

"Thorik?" Grewen said, waking the Num from his trance. "One way or another, it's time to end this."

Pulling back his shoulders and straightening his back, Thorik nodded with conviction. "Agreed." Removing his backpack, he reached in past his wooden coffer and pulled out a flint and the sack of Runestones.

Grewen glanced around one more time for the E'rudites as well as any more spheres. "Are you sure this can be done?"

Reaching into the sack, with Bakalor's green flames glowing from behind him, Thorik felt the ridges on the Runestones to find the right one. Long ago, his grandmother had instructed him to learn how to know each Runestone without needing his eyes. The skill had come in handy many times. "No, I'm not sure. I've never tried it before, but I don't see why it wouldn't work."

"You know you're risking your life on trying this."

"I'm risking my life just being here." With that, Thorik placed the sack back into his backpack and handed it to Grewen. "If I don't make it, please give the coffer to Avanda so she can know the truth about my feelings for her."

Grewen took the sorry-looking pack of torn fabrics holding items that peeked out of ripped seams and punctured holes. If he didn't know better, he would have assumed it was a bag of garbage.

Before Thorik could make a few steps into the clearing, the Mognin lifted him up with his free hand and brought him up to his chest for a strong hug. "Good luck, little man."

The warmth of the Mognin's giant over-sized hand around him and the natural heat radiating from thick leathery chest reminded the Num just how comforting a hug could feel. "Thank you for being at my side. You're a dear friend."

"Enough with this!" Bakalor announced as his flames gave a momentary burst of increased height and heat. His impatience needed to be fed with some action. "It's time to show my superiority so I can begin my reign over the all the lands." The rocks around his mouth tilted just enough to appear as a slight smile while his eyes widened in excitement so large it appeared the massive diamond eyes would fall right out of his head.

Grewen set Thorik down and watched him enter the Govi Glade, like a parent would watch their child on their first day of school. He nodded with respect as to what the Num needed to do.

A hot flaming rock hand grabbed Grewen's shoulder and pushed the giant Mognin to the side, allowing Bakalor the clearance he needed to enter the grass field without having to overturn any more trees. The path they had used from the mountain was now littered with trees knocked over or burnt by the demon's passage.

Grewen didn't resist and casually moved to the side. His thick hide-like skin protected him from most flames, so he allowed the green flames, from the oily residue left on his shoulder, to burn out naturally. It was actually a pleasant and relaxing feeling on the cool night.

Walking with conviction to the center of the Govi Glade, Thorik was followed by the massive rock creature as it lit up a large part of the grassy field. It took a Thorik six strides for every one of the demon's steps in order to keep a healthy distance.

Arriving in what appeared close to the center, Thorik stopped and held up a single hand, stopping the rock creature in his path. "Let me know if you see anyone show up."

Bakalor's grin was obvious by now. Placing one of his stone feet up on a sturdy tree trunk, he straightened his back and stretched out his arms as he waited for anyone to approach Thorik. Within minutes the tree trunk was in flames, but unnoticed by the demon.

Taking a deep breath, he held two Runestones out before him. The Freedom Runestone and the Endurance Runestone. "And watch out for spheres. They come out of the ground and will swallow you up whole."

The demon glanced down at the tree trunk and near his other foot to see if he could see any signs of such an occurrence. "Understood." Looking back up and around, he took time to glance down periodically.

"And keep an eye on any spheres coming my way while I focus on the Runestones."

Gathering his thoughts, Bakalor spent a moment looking about the glade for E'rudites, before looking to the soil beneath him for changes, and then peering up to ensure no spheres were heading toward Thorik.

Holding the two stones out before him, he stretched his neck and tried to relax. "Can you also keep an eye on-"

"No!" shouted Bakalor, interrupting the Num. "I am here to dispose of your enemies not to be your servant or caretaker." He stopped all motions except his first which was to search out any intruders to the glade. The thick tree trunk he rested his foot on began breaking apart from being on fire as it moaned from his weight. "Now get on with it!"

Realizing he was pushing his luck with the demon, he quickly nodded and went back to work. Holding the two Runestones back to back, one facing up and one facing down, he placed his hands on both sides and wrapped his fingers around them. His thumbs resting on each side of the top Runestone while his forefingers pressed on each side of the bottom one.

Thorik had never tried to activate two Runestones at the same time. It was often difficult to control one at a time, let alone a second. "There's always a first time for everything," he mumbled to himself as he closed his eyes and began to concentrate.

Normally he would focus on the symbol on the top of the Runestone and just allow the energy trapped inside to utilize his body as an outlet, but with two stones he struggled to figure out how to give himself to them both at the same time.

Just by the energy that Thorik and Bakalor gave off, the Govi Glade began to come to life with a few more spheres rising from the ground and floating upward a dozen yards before falling back into the earth, changing the season of the grassy area it touched. If a winter blizzard swirled with a sphere, it left a thick coating of snow upon the grass and trees it touched along its journey.

One by one the amount of spheres increased across the entire length of the field, never to stray outside of the boundaries, never to climb up higher than an arrow could be shot, never to end the cycle of reliving the past or future within today's world.

Electrical tingling finally began to surge up one of Thorik's arms. However, instead of racing up one and then across his chest and back down the other arm to complete the connection, an electrical tingling began flowing up his other arm at the same time.

Unsure how this new sensation would end, he tried to relax and trust his training to keep focused as the tingling from both sides reached his shoulders and then made their way across his chest, crossing paths over his heart.

Thorik's heart stopped beating. It froze from the shock, along with his body, as a shockwave of energy shot out in every direction.

For a few moments every season and every event that ever took place within the glade was simultaneously happening and in full view as they intersected and overlapped in the same space. Thunderstorms and forest fires shared the same trees at the same moment. Battles of E'rudites and Alchemists lobbed magic at each other concurrently with families of deer and other wildlife grazing in the peaceful meadow. A shack was built, grew old, and then destroyed all at the same moment. For this brief moment, time's long linear length had snapped like Bakalor's chain and compiled upon itself in one lump mass.

So true was this metaphor that it, like the chain that once held Bakalor, the snapping of the taut links of time knocked both the demon and Grewen off their feet and onto their backs.

Blinking back to consciousness, Thorik's heart jolted back to life again as though it had never missed a beat.

It was impossible to say how long they were out with the flux of time being different for each one of them, but as they all opened their eyes, they witnessed a sight never seen by anyone or any creature ever before.

Thousands of spheres filled the sky above the glade. Each filled with different times of the day and season, each in their own year that spanned millenniums. Every sphere that existed in the glade now hung over the area, over Thorik and Bakalor's head, as Grewen watched from the edge of the forest.

The slight movement of the spheres caused a few to spark from soft collisions, which forced them to increase in speed and cause larger impacts and faster speeds. Before long, the sky became a chaos of movement, sending many of the spheres down toward the glade at incredible speeds. Crashing to the earth, the ground thundered from the shock of the forceful impact as the sphere disappeared like normal but left the terrain sunken by a foot.

Bakalor stood back up and held his ground, watching above to see where the next sphere would be shot like a cannonball down out of the sky. It wasn't long before one headed his direction. Leaping to the side to get out of the way, he turned to witness his tree stump explode into splinters upon the impact. Seeing them up close, he realized they were large enough to swallow him whole.

"Thorik! Get out of there!" Bakalor yelled out. "You will be no good as bait if you are already dead."

Unfortunately, Thorik could not hear him. Between the colliding spheres above them and the ones crashing upon the ground, the noise levels were tremendous. And even if he had heard the demon's warning, it would have been too late to take any actions as a sphere filled with ocean water hurled down toward him faster than an arrow's flight.

The rocketing sphere made its way toward the Num, exposing the contents of the ocean life as it raced deeper into its reality in its own time. Once it hit Thorik, the Num would be instantly displaced into the bottom of the ocean that was being displayed, assuming he survived the impact.

Grewen wondered if his eyes were playing tricks with him in the nighttime field lit by the electrical storms in the spheres floating above. He hoped the final impact point would be in front or behind his good friend, anything other the direct hit that it appeared to be. Nevertheless, his poor eyesight had seen it correctly.

The large bubble filled with water slammed down upon Thorik Dain of Farbank while he was still focused on both of the Runestones and totally unaware of the threat. The mass and speed of the collision caused a thunderclap in the air and tremor in the ground as it struck hard and left a crater in the ground a few feet deep.

The destructive force flattened all the grass and compressed the ground so densely that it nearly turned into a rock. It would take many years before life would grow in most of this location again. There was, however, a small circle within the impact sight that had escaped the pressure. This small yard wide circle surrounded the Num as he continued to keep his eyes closed and his hands on the Runestones. The Freedom Runestone had protected him from the spheres, which were creations of E'rudites and Alchemists. The Num had speculated such effects, and was relieved that his gamble had paid off.

The Endurance Runestone had created the energy to give life to the Govi Glade in order to coax the E'rudites to show themselves. However, just as before, the energy it gave the glade was quickly depleting his own vitality.

Looking up from his Runestones and then at Bakalor, Thorik nodded to indicate he had survived without harm. "The plan has worked so far," he told himself as he kept the focus on the Runestones. "All we need now are…"

As if he had been waiting for his queue, Lord Bredgin walked out from the tree line and into the glade from the far side.

Removing his fingers on his left hand from the lower Runestone, he allowed the Endurance Runestone to end its power. The conflicting energy surges, racing across his body, stopped and began flowing in a single direction, relieving the Num of some great discomfort.

Bredgin's cloak of darkness trailed behind him as he headed directly toward Thorik, while spheres rained down upon the glade, hammering the ground with shockwaves of noise and momentary earthquakes. Uncaring about his environment and the plummeting objects from above, he made no deviations to his path, leaving a yard wide path of dead grass and unfertile soil.

Approaching the Num, the E'rudite raised his hand up toward him, as to focus his energy in a tightly focused location and release it out of his fist at Thorik's head. The dark aura that normally surrounded Bredgin's body traveled up his legs, torso and then out to the end of his arm, ready for a single fatal attack. His focus was so intense that he completely ignored his own safety as a rock creature four times his size came upon him.

Swiping his hand over the grass field, Bakalor snatched up Bredgin within his palm and lifted him up to his own face. "I will crush you like a bug," he said, pleased how easy this battle ended up being.

Diverted from his attack on Thorik, Bredgin exploded his fury upon the demon, blasting his face with his E'rudite power of darkness.

A cloud of thick black vapors enveloped Bakalor's head, preventing anyone from seeing his face. Oils that normally dripped off his head and onto his shoulders dried up and stopped flowing, ending the flames above his shoulders. Essentially, the demon's head was lifeless and his body went rigid. Even after the veil of darkness faded from his head, the oil continued to burn with the ill-green light everywhere except his head and the hand which the E'rudite firmly held him in.

"No!" Thorik shouted, but his voice was drowned out by the drumbeat of the spheres showering down upon the glade. His plan to hide within his Runestone protection while Bakalor battled the E'rudites had failed, and he needed to determine his next step.

Not only had his planned failed against Bredgin, but it was now worse, for Darkmere stepped out of the woods and into the field. His always calm demeanor caused Thorik's nerves to be on edge. With Bakalor out of the battle, how could he possibly continue the fight with Darkmere and his son? He had to think quickly.

Grewen also saw the dilemma and began to enter the minefield of falling spheres, until he saw Thorik motioning him to stay back. Against his desire to help, he had to trust his friend and step back out of the dangerous field and into the edge of the forest.

Bredgin eventually freed himself. Making his way back down to the ground, the E'rudite composed himself, ready to put an end to the troublesome Num. Smiling for the first time in a very long time, the bald tattoo-headed man stretched his fingers to prepare for his final assault.

Sparks and flashes of green light began to dance about behind the E'rudite, causing a swaying shadow upon his soon-to-be victim. However, he would have to wait to eliminate Thorik, once again.

Flames from the oil that coated Bakalor's joints increased in random flares across his body until the sparks worked their way up his wrist and to the inert hand that Bredgin had sat in and drained of vitality. Within seconds, the hand came back to life. The same was true as the sparks worked up the demon's neck and up the sides of his head until a single burst of flames exploded in every direction with a fierce strength. Bakalor was once again alive. "ARRR," he screamed in anger over the E'rudites attack. The demon was now furious.

The darkness surrounding Bredgin had protected him from the demon's outburst. It had also blocked the flames from anything in his shadow, which included Thorik.

A giant backhanded swipe from Bakalor sent Bredgin sailing across the field, landing in a recently made sphere crater. Blood escaped out of multiple cuts across his body and face, exposing the color red against his normal shades of gray. He was injured. He was vulnerable.

Lifting the tons of rocks in his body, the demon raced forward and threw himself in the air to land upon the man to crush him.

Bredgin had never moved so fast in his life as he leaped out of the way to safety just as the boulders smashed into the already compressed terrain. Turning back around, the E'rudite placed his hands upon the demon's side and pressed his dark forces deep inside the rock creature. Shades of gray washed away any hue of his own blood, returning him to his normal menacing self.

The flaming oil acted as the lifeblood of the rock creature and the external, as well as internal, flames were quickly being extinguished, causing Bakalor to sample the unpleasant taste of death upon him as the demon fought his way up to his knees. He again backhanded the man away from him before laboring his way back up to his feet and igniting all his flames once again.

Bredgin was bloody and hurt from the attacks. He had always used his power over the darkness to do his bidding, not mend the physical nature of his body. New sensations of pain ranged from a broken arm to a concussion among the other cuts and bruises caused by being batted about by a twenty-four foot rock monster. Attempting to shake off the dizziness, he looked up to see Bakalor step next to him. Towering over him, Bakalor lifted one of his huge feet above Lord Bredgin's body.

Using the remaining powers that he could still gather, he pushed up his dark thoughts and put out the flames on the bottom of the rock foot, but the weight of the solid stone would still be enough to crush him.

It was then that he finally realized his mortality as well as the dangers of the Govi Glade. One of the many spheres that hailed down upon the area collided with the demon before Bakalor could crush Bredgin. In that instant, the sphere drove the demon's upper body deep into the ground, leaving only his feet visible with his toe pointing to the sky.

Bredgin had survived the demon's attack. However, his body was damaged and his orientation was in disarray while he lay in the glade in agonizing pain.

Oddly, Darkmere continued to watch the events from afar, never lifting a hand to assist or stop any events playing out before him. He was simply an observer.

Thorik took the opportunity to end Bredgin's life of terror once and for all. Dodging the aerial attacks on his way over to the man, while the E'rudite was still disabled from his battle, the Num approached him and stood above him. His anger grew as he looked down at the injured man who had caused so many people so much pain over the years. And yet, he struggled to convince himself to make the final blow that would end the man's life.

Tinges of color washed in and out of the E'rudites skin as Bredgin attempted to gain control of his faculties. As he did, he saw his moment and summoned any remaining dark forces he could pull from. Grabbing the Num's ankle, he pushed out his powers to cripple Thorik by sucking the life out of his leg to the point that it was nothing but ashes. However, to his surprise, his powers failed him.

Keeping his focus on the Runestone, Thorik glanced down at the man's hand grasping his ankle with a sigh of relief. It had continued to prevent any E'rudite forces to affect anything near him or touching him. Kicking his leg free, he asked Bredgin the obvious question as the thunder of crashing spheres continued around them. "Why? Why do you wish me dead?"

"There he is!" shouted Ambrosius' voice from behind Thorik. He had suddenly appeared within the glade utilizing his son's power to transport between locations. Letting go of Ericc's shoulder, he raced toward the Num waving his staff overhead like a madman.

A near miss of a sphere slammed down between the two, sending the old E'rudite to the ground. Rolling to a stop on his back, Ambrosius' anxiety rose as he saw another sphere heading right for him like a cannonball shot down by the gods. With no time to move, he used the split second of time he had to react, depleting all of his powers to bat the sphere as hard as he could back up into the air.

Unfortunately, the force used was so powerful and so focused that it penetrated the surface area and exploded the sphere in midflight, tearing the fabric of time and causing a vortex to form in its place above them.

Realizing the event hanging over their head was potentially more dangerous than the events taking place on the ground, Ambrosius rolled up to his knees. "Get out of here! Now!" Standing up, he rushed forward at Thorik and used his powers to push the Num away from Bredgin in his attempt to escape the glade. To his surprise, Thorik never moved. In fact, his powers never reached the Num.

"I won't let you prevent my birth!" Thorik shouted in defiance.

"Have you lost your head? I'm not trying to obstruct your existence!" Ambrosius was still confused as to why his powers had failed him.

Thorik stood his ground as the falling spheres began being sucked into the vortex. "I won't let you kill me, either."

"If I had wanted to kill you we wouldn't be having this conversation! I've been striving to modify your existence in order to prevent Bredgin's attempt to thwart your birth." Frustrated at the Num's words, he continued to look over his shoulder at the danger and chaos around them.

The hundreds of spheres that had been shot to the earth were now slowly starting to rise back up from underground from the pull of the vortex.

"Bredgin's the one trying to prevent me from being born? But I heard you clearly say that the strategy was to do this," he yelled over all the noise in the glade.

"Yes! After countless years of equations and theories, I finally figured out *his* strategy."

"I thought you were talking to an invisible friend in the corner of your home."

"A decade of solitude and research will play havoc with one's mind, and mine wasn't exactly on social etiquette during your visit. Have I earned no trust from you after all these years?" Ambrosius was in no mood to wait for an answer. "If you hadn't existed, who would have found and saved me in the woods, north of Farbank? Who would have prevented the sacrifice of my son? Must I go on?"

The Govi Glade's danger had changed from a thunderous hailstorm of translucent orbs to an eerie silence of rising spheres as though dead spirits were awakening from their graves. There were fewer safe locations to stand in the grassland than there were dangerous ones. Survival would be unlikely if they stayed in the area much longer.

"We need to leave!" Ericc yelled as he raced around a rising sphere and then up to them.

"Not so fast," said a new voice to the group. Darkmere was now standing just a few feet away. "I am in agreement to the idea of preventing Bredgin from averting Thorik's birth, for it would prevent many opportunities for me. However, Thorik Dain of Farbank must die after killing the Mountain King, before the truth is discovered and disrupts our timeline."

Thorik raised his hands up toward the E'rudite in white, knowing that Darkmere's powers couldn't hurt him as long as his Runestone was still activated. "The Mountain King? He's long since deceased. And even if he wasn't, I would refuse to kill anyone for you!"

Reaching forward with unexpected speed, Darkmere used his own staff to knock the Runestone out of the Thorik's hands, ending the Num's safety from E'rudite powers. "You already have." The dark lord's voice was thick with pleasure.

Thorik jumped to the ground to pick the Runestone back up as Darkmere launched his attack on the now vulnerable little man.

Ambrosius stepped between them and blocked his powers, pushing both the elderly E'rudites back away from each other.

Summoning what little strength he had left, Bredgin fought through his own pain to take his last opportunity to stand up and leap at Thorik.

Seeing the events unfold, Ericc jumped forward and grabbed the Num, only to have the two of them disappear and then reappear several yards away, out of Bredgin's reach.

As a new battle of E'rudites unfolded, spheres falling to the earth were either sucked into the vortex or pulled by its forces so strongly that they rotated around the vortex before entering. This rotation ranged from the small to the wide. Larger diameter rotations grazed the glade itself before spinning around the vortex a few more times before being pulled in.

Spheres were pulled from the earth up into the vortex and often collided with others swirling around it, sending sparks in every direction. It was mass chaos as the crashing of hundreds of spheres prevented any location from being safe. And yet, in the center of the field stood four E'rudites and one Polenum.

Thorik ran from his new location back into the action to find his Runestone that had been knocked from his hands. Oblivious to the danger, he felt compelled to regain his protection against all of the forces around him. He knew he didn't have a chance without it.

Bredgin and Darkmere took the opportunity to attack Ambrosius and were immediately successful in overpowering him. Ericc appeared behind Darkmere to relocate his uncle to a distant location. Upon grabbing him, Darkmere stopped his attack on Ambrosius and changed the flesh and muscles in Ericc's hand into sand, which crumbled and fell away.

Ericc screamed in pain, staring at his missing hand, while Darkmere turned back to his brother in time to receive a blast of Ambrosius' powers across his face, nearly ripping his head off.

With the E'rudites fighting each other, Thorik had the time to find and activate his Freedom Runestone in the tall grass near a large stone to protect himself from their powers as well as from the ever-increasing spheres. And it was a good thing he did, for just then a sphere rose from the ground underneath him. Concentrating on the Runestone preventing him from falling inside, instead, he was gently pushed to the side as it lifted. However, as it did so, it also lifted the large group of stone boulders that he was leaning up against.

The earth remained in place, but the stones lifted out of the ground as they rode upon the outside of the sphere's surface. These were no ordinary stones, these were arranged in a pattern that appeared to be a two-legged and two-armed creature. Bakalor's body had been lifted from the depths into the madness of the E'rudite battle and sphere collisions.

Lifting the demon back up to his feet, the sphere slowly floated up toward the vortex.

Thorik turned his back from the fighting E'rudites and ended the use of his Runestone. Knowing he was in great danger for doing so, he grabbed his flint and began making sparks against Bakalor's legs. Starting a fire had never been his forte; however, he knew all he had to do has get enough sparks to ignite a drop of oil in order to carry out his idea.

Within moments, a single spark landed just right on the demon's leg and began to spread quickly across his body. Within moments Bakalor had returned and Thorik had his Runestone activated. They were back in the battle.

Among the crashing spheres and attacks from each other, not one of the E'rudites saw him coming as Bakalor reached down and grabbed all four of them with his two hands. He then immediately launched them straight up into the air to be swallowed by the vortex above the glade.

And just like that, the E'rudites were gone.

However, the glade continued to spin spheres around and pull them from the air as well as the ground until every last one of them were sucked into the vortex.

Thorik had managed through it all by standing still and focusing on his Runestones, while the demon was pushed around the glade until they had stopped.

After the very last straggling sphere rose from the ground, the vortex imploded upon itself, sending a shockwave across the glade and against the trees.

All stayed silent. Even the sounds of forest animals and insects had halted. Not even the sound of trees blowing in the wind could be heard for several moments afterward.

Enjoying the moment of calmness after the battle, Thorik welcomed the sun as it began to rise over the distant mountains. Taking in a deep breath and let out a heavy sigh, he watched Grewen make his way toward him.

Bakalor was still furious about being buried alive and his flames extinguished. Yet his ego increased even more than before about his ability to defeat anything that would challenge him. "I truly am the most powerful creature ever created," he said with confidence. "Nothing can stop me from ruling all and destroying those who oppose me!"

Uneasy about his comment, Thorik needed to correct him. "Except, of course, those who wish to leave these lands with me…as we agreed."

"I have just proven my powers are above all others. I need not make or carry out agreements. I do what I wish when I wish. I am now your god and ruler."

"We had a deal. You wouldn't be here now if I hadn't freed you!"

"I owe no one! I am all powerful!" Bakalor roared with excitement over his victory and start of his new reign, as he welcomed the distant light reach over the mountains and bathe the glade with a greeting to a new day. "What is this light source?"

Thorik searched past Grewen slightly confused. "You mean the sun?" The warm rays began to play on his pale Num face. It felt good, in spite of his dilemma with the demon. "It brings life to the land. It rises in the morning and falls every evening."

"I've never seen the sun before. However, I shall rule the sun and it will rise and fall upon my command."

"How can anyone have never seen the sun?"

"Deleth hasn't exposed me to it, yet." He realized the importance of his words just as the stinging pain from the sun's rays showered upon his body. "What have you done to me!"

"Done to you? What are you talking about?"

Steam rose from the building blocks of Bakalor's body as he screamed in pain and ran for shade within the trees. "You've tricked me! You knew Deleth hadn't protected me from the sun yet. And by exposing me to it prior to his treatment, the sunlight will kill me!"

Thorik looked back and forth from Bakalor and Grewen. "I had no idea," he told his friend.

Grewen grinned. "I actually thought it was very clever, little man."

Turning back, Thorik could see Bakalor reach the forest and attempt to hide under the forest's canopy. "I promise. I had no idea!" the Num explained.

Letting out a war cry of pain, the demon was unable to obtain enough shade to prevent the sunlight from slowly killing him. "You've stolen my opportunity to rule to world. I'll never forget this! And I'll never forget the name Thorik Dain of Farbank! I won't rest until I see you suffer!"

As Bakalor hid in the shade of the forest canopy, he slammed his fist through thick tree trunks. In his fit of rage he tossed parts of trees and large boulders out into the Govi Glade toward Thorik. Fortunately for the Num, the demon was a very poor shot.

Still agitated, Bakalor realized he needed to escape before the sunlight finished the job it had started. Covering his mouth and one nostril, he blew hard and long out the other nostril. After a few moments, his tantrum began again as trees were broken with his fist and then tossed out of the forest.

It wasn't long before a hole in space formed in the forest, near the demon. Growing in size, the hole became a large portal leading to the inside of the Temple of Surod.

Stepping out of the portal, Deleth was obviously disappointed as he gazed at Bakalor hiding from the sunlight in the forest. "You requested my assistance?"

The demon roared with anger at his master. "I didn't know about the sun! Why didn't you prepare me for it! I was tricked!" The massive rock creature shook in pain from the slight rays of light that seeped between the leaves and burned his rock skin while diminishing his flames. Parts of him began to crystalize, crack, and flake off.

"You're an idiot," Deleth said calmly. "It appears you no longer will rule the land." After a moment of contemplation, he continued. "Instead, I will teach you how to travel through rock and earth. You will rule the underworld for me."

Turning, the Overlord increased the size of the spatial portal to support the demon's massive size. He then led his creation out of the forest and into a dark temple before closing the gateway in space behind them.

And in a flash, Deleth and Bakalor vanished from sight.

Relieved it was over, Thorik glanced back toward the mountain, only to see a collection of various species flowing out of the forest and into the open field. The citizens of Dolor had escaped the city. They had survived. And leading them out of the forest was the most amazing creature he had every wished to see. Avanda. It was a sight he thought he would never see again.

Just as Thorik's face flushed with delight, he witnessed the horror following her. The Blothrud, Savroc, stepped out of the woods and looked directly at him. It was as though he knew Thorik was looking at him, and a sudden fear ran down his spine.

Before Thorik could react to warn Avanda of Savroc's arrival, the citizens of Dolor continued to flow out around the Blothrud and into the field, along with several Mognins carrying the Keystone on its framework. Brimmelle and Revi helped Narra with the long hike, and Chug limped his way into the light with a small green dragon coiled up on the back of his head, between his ears. On Chug's backside sat a funny looking orange and red bird who chatted to anyone that came near her, just as Gluic always did. Meanwhile, Avanda helped everyone out of the cool forest and into the warm field filled with sunshine. Tattered and torn, they had survived.

With a deep sigh of relief to see them, Thorik nodded at his Mognin friend as he glanced about at the rest of the calm glade. For the first time, he saw the Govi Glade as a normal field of grass with scattered boulder outcroppings and a few stray trees. "Isn't this peaceful, Grewen? Not a single sign of the E'rudite and Alchemist Wars. You'd never know that thousands of years ago there was a battle of magical powers that rivaled all others."

Grewen handed Thorik's pitiful looking backpack to him. "Yes. And if we didn't know better, we'd never have guessed that this was where Wyrlyn and Irluk's armies battled for untold years, causing an endless loop of time and space distortions. I always wondered what caused him and his apprentice, Irluk, to be so opposed to each other that it would start a war."

"I always questioned the same thing." The Num took another moment to enjoy the scene before them. "Do you think that this is what it looked like prior to the Alchemist and E'rudite War?"

Grewen chuckled at the thought. "There is no way for us to really know unless we were there, little man."

"True," Thorik said, seeing movement in the forest, opposite that of where the Dolor citizens were arriving from. "Grewen, all the E'rudites are gone, right?"

"I saw all four of them go into the vortex with my own eyes. Why?"

Nums' eyes were naturally better than Mognin's, so it wasn't of any surprise that Thorik had seen the wagon first. "Let me know when you see what I see."

Grewen squinted to see the distant movement of a wagon being pulled by a typical two-legged thick-necked Faralope. The two riders in the wagon appeared to be travelers as they showed no signs of royal flags, armor, or weapons of any sort.

"Anyone you know from Dolor?"

Thorik cleared his throat with a slightly worried expression. "No. I'm sure they aren't from the city."

As the wagon came across the field toward them, Grewen chuckled at Thorik's reaction. "Ever since I met you, you've always overreacted to the unknown."

The tall Mognin stood in the glade, towering over the Num, in an almost comical appearance to the two new arrivals as they stopped their wagon before passing by. "Greetings. Do you need assistance?" the male driver asked, while the female next to him sat quietly next to him reading a large book.

With his mouth hanging open, Thorik gazed at the sight, unsure how to answer. "No. Well, yes...I am Thorik Dain of Farbank and this is my friend, Grewen."

"Interesting. I know most cities, but I've never heard of Farbank," the man replied. "I am Wyrlyn and this is my apprentice, Irluk."

Gently closing her book, she exposed a young black panther lying at her side. Glancing over at both of them, she pet the black panther kitten next to her. "Greetings," she said with little interest. "So, is your answer yes or no? It wasn't clear."

"Be civil," her master instructed. "They are not accustomed to people such as we."

"We need to keep moving, master. If we stop to visit with everyone we meet along the way, we won't witness the installation of the Keystone in the Lu'Tythus Tower. This crystal's powers to brace the Weirfortus Dam will give birth of a new age. It is important to my research."

"Grewen," Thorik said calmly. "I think I may have made a wrong assumption."

The Mognin grinned. "May have?"

Pronunciation Guide

CHARACTERS
Ambrosius: aeM-brO-zee-ahs
Avanda: ah-Van-Dah
Bakalor: Bah-Kah-Lor
Bredgin: Brehd-gehn
Brimmelle: Brim-'ell
Chug: Chug
Darkmere: Dark-Meer
Deleth: deL-'eth
Ericc: ehR-iK
Feshlan: FehSH-Lahn
Gansler: Gan-sler
Gluic: Glu-iK
Grewen: Gru-'en
Irluk: uhR-luhK
Narra: Nair-Rah
Ovlan: ahV-lahN
Pheosco: Fee-ahs-kO
Revi: Reh-Vee
Rummon: Rum-mahN
Savroc: sahV-roK
Thorik: Thor-iK
Trewek: trU-ek
Vesik: Ves-iK
Wyrlyn: Wer-Len

LOCATIONS
Cuev'Laru Mountains: Koo-ehV Lah-Roo
Cucurrian River: Koo-kuR-ee-uhn
Dolor: Do-lour
Govi: Gah-Vee
Lu'Tythis: Loo-Tith-is
Pwellus Dementa': Pwel-uz Dee-men-tAY

Pronunciation Guide

SPECIES

Blothrud (AKA Ruds): BlahTH-Ruhd
> *7' to 9' tall; Bony hairless Dragon/Wolf-like head; Red muscular human torso and arms; Sharp spikes extend out across shoulder blades, back of arms, and back of hands; Red hair covered waist and over two thick strong wolf legs. Blothruds are typically the highest class of the Del'Undays.*

Del'Unday: DeL-OOn-Day
> *The Del'Unday are a collection of Altered Creatures who live in structured communities with rules and strong leadership.*

Fesh'Unday: FehSH-OOn-Day
> *The Fesh'Unday are all of the Altered Creatures that roam freely without societies.*

Gathler: GahTH-ler
> *6' to 8' tall; Hunched over giant sloth-like face and body; Gathlers are the spiritual leaders of the Ov'Undays.*

Human: Hyoo-muhn
> *5' to 6' tall; pale to dark complexion; weight varies from anorexic to obese. Most live within the Dovenar Kingdom.*

Krupes: KrooP
> *6' to 8' tall; Covered from head to toe in black armor, these thick and heavy bipedal creatures move slow but are difficult to defeat. Few have seen what they look like under their armor. Krupes are the soldiers of the Del'Unday.*

Mognin (AKA Mogs): MahG-Nen
> *10' to 12' tall; Mognins are the tallest of the Ov'Unday.*

Myth'Unday: Meeth-OOn-Day
> *The Myth'Unday are a collection of Creatures brought to life by altering nature's plants and insects.*

Ov'Unday: ahv-OOn-Day
> *The Ov'Unday are a collection of Altered Creatures who believe in living as equals in peaceful communities.*

Polenum (AKA Nums): Pol-uhn-um
> *4' to 5' tall; Human-like features; Very pale skin; Soul-markings cover their bodies in thin or thick lines as they mature. Exceptional Eyesight.*

64193989R00143

Made in the USA
Charleston, SC
28 November 2016